THE PRODIGAL

Nicky Black

COPYRIGHT

This edition 2015

1

First published in Great Britain by
Hard Place Publishing Ltd

Copyright © Nicky Black 2015

Nicky Black asserts the moral right to be identified as the author of this work.

This novel is entirely a work of fiction. The names, characters and incidents portrayed in it are the work of the author's imagination. Any resemblance to actual persons, living or dead, events or locations, is entirely coincidental.

All rights reserved. No part of this text may be reproduced, transmitted, downloaded, decompiled, reverse engineered, or stored in or introduced into any information storage and retrieval system, in any form or by any means, whether electronic or mechanical, now known or hereinafter invented, without the express written permission of the author.

For my big brothers, Alan and Trevor
Taken from us too early
Be at peace

Other books by this Author:
The Rave (2018)
The Flower House (2024)

PROLOGUE

Newcastle upon Tyne
October 1977

There was an angry wind that day. It whipped the rain around his head, his freezing hands struggling to fix the transformer into place. He shook the rain from his face and felt the harness loosen a notch. Gasping, he grabbed at the slippery wood as the transformer fell from his hand.

Then he, too, was falling.

Frank Jamieson hit the sodden ground with a thud that reverberated through every bone in his body. He lay on his back and blinked up at the telegraph pole, the harness swaying in the wind. Broken. Perhaps he hadn't fastened it properly. Perhaps those birthday pints at lunch time had been a mistake.

He knew at that moment that his journeyman days were over. But never could he have imagined the cost to his family – Jackie and Lee, his wife and son.

With bowed heads, the groundsmen confirmed at the inquest that they'd all taken a drink that lunch time. No compensation due. Gross negligence: next case please.

That day changed everything. It was the day Frank Jamieson changed from the strong, silent type to the sullen, bitter type, his back and his spirit broken. The day his wife changed from liking a drink in Turners on a Friday night

1

with her pals, to liking a drink any time of the day, and often alone.

And Lee. Only nine years old and homeless, the mortgage on the cosy, terraced house in Kenton no longer affordable, the boy subjected to the stench of his grandad's tiny flat while his mother stubbornly rejected house after house offered by the Council. She was way too good for some sink estate riddled with roaming dogs and shopping trolleys. She'd hang on, she said. She'd wait for an empty house on a nice new estate that would never come.

The reek of five cats and old man incontinence permeated their clothes and hair, clinging to Lee's school uniform so that bullying and tears became a daily occurrence.

Eventually, they were left with no choice, and they moved onto Valley Park Estate within the year.

There were plenty empty houses on Valley Park.

ONE

Lee dragged himself out of a deep sleep as the train steward announced that the next station stop would be Newcastle. He peered through a misty window that had the word twat etched deeply into it. There was a knot in his throat. Fear, nerves or anticipation: he couldn't tell.

He dug into his pocket to check how much cash he had for a taxi. As he opened his wallet his eyes fell on the small, creased picture of a dimple-cheeked child of about seven. Grinning. Toothless. Gorgeous.

The child he'd been denied.

It was the only picture Debbie had sent him – must be eight years ago now. He didn't blame Debbie, not really, but she could have told him. She could have found a way to tell him she'd had the baby and not got rid of it like everyone wanted. Instead, he had to find out years later from Hoots, his old drinking pal, so-named because of his Scottishness and love of battered haggis.

'What, she never telt ye? Aboot the bairn and that?' Hoots had come to London to look for labouring work, but one nip on the arse from a skinny rent boy at King's Cross and he was in a cell awaiting assault charges. Lee, a beat officer fresh out of training, had brought him a cheese sandwich and a cup of tea. Christ, they'd laughed. The things they'd got up to: Jesus. Lee had laughed long and loud until he'd learned of the baby – seven years after the fact. Louise she'd called her. She would be fifteen now, a young woman. A young woman he'd been denied.

As the train slowly crossed the river approaching Newcastle, he looked with aching nostalgia at the Tyne Bridge. It frowned at him, green and resplendent. He searched beyond the bridge, not at the derelict warehouses and breakers' yards he was expecting, but at a gleaming river, light bouncing off the water from the windows of smart offices and flats which now hugged the Tyne. Couples strolled hand in hand down the quayside; people tied their bicycles to elegant lampposts.

Twisting awkwardly in his seat, he rested his forehead on the window to get a last glimpse of the scene before it disappeared from view. He looked around him expectantly, wanting to share the spectacle, but people were on their feet, retrieving their bags and putting on their coats. They'd seen it a hundred times, watched the change happening slowly. Like growing old, they just didn't notice it.

Whatever the feeling was in his throat, he could now put a name to it. Excitement. He felt like a child about to arrive at Butlins. Only this was going to be no holiday.

***

Nicola Kelly checked herself in the full-length mirror at the bottom of the stairs, admiring her shapely figure in her new clobber. Leaning into the mirror she scraped the mascara gunk out the corner of her eyes with a little fingernail. She checked each profile and gave her shoulder-length brown hair a quick finger-comb. The make-up was good. Not too much to make a fuss. She sighed and looked at her watch. He'd said he'd be back by seven.

Hearing a car door slam outside she stood tall, pushed up her boobs and pulled on her jacket, hoping to get out of the door before he could say anything. But Micky Kelly stood in the doorway already. *Where are you going?* his marble eyes asked.

It was over in a nanosecond. He took in her lipstick and clothes in the blink of an eye. She stiffened, the memory of the face being scrubbed off her with a nail brush over the bathroom sink still fresh in her mind. She looked back into the mirror, this time flattening everything down and pulling the top up over her cleavage.

'Come 'ere, man,' said Micky, putting his thick arms around his wife's waist. He hated it when she flinched in his arms. 'You're fucking gorgeous.' He kissed her, pressed himself against her, breathing out heavily and reaching down to her firm, round backside with his hands.

Nicola felt his hot breath on her face and pulled back. 'Margy'll be here in a minute,' she said, looking around for her handbag. 'Why don't you come later?'

Spurned, Micky turned away and headed for the kitchen, emptying his gym bag onto the floor. Why would he want to spend his evening with his wife's sorry excuse for a brother?

Nicola swallowed her anxiety. She needed to see Mark. Her brother's trial was only a week away and he wasn't coping. He was jumpy and fractious, thin as a rake and black around the eyes from lack of sleep. She knew the signs when he was about to fall over the edge.

She weighed up her options, every little decision needing an assessment of the consequences. Walking into the kitchen, she sidled up behind her husband, her arms going round his great stomach. She purred a little: 'The kids'll be staying next door, so if you can get off work and come later ...'

He cleared his throat. 'We'll see,' he said, feeling himself harden. But by the time he'd turned around, Nicola was heading back to the living room.

Their two boys sat on the floor with sherbet dips watching *The Lion King,* Liam's favourite film. Six-year-old Michael was showing little Liam how to lick his finger and dip it in sherbet. As she stroked Michael's hair she noticed her handbag lying on the floor next to Liam. It had become his favourite toy of late - taking everything out and putting everything carefully back in. She kissed them on their heads, picked up her bag and headed for the hall just as she heard the doorbell chime.

As she opened the door she heard Micky yell, *'And don't let that fat bitch get you pissed!'* She stared into her friend's unyielding face. Margy sucked in one round cheek and glanced over Nicola's shoulder at her fuckwit of a husband, her arms folded over her huge breasts.

'Hiya, Margy,' Micky shouted pleasantly.

Margy sighed and curled her lip. She couldn't be arsed with fuckwits. 'Howay,' she said, and turned from the door as Nicola shouted her goodbyes.

Nicola caught up with her friend who was taking an envelope from her bag.

'Here, this came to the centre for you,' said Margy.

Looking over her shoulder to make sure Micky had closed the door, Nicola opened it and read it. Her computer qualification: a distinction in word processing and spreadsheets. Her face spread into a smile: 'Eeeeh, Margy, I'm not thick! I'm not thick!' she said, waving the paper in the air.

'Aye well, give it back here. If Him Indoors finds out, he'll have you locked in the shed for a fortnight.'

Nicola handed the envelope back to Margy with a grin. Her first ever qualification. It felt good, and as she walked briskly down the street, shoulder to shoulder with her best friend, she pulled the top back down and pushed her boobs back up into their rightful position.

***

Lee ordered a large Scotch with ice from a waiter in a white pinny. He observed the straight-haired women in glittering heels sipping cocktails and the rosy-cheeked men drinking beer out of bottles, their shirtsleeves rolled up to the elbow, their voices carrying crystal-clear and unself-conscious. This wasn't the Newcastle he remembered. But then, his life had been on Valley Park – his school, his friends, his enemies, the Nags Head where they all drank underage and freely.

The only thing that hadn't been on Valley Park was Debbie. Debbie was from Jesmond Vale – the posh end. She'd wanted to defy her round-bellied philanderer of a father and show her tight-arsed mother that girls could have fun if they wanted. It was the 1980s, and freedom was rife. They'd met just days after his sixteenth birthday in Eldon Square Shopping Centre where she was looking for earrings and he was looking for girls. Lee was the handsome one: his perfectly wedged hair and brown Bambi eyes meant he wasn't short of girlfriends. His mates, Hoots and Dinger, were spotty and skinny with lank mullets to their shoulders. They would have to make do with the ugly mates, but they were happy for anything they could get, let's face it. Debbie was with her friends, twin daughters of dentists, both with mouths full of metal and shoulder pads out to here. Lee had sat opposite her with his Big Mac. She'd grinned a gappy, imperfect grin at him over the straw of her milkshake and he'd nearly come in his stone-washed denims. It wasn't long before he was coming inside her on Tynemouth beach and Louise was made.

At sixteen, Lee had walked away from Valley Park, never to return. The news of his impending parenthood had sent his own embittered father into one of his unearthly rages. Bruce Turner's kid? *Debbie Turner?* Bruce Turner had given Frank a job, a chance, for Christ's sake. It might just be part-time, but he could sit in a chair and seal boxes. And now his own son had got the man's daughter up the spout? Did he know who this man was?

Lee knew who he was, the mighty Bruce Turner with his box at Newcastle United and his scrapyards and factories all over the place. Yes, he gave the odd cripple a job to help him get his jowly mug on the local news, but he didn't have a philanthropic bone in his body.

Lee had never returned to Valley Park after that. But it was Frank who had said never. Never wanted him in his house again, never thought he'd amount to anything, never wanted to see him again. His father's sticks had beat the words across his back.

Finishing his whisky, he looked at the row of taxis outside the hotel bar window. He should do it now. Get it over with.

***

When Nicola arrived at the pub with Margy, her brother Mark and his wife were already there. Mark's wife, Kim, was looking a bit rough. Normally she'd have her make-up perfect, and her hair washed and styled, but tonight her face shone and her blonde hair was brittle and dark at the roots. She'd lost weight since the baby was born. They both looked worn out, but they were still in love, Mark and Kim. It made Nicola feel lonely inside. It made her want the old Micky back. She wanted it to be like it used to be, before he started to blow everything out of all proportion.

She loved the bones of this boy, her little brother. They were extensions of each other. They looked alike, same dark, shiny hair, freckled noses and heavily lashed, green eyes. Of course, his hair was shorn now, the edge of a tattoo of some beast from his back reaching up and round his neck. It was never questioned that they wouldn't be near each other for the rest of their lives. She'd looked after them both when it became obvious that their mother didn't care if they went to school or not, if they were loved or not. But, unlike Mark, it had made Nicola tough. He needed her, and she would always protect him.

She watched him now as he sucked on the end of a cigarette like it was his last. He was a nervous wreck. She took in the long scar above his left eyebrow, reaching down to his temple, the mark of the baton of some flat-faced policeman. The police had made his life hell for years, and Nicola felt her blood boil whenever she saw a uniform or a squad car. They'd got their way this time. She wanted to spit on them, the shitheads. Everyone knew Mark wasn't into drugs anymore. And even if he was, he wasn't thick enough to keep them up the kitchen drainpipe where the slimy hands of some greasy copper had no doubt put it. Mark was terrified of going to prison, of being cooped up, unable to breathe, and if he ended up inside, she knew the scum would have got just what they wanted. She was frightened too. She knew it would ruin Mark's fragile life at best, and kill him at worst. She hated every last one of those pigs, and when her husband drank with them and shook their hands she wanted to kick him hard in the balls.

Margy interrupted her thoughts with a nudge in the ribs.

'It's the band,' she said, pointing at four large, hairy men lugging instruments.

Nicola grunted and Margy raised her eyes to the ceiling.

'Well, go on then. Get the bliddy drinks in,' she said.

***

The taxi dropped Lee at the edge of Valley Park, the driver not wanting to venture anywhere near the Nags Head. 'Nowt but trouble,' he growled as Lee handed him a fiver then watched the taxi speed away without the offer of any change.

He walked towards the pub, everything around him frighteningly familiar, yet different, smaller than he remembered, quieter and darker. As he pushed the door to the pub open and walked up to the bar, he recognised the barman, Scotty, now in his fifties and sporting a beer belly the size of a small country. A band was setting up on the stage and people were whooping and cheering the big, bearded blokes in Dubliners T-shirts. He took in the faces around him: Scotty, the old, toothless drunk at the end of the bar, swaying like long grass. That's when he noticed her. She stood next to him, and he glanced sideways at her for a second, feeling himself redden a little. A few seconds later, his head turned as he felt her move next to him, his eyes drawn to her, like an addict is drawn to their drug of choice.

There was no recognition in Scotty's eyes when he asked Lee what he wanted. Lee shook his head.

'She's next,' he said.

He heard her order a pint and three lemonades, throwing her hair back from her shoulders then looking at him. He saw something in her face, a flutter of recognition maybe. Her green eyes blinked at him for a second and he opened his mouth to speak, but she turned back to Scotty to pay for her drinks, then walked back to the table she shared with a big, matronly woman, a puny man with a neck full of tattoos, and a childlike young woman with frizzy blonde hair in a small ponytail.

Nicola set the tray on the table and blew her fringe from her face. As she'd stood at the bar, her arm a few millimetres from that of a man she thought she recognised, she'd felt a flicker in her tummy like she did when her babies first moved. It didn't show, obviously, she'd made sure of that.

Sitting down, she drank the top inch of lemonade from her glass and glanced at Lee: maybe she knew him from school, or maybe he was off the telly or something. He was dressed well, good jeans, expensive shirt tucked in with the sleeves rolled up, and the shoes shone. She soon realised, though, that she simply recognised one of her own when she saw it, no matter how much their shoes cost. She knew everyone on this estate, knew every face in this pub, but not this one. She watched him light a cigarette, both hands wrapped tightly round his lighter, not behind one hand like the posh people who often had their cigarettes lit for them. The skin was lined, his teeth a little out of kilter, and his nails bitten to the quick; his joints and knuckles had the roughness and scarring of a man who'd worked outdoors and, though he stood up straight, his shoulders were a little hunched like someone who'd stood in the cold many a night. This was a local boy made good. And handsome, too.

'Jesus, a lass could die of thirst.' Margy's hands sat on her wide hips and Nicola, jolted back to reality, quickly reached under the table. She took a bottle of vodka from her bag and poured it into her glass of lemonade under the table, making sure Scotty couldn't see. She passed the vodka under the table to Margy, who took it with a sincere expression. 'You are the best friend in the fucking world,' she said to Nicola, who smiled, the first few sips of vodka warming her already, her spirits rising as she relaxed into her night out, surrounded by the people she couldn't live without.

The band started 'Whiskey in the Jar', and women were on their feet already. Big women with sparkly tops and white, bruised legs; little women with teeth missing.

Nicola felt the brown eyes of the man at the bar on her. She knew he was watching, and she liked it.

***

Micky pulled his black jacket around him as the night air took on a chill. It was ten o'clock and the club was filling up with people taking advantage of the free entry before ten-thirty. He sniffed often, eyes like a hawk's, not missing a trick. He looked like a human Titanic, the long dimple in his chin curving aggressively like an exclamation mark.

'Jeez, look at this lot,' said Stevie, Micky's door mate for the night.

Micky braced himself as a group of lads wearing pink Afro wigs approached them. 'No stags, mate, sorry,' said Micky to the lad at the head of the group.

'Ah, well this isn't a stag night, see,' the lad replied, 'it's a divorce night. My mate Alan here—'

'Do I need to say it again?' said Micky, not looking at him, but keeping his eyes on the rest of the group.

Stevie stepped up next to him. An ex-boxer like Micky, Stevie always found himself at the beck and call of the better of the two fighters. Everyone knew Micky could still knock a bloke out with one punch.

'*Let us in, you fucking twat,*' shouted a drunken skinhead from the back.

'Please?' said Alan the divorcee to Micky, pleading with his hands, 'we're not that drunk. Honest, guv.'

'Listen, lover boy,' said Micky, getting close to Alan, 'you seem like a sensible bloke. Now take your mates up the road to Legends or something, or you'll not be getting another wife anytime soon, right?'

Alan looked around at his friends.

'I'll count to ten,' said Micky, stepping back.

'Howay lads, looks shite anyway,' said Alan. They all hesitated.

'In my head,' added Micky.

Alan began rounding everyone up, but as they started moving on, the skinhead turned on his heels and headed back towards Micky. 'Who do you think you are, eh?' He stood about three feet away from Micky, pointing at him, spitting out the words. Alan pulled at his friend's T-shirt, sensing what was to come. 'Think you're a fucking hard man? Well, I know people, me, who are fucking harder than you, you lardy—'

Micky's head rammed into his face, a couple of girls waiting in the queue squealing as blood gushed from the skinhead's nose and he fell to his knees. Micky took a handkerchief from his top pocket and wiped his forehead while Alan dragged his friend away.

'There's CCTV,' Alan said, pointing to the camera up high on the side of the building, 'I'll get the police, you watch.'

'Aye, whatever,' Micky said to himself.

Stevie was handing out bits of paper to the girls in the queue who were clinging to each other. 'First drink's on the house, lasses,' he said as he ushered them inside.

'As soon as Mooney gets here, I'm off,' said Micky, composing himself.

'All right for some,' said Stevie. It pissed him off that Micky seemed able to pick and choose where and when he worked. They were still equals in his mind, but it was obvious that Micky was being primed by Tiger to move up the syndicate into a more senior position. Still, the boss knew best.

Micky sniffed once more. He couldn't be arsed with the jealousy and the 'team dynamics'. He just wanted to make money so his kids didn't grow up wanting for basics. And Nicola. She'd get a nice house off Valley Park with a dishwasher and a walk-in shower. He would make sure she was better off with him than with anyone else. It was just taking longer than he thought.

Micky was under no illusion. Nicola was out of his league, but she loved him – she'd married him, given birth to his kids. She was ten years his junior, and even better looking now than eleven years ago when they met. Her body was still shapely, slim at the waist but ample around the tits and arse, just how he liked it. Now thirty-seven, Micky had piled on the weight. He had always been stocky and muscular, and he worked out constantly at Tiger's gym, but the years of steroids and protein enhancers had taken their toll. His hair was gone, his eyes shrunken. He was mammoth, but he liked it that way. It made him threatening, and threatened people did what they were told and didn't question his opinions and make him feel stupid. Nothing made him angrier than being made to feel stupid.

By the time Mooney got to the club, it was almost ten-thirty.

'Where the fuck have you been?' Micky towered over him.

'Down the Quayside, load of footballers in, sold a mint.' Mooney was his usual twitchy self. At barely five feet tall, he couldn't control the ticks that ravaged his pock-marked face. His head was a mop of curly, greying black hair, greasy and uncombed, and his blue eyes bulged like those of a newly hatched chick. There was a smell of dampness about him. He repulsed women and he hated every last one of them for it.

'Should've seen all the sluts hoying themselves at them.' Mooney jogged on the spot, completely hyper.

'Well, there's plenty more sluts inside. And here, don't come out till you've taken at least five hundred.'

'Yes, boss.' Mooney's face lit up at being offered a club again rather than the second-rate pubs and bars that were his usual haunts. He saluted Micky and winked at Stevie as he went in the door, Stevie flaring his nostrils as if he'd smelled something rancid.

'Right, I'm off,' said Micky.

'So I'm on me own, then?'

Micky gave Stevie a look that told him to back off as he hailed down a passing taxi. 'Tiger's sending someone over,' he announced as he slid into the back seat of the cab.

The driver sat upright. 'All right, Micky lad,' he said, but Micky couldn't be doing with pleasantries. He'd been getting more and more itchy to get back to Nicola over the past hour.

'Valley Park,' he ordered and, knowing when to stay quiet, the driver pulled off.

Micky called Nicola's mobile. He called again, and then again. She hated that phone, and he hated that she never took it out with her. That was the whole point of the damn things.

As the taxi crawled through the traffic, he could feel the anger bubbling in his chest. She'd looked stunning earlier. It had taken every inch of control he'd had not to rip her face off so no one else would look at it. She'd be the best-looking bird in that pub by far, and if she was pissed, her lard-arse mate would have her up dancing and the blokes would be thinking their luck was in.

The queues of taxis heading around town was dense. He could have walked quicker. He covered his mouth with his hand, breathing deeply to fight off the frustration. He clenched his jaw and dialled her number again. He'd ram that fucking phone down her throat if she didn't answer this time.

***

Lee soaked up this long-lost haunt from his past. The upholstery was a soft green now, rather than the tan-coloured leather of the 1980s. He could remember sinking his fingers into the cracks of the leather and pulling out the stuffing while his dad moaned about people leaving green crisps in the ashtrays. Frank had brought him here for his first pint on his sixteenth birthday. You didn't wait until you were eighteen on Valley Park. Sixteen years later he was in the same bar, staring at a woman as she danced to

'The Irish Rover'. He watched her hips move. She spun around on one foot, propelling herself with the other, her hands above her head. His eyes burned from lack of blinking. She stood out somehow, her skin too clear, her eyes too bright, her smile too white – dare he say it, too good for the place.

The song came to an end and the pub was full of cheers. The band moved on to 'The Twelfth of Never' and couples got up to slow dance. Nicola fell into her seat, out of breath, her hair wet at the fringe with sweat. As she pulled at her top to cool herself down, she stole a look at Lee, took in his tall, slim frame, brown eyes, the fair, wavy hair receding slightly at the temples. When their eyes met, he smiled, his face creasing into ripples of skin across his cheeks right up to his ears.

Margy peered suspiciously at Lee over her glass. This could go one way or the other, and she hoped it wasn't the other. Although she would happily see Nicola free of that dickhead husband of hers, she also knew how much danger something like this could put her in. Just the fact that someone else was looking at her like that could throw Micky into a frenzy, and Margy knew what he was capable of. She looked to Mark, wondering if he'd noticed the silent flirtation, but Mark sat straight and unmoving, his eyes piercing something in the near distance. She followed his gaze to the bar, and nudged Nicola gently. They all stared at the back of his fiery red head. Tyrone Woods.

Nicola put her hand on Mark's arm, but he was up and out of his seat, not noticing Kim's drink falling to the floor.

It was a few seconds before Tyrone sensed the breath on the back of his neck. He turned, started, and tried to move away, but was hemmed in by men wanting their drinks, their women waiting thirstily at their tables.

'A word,' said Mark, his fists tight at his sides.

Tyrone wiped his young, lipless mouth, his eyes darting around the pub. 'Nar, you're all right,' he said tensely in a drawling Derry accent.

'Still gonna do it?' Mark said in Tyrone's ear. 'Still gonna lie for the filth?'

Tyrone's tiny blue eyes were normally daggers, a warning to stay the hell away. But the boldness Mark was used to in this boy was gone. Like Mark, he was anxious and frightened. Tyrone's eyes shot towards the exit, but Mark put his head in the path of any gaze that wasn't directed into his own face.

Lee, sitting just a few feet away, noticed the change in atmosphere. The red-haired kid at the bar looked scared out of his wits, and Nicola and her two companions no longer smiled and laughed and drank their vodka. They sat huddled together, watching, finding comfort in each other's hands.

Nicola watched in alarm as she saw Tyrone's older brother, Gerry, emerge from the men's toilets and stride towards his brother and Mark. His long, bandy legs, round shoulders and hawklike face gave him a grizzly, cartoon-like appearance. Gerry Woods was ugly, and he had a reputation for not stopping until his opponent was either unconscious or dead.

'Back off, cunt.' Gerry's hand pushed at Mark's chest, forcing him backwards into the drink of the toothless, grinning old drunkard.

Nicola was there in a flash, despite Margy's attempts to keep her in her seat. Mark pushed her to one side, but Nicola stood her ground and looked up at Gerry with narrowed eyes, pointing a warning finger at him over Mark's protective arm.

'You lay one finger on him, and my husband will kill you.'

On Mark's persistent orders she went back to her seat reluctantly and glared at Tyrone's anxious face. Tyrone Woods, barely seventeen, not a millimetre of his face free of a freckle, and the key witness in the prosecution. Next week he would swear under oath that Mark had sold him ecstasy and cocaine and offered him heroin out the back of the youth centre where Mark used to volunteer on Wednesday and Friday nights before his arrest.

Gerry seized Mark's T-shirt at the neck and threw him back against the bar. 'Don't be messing with witnesses now, Mr Redmond. Might add a few years to your sentence.'

'I just wanted a word, mate,' said Mark, struggling to keep his cool.

Gerry's body forced Mark's back against the ledge of the bar until his stomach heaved. He swallowed some vomit but showed no emotion.

'I am not your mate,' said Gerry, his Irish accent even thicker than his brother's. He pointed to Tyrone who stood tensely at the bar, smoking, his eyes on his pint. 'Leave him alone, or I'll fucking waste you before they can bang you up.'

Lee glanced at Nicola, biting her nails. She stole a look back at him and, realising he was scrutinising the situation, took her fingers away from her mouth. She sighed, feeling calmer, safer. No way would Gerry Woods dare hurt Micky Kelly's brother-in-law.

The song came to an abrupt end and the band announced they were taking a fifteen-minute break which was met with humorous moaning and booing from the rest of the customers, unaware of the rising conflict.

'See you next week then, *mate*,' said Gerry, letting go of Mark's T-shirt as people's attention turned from the band to the bar. 'Now we'd like to enjoy our beer, so fuck off.' He pushed Mark back once more for effect before making his way back to his little brother.

Mark wiped down his T-shirt and looked over at his sister's worried face, feeling the humiliation burn his neck, sensing the world crushing in on him from all sides. He'd never been able to fight, but he could run. Fast. And there was nowhere to run this time except all the way to jail, a jail full of men like Gerry Woods.

The searing heat reached his cheeks. His ears pounded; his eyes filled with seething water. He moved slowly to the middle of the room and raised his voice above the chattering drinkers.

'What've they got on you, Tyrone, eh? What they paying you?'

Older brother Gerry slammed his pint down on the bar and turned slowly like a witch at Halloween.

Silence fell on the pub and all eyes turned towards Mark.

'I never thought they'd turn you, mate,' Mark said. 'Never thought they'd turn you into a *fucking liar*.'

Gerry lunged and Mark was round the back of the bar in seconds, Scotty holding two pints above his head. They were soon knocked out of his hands as Gerry got round the other side, staggering, and slipping on the wet floor.

'Come on, lads, take it outside,' pleaded the barman.

There was chaos. Women were screaming, men shouting. Lee jumped from his bar stool, but the alcohol and rush of adrenalin made him sway and lose his footing. He fell to the floor and someone ran into him, knocking him onto his back. He told himself to get a grip, but he felt completely useless. Standing up with the help of Scotty, he got his bearings. Nicola was on her feet, not knowing where to put herself while Margy sat on the edge of her seat with a protective arm around Kim, the other hand firmly grasping her drink.

Mark, knowing that going outside would be the end of him, ran circles around the pub, leaping over chairs and dodging Gerry at every turn. Lee searched his pockets for his mobile, found it, but heard fresh screaming before he could get a proper hold of it. He caught the glint of Gerry's weapon and instinct took over.

He was behind him before he knew it and had Gerry in an armlock and on the floor a few seconds later. He wrestled the knife from his hand and it fell onto the sticky carpet, but another hand had snatched it away before he could get a grip of it. He looked up to see Nicola holding the blade, then the boot hit his face and he was flying backwards. He rolled over, crouching on his hands and knees, blood and spit falling to the floor. He blinked up at Tyrone, his adolescent body in a fighting stance, his pink face riddled with terror.

Lee coughed and turned his head, the noise around him blotted out with pain. He blinked, trying to focus. He could see the toothless old man at the bar behind him, one hand held to his chest, the other outstretched as he burst into 'Danny Boy'. Ahead of him, Mark was on the floor in a ball, being kicked to shreds by Gerry, Nicola throwing herself at her brother's assailant, knife in hand, only to be tossed to the floor every time. To his right, Scotty stood by the singing old man with a baseball bat held aloft.

The band's singer suddenly appeared and grabbed hold of Tyrone, his arms up behind his back in a jiffy. Lee recognised the move and an ex-copper when he saw one. Gerry, hearing Tyrone's cries for help, gave Mark one last kick and strode towards his brother. Snatching the baseball bat from Scotty, Lee stood between the two siblings, the blood from his nose running into his mouth. Gerry scoffed, and Lee held up the bat in defence while Nicola stood next to the crumpled Mark, the knife still hanging loosely in her hand.

Mark saw his opportunity and snatched the knife, staggering to his feet as Tyrone shouted a warning to his brother. Mark lurched up behind Gerry, who turned around to face him.

Gerry felt the edge of the knife penetrate his shirt and break the skin of his belly before Mark hesitated at the sound of Nicola's screams. The pub had completely emptied out. Only the toothless, old man remained, sniggering through wet lips.

'You're fucked, Redmond,' said Gerry.

Nicola heard her voice in her head, but her lips remained frozen, her screams silenced by fear. *Don't do anything stupid.*

Mark teetered, his eyes bloodshot, his face dripping with sweat and blood, his ribs shattered. His hand tightened around the knife. Just one thrust. 'If I'm going down, I might as well take out one of you while I'm at it.' He spoke through gritted teeth, the knife pointed at Gerry's liver.

Lee, realising he would have to come clean, slid his hand into his back pocket to retrieve his police ID, but before he could bring it out, they were joined by an impressively heavy man with a shaved head, black suit and white shirt. He was a bruiser, the folds of fat on his thick neck pouring over his shirt collar. Everybody stared at him like he was Christ or something.

'Put your fucking toy away,' Micky ordered Mark.

Mark didn't move and Micky walked up to him, held out his hand, nodding towards Nicola. Looking at his sister's streaked, petrified face, Mark gave Gerry one last glare and stepped back, handing the knife to Micky who squared up to Gerry, his face an inch away from his.

'Fuck off, you Fenian piece of shit.'

Gerry curled his lip, spat on the floor at Micky's feet, and looked around him before walking towards the exit, picking Tyrone up off the floor on his way.

Micky watched them leave through pinpoint eyes, then he turned and marched up to Lee.

'No, Micky.' Nicola held his arm. 'He was helping.'

'We don't need your help,' Micky said, ripping the baseball bat from Lee's hand and motioning to Nicola and the others to follow him outside. They all responded without question, quickly gathering bags and coats, Margy helping the wasted Kim to her feet. Micky put his arm around Nicola and she leant into him, Lee watching, trying to get his coat on with Scotty's help.

'Why did no one call the police?' Lee asked him.

The barman scoffed and shuffled away.

Outside, Nicola eased her arm from Micky's grip. 'My phone,' she said. 'I must've left it on the seat.'

'If you've got your phone, why didn't you fucking answer it?' asked Micky sharply.

'Jesus, Micky, calm down, I don't even know how to switch the bloody thing on.'

'I'll get it,' said Micky, irritated.

'No,' she said with an authority her husband didn't like one bit. 'Don't leave them out here on their own. I know where it is.'

Micky's eye twitched, but as Mark fell to his knees again, he sighed, looked heavenward, and nudged his head

23

towards the pub door before leaning down to pick Mark up.

Nicola hurried back into the pub and walked up to a bleeding Lee who finally had his coat on. She stood in front of him, her swollen, blackened eyes locked onto his.

Glancing down, Lee noticed her wedding ring as she subtly took hold of his little finger. His eyes darted to the exit door, beyond it to the bouncer with the attitude. He looked back into her eyes.

'Thank you,' she said. And she was gone.

TWO

At 8.45 on Monday morning Lee emerged from his hire car outside a towering, Victorian red-brick building, incongruous amidst the surrounding grey concrete flats and metal-shuttered shops. Hundred-year-old police lamps stood at the top of a broad staircase, standing to attention on either side of the double glass doors. Lee imagined an old Dickensian gentleman in a battered top hat lighting them with a burning torch.

He walked up the steps and through the doors into a silent, bleak station, green plastic chairs lined up on either side of the fortified-glass reception. Posters adorned every inch of the walls, advertising helplines for drug users, victims of domestic violence and the homeless. It could have been any police station in any city from the inside.

Lee shivered despite the warmth of the sun outside and approached reception. He was keen to get started. The job was in the east of the city, a place he was unfamiliar with, its sprawling estates and flat landscape a world away from the West End's steep streets and protracted views of the industrial landscape of Gateshead. He was invited by a laminated sign to 'Press the buzzer ONLY ONCE and WAIT'. He was about to press it a second time when a slim young woman in jeans and a hooded sweatshirt, brown hair in a ponytail, appeared at reception carrying a cup of coffee. She smiled at him. She couldn't have been more than twenty-two or three.

Lee bid her good morning and she replied likewise, jumping to sit on the high swivel chair behind the glass. She blew on her coffee and took three quick slurps, looking up at him with curious eyes.

'DS Lee Jamieson,' he said, 'I'm starting here.' She looked at him over her mug, expressionless. 'Today,' he added, 'to work?'

She blew on her coffee once more and took another sip. Lee fished his ID from his inside pocket and pressed it to the glass, the young woman turning her head to one side to read it.

'Through that door,' she said.

Lee heard a click and a buzz to his right, and when he headed through to the back of the reception the woman held out her hand.

'DC Thompson,' she said.

He shook her hand, and she pointed to a door sporting a 'Staff Only' sign.

'The boss is waiting for you,' she said. 'Turn right, second door on your left.' Her eyes followed him through the reception area to the door, a private smile on her face. About time there was some eye candy around here.

Lee walked into an open-plan office, pairs of eyes looking up at him without acknowledgement. He nodded a greeting anyway, taking in the leaning towers of files and straining his nostrils against the sickly smell of disinfectant. He looked around for an office and, spotting a line of three doors, headed towards them. He knocked on the second door just beneath a sign reading 'Detective Inspector Carole Meadows'. On her *Come in,* he entered the office. His gaze fell on the gently lined face of a woman in her late forties wearing a grey trouser suit and white, open-necked shirt, standard uniform for women DIs, it seemed.

The DI stood as he entered. She was the shape that countless women complain of, flat-chested and wide-hipped, her blonde/grey hair cut into the severe shortness of a woman who just didn't have time in the morning. Her spectacles were a little too wide, giving her a slightly cross-eyed look. She walked around her desk and greeted him warmly, offering a handshake.

'Welcome home,' she said, 'Sit, sit.' She indicated one of the two chairs opposite her desk.

Lee sat and watched her eyes scan the bruised cheekbone and cut over one of his eyes. He touched his face.

'Coffee?' she asked, walking to a percolator full of treacle-coloured liquid.

He declined and she poured herself a large mug then walked back to a desk that was completely in order, the out-tray empty and a few pieces of white and pink paper in the in-tray. Her computer was devoid of Post-it notes, a box of tissues to one side, and a single pen, pencil and ruler stood perfectly straight in a desk tidy.

'So, no need to tell you what a great city this is,' she said. He tried to place the accent. West country? He nodded his head in agreement, clasping his hands together on his lap, wondering what exactly the greatness was he'd left behind sixteen years ago. 'We've got big plans for this city,' she said earnestly, 'but some places are out of control. That's why you're here.'

'Looks amazing – the Quayside, the city centre—'

'Completely transformed,' she finished his sentence for him. 'But there are problem areas, like I said, serious problems that we need help with.' Lee knew it – Byker, Walker ... 'And there's none worse than Valley Park Estate.'

Lee crossed his legs and shifted in his seat. Surely not.

'Here are the crime figures.' She pushed a bound document towards him. 'They're a shocking read.'

Lee took the document but didn't open it.

'We want the estate turned around, big regeneration plans.'

Lee wondered who 'we' was. 'But Valley Park is West, the job was an East End ...' He tapered off when she regarded him as if he'd just told her the most obvious thing in the world. Her eyes flashed with annoyance. This was a woman who did not like to be challenged.

'So why now?' asked Lee. 'Why not just bulldoze the place, start again?'

'Oof, too expensive.' She waved her hand as if swatting a fly. 'The Council have just got their hands on millions to tart the place up, but they need to show they've got the support of the residents before the cash flow starts, and the crime rate's got to come down so they can mix it up a bit, you know, tenure-wise – bring in the private sector, build some nice flats, a few young professionals, maybe a Pizza Hut or something. But at the minute, no young city dweller with any sense is going to buy a flat anywhere near the place.'

Lee turned the ends of his mouth downwards and nodded. Damn right.

'We're all working in partnership these days,' she said. 'Pain in the neck, but it's the only way to get any money out of anyone. It's partnership money that's paying for you, so they'll want their money's worth.'

'They' now, not 'we', Lee noticed.

'So.' She opened a drawer to her right and brought out a thick glossy document, considered it for a moment and passed it to Lee. 'A socio-economic study. Read it.' She reached into the drawer again and brought out another, smaller but equally glossy document. 'Residents and Stakeholder Survey,' she said, passing it to him. It was quickly followed by a Regeneration Delivery Framework, Strategic Health Needs Assessment, SWOT Analysis, Housing Forecasts, Spatial Plan, and a Crime Reduction Strategy. Lee held them all on his knee knowing what they would say without even looking at them. Valley Park was poor, sick, neglected and forgotten. It was in crisis, and no one could afford more riots.

'There's a meeting tonight at the community centre on the estate,' she said, supping the coffee and wincing at its coldness. 'I'd like you to go. No one will know who the hell you are so for God's sake, don't let on you're one of us. Not yet, anyway. And try to cover those up before you come in next.'

Lee touched his face again and was about to offer some feeble explanation, but DI Meadows was picking up her phone.

'Let's meet the team,' she said, 'and please: help yourself to coffee.' It was an order rather than an offer.

***

A few minutes later, Lee was holding a cup of treacle, surrounded by what appeared to be the Addams Family.

'Everyone, this is DS Jamieson who is taking over the team, from today.' DI Meadows was standing next to Lee in front of the desk. 'Lee, this is DC Clark, recently moved over from the Drug Squad.' A ginger drip in his mid-thirties,

Clark smiled crookedly, his teeth all over the place, his eye contact non-existent. 'And this is DC Gallagher. Paul.' Lee was approached by a beer-bellied man of about forty wearing a red-checkered shirt bursting at the waist and a blue-striped tie, both of which had seen better days.

'Welcome to Little Beirut,' said Gallagher offering his hand. Lee shook it, noticing the smell of stale tobacco, alcohol, and something else funky he couldn't quite decipher. Next to be introduced was Jane Thompson whom he'd met at reception, a reasonably attractive rookie with clear skin and hazel eyes.

'DC Gallagher's been acting up, until we filled the post,' DI Meadows informed Lee.

'Always the bridesmaid,' mocked Gallagher. 'A bit like you, eh, Thompson?'

DI Meadows stepped in. 'Jane, why don't you show DS Jamieson around the patch,' she said, seating herself back behind her desk, ready for the next task at hand.

'My pleasure,' replied Thompson, giving Gallagher a derisive smile.

'I can manage,' said Lee.

'Best have the guided tour,' replied Meadows, adjusting her glasses and not looking up from the papers in front of her.

Lee wasn't going to argue and Thompson indicated with her head, 'this way.'

***

DC Thompson waited impatiently at traffic lights on the West Road.

'So, how long is it since you've lived here?' she asked.

'About sixteen years.'

'You might be in for a shock.'

They drove in silence for a few minutes. At the cemetery they turned left down a steep hill, a narrow road of terraced Tyneside flats, every fifth one of which, despite brand new front yard walls and railings, was boarded up. The view was stunning, looking down the hill to the river and Gateshead beyond. Anywhere else and people would be snapping these up and making a small fortune.

Halfway down the hill, Thompson turned right and Lee felt the recognition like a slap in the face.

'Hang on, pull over here,' he said, leaning forward to see more clearly through the windscreen.

Thompson screeched to a halt not far from a group of young lads of about fourteen or fifteen playing football on some spare ground. They jeered at Thompson's bad parking, and as she ground the gears in an attempt to straighten up, the lads cheered and laughed even louder.

Lee got out of the car, drawn to a burnt-out house nearby. He surveyed the street, recognised the corner shop and headed to it, frowning at the cock and ball graffiti on the wall, next to it the words *Fucking Fuck Off Paki* in red.

In the shop Lee waited, holding a can of Tango behind a couple of spotty girls with toddlers in buggies buying lottery tickets.

'I want me hair like that for me wedding,' said one pointing to a *Hello!* magazine on the counter.

'You gonna sell your photos for a million, eh?' asked the shopkeeper cheerily.

'Aye, friggin' gorgeous, me.' The girls laughed, turning their buggies and banging the wheels painfully into Lee's leg. He let them past graciously.

'Divvy cunt,' one of them said.

'*Divvy cunt!*' one of the toddlers repeated, and the girls laughed louder.

'*Divvy cunt! Divvy cunt!*' the kid repeated, loving the attention.

The door closed and Lee passed a pound coin to the shopkeeper who was shaking his head, half-smiling, half-disgusted.

'Have you reported that graffiti?' asked Lee. 'They'll come and remove it.'

'Ach, no point, it would just be there again the next day,' he replied. 'I wouldn't care, but I'm from Bangladesh me, I ain't no fucking Paki.' He thrust the change at Lee, who took it with a raised eyebrow before leaving the shop to find Thompson waiting outside, watching the young lads closely. He stood next to her, shielding his eyes from the sun.

'Didn't you play out on the streets when you were young?' he asked.

'This lot don't play, they do business,' replied Thompson, eyeing them suspiciously. 'You know this street?'

Lee nodded. 'See that burnt-out house?'

Thompson looked up the road to a gaping hole in the terrace.

'My grandad lived there,' said Lee, 'with five of the deadliest cats you've ever had the pleasure of smelling.'

***

Lee had been sitting in his car outside the house in High Heaton for half an hour when the black couple emerged, laughing, off out to the pictures or to meet friends for dinner. They climbed into their silver Golf and drove off. Switching on the internal light, he looked at his list. This was the second house he'd stalked this evening. He'd spent the afternoon looking up all the Deborah Turners he could. Being an officer of the law had its perks, access to information being one of them. Of course, it was likely she was married, living somewhere else even, but Lee believed in starting at the beginning. If this didn't work, then he'd check the marriage records, births, deaths, whatever it took.

There were seven Deborah Turners of the right age living in Newcastle. The first house he'd sat outside was a West End dive, a student house with dirty windows and holes in the roof. The property he looked at now wasn't the right one either. Wrong ethnicity. He checked his A to Z and set off with a determined sigh.

Ten minutes later, he sat outside a standard semi-detached house near the Freeman Hospital with wide bay windows and a trimmed garden to the front, a green Renault Clio in the drive. A woman's car.

Lee looked at his watch, it was 6.36 p.m. It was a squally evening, the sky dim and moody almost like night, and the house he stared at was in darkness. This was the sort of home his mother had yearned for. Forever going through the Homemaker section of the Saturday *Journal*, she'd ring houses with a pen, commenting on the prices, how long it would take to save up for the deposit, and how much they would need to earn to pay the mortgage. She was dead some fourteen years now – ravaged by drink, but it was the cancer that got her in the end. He hadn't found out until six months after she'd gone, his father choosing to cremate her alone without Lee or her smashed friends hanging around, reminding him of his failures. Frank had gone a year later, a letter from a solicitor giving Lee the details of his fatal pneumonia and the two thousand pounds he'd left to the

British Legion. At the age of nineteen, Lee had felt utterly alone.

A light came on in the front room of the house and he opened the car window to get a better view. Inside, a slim woman in her thirties with a straight, blonde bob wearing a red tracksuit walked to the side of the room and stopped, messing with something on a shelf. A young girl joined her and started leaping about, spiky, dyed red hair and dressed in a tieless school uniform. The woman joined in and they both danced around the lounge to the silent music.

After a minute or two, she came to the window and he saw her clearly as she took a curtain in each hand and snapped them closed, shutting him out. Lee turned to face forward, winding up the car window.

Debbie.

Looking at the dashboard he noticed the time. 6.55 p.m.

Shit. The damned public meeting.

***

The rain was falling in sheets when Lee arrived at the community centre. He expected to see a hall full of buzzing residents, as was his experience in London – tell anyone you're going to be knocking down a few houses and they would be out in force, arguing for a brand spanking new youth club as compensation. He entered a large, dank room brightened only by the orange and purple drawings of toddlers. Hundreds of chairs had been set out theatre style, but only around twenty people occupied them, facing a line of men of various sizes and ages sitting at a trestle table at the front of the hall.

Lee took a seat at the back and picked up a glossy leaflet from his chair entitled *Valley Park: Your Lives, Your Future.*

He yawned and sat back while a lanky Council worker in his fifties, an identity badge hanging from his neck, stood up and addressed the room over the top of his glasses. Lee lost him at *Director of Regeneration*, his monotone voice and annoying flat 'r' causing his eyes to close. Feeling himself nod off, he straightened up in his seat, his eyes falling on the back of two heads a few rows from the front. He sat up a little straighter, suddenly alert – it was her, with her matronly friend.

Lee's attention turned back to the top table. After introducing a couple of boring-looking planner types, the Director turned his attention to a young man sitting to his right, a consultant of about twenty-five, wearing a sharp, grey suit, Armani glasses and a shaggily precise haircut. He reminded Lee of the guys drinking in the bar of the hotel. Clean, educated, ambitious. Matt was his name. *Figures*, thought Lee, *would have to be Matt or Dan or Sam.* The short but smart names of the middle class.

The show kicked off with a slick presentation on a screen which Matt operated via remote control. It showed smiley, happy, virtual people in clean, tree-lined streets, pushing buggies, carrying shopping bags and talking on their mobile phones, having lovely lives. A glass, high-rise block of balconied flats, with a cafe at the base, slim people of all colours and creeds drinking cappuccinos and glasses of white wine, or working on their laptops. Matt talked of outcomes, of improved health, more jobs and better GCSE results. Social capital. Community engagement. A safer, cleaner, greener life for all. The residents watched, unmoving, frowning in mass concentration until the Director thanked Matt and invited questions.

Silence.

Margy spoke to Nicola under her breath, 'Snog, marry or suck off.'

Nicola's laugh was loud in the soundless room and she stifled it with a hand, nudging Margy to shut up.

Margy grinned at her. 'I reckon I've had him,' she whispered, nodding towards one of the planners, 'On the Town Moor. Spotty arse.'

Nicola scraped her chair away from Margy who giggled naughtily, told her to 'watch this', then stood up, taking on a commanding air.

Lee ducked down in his chair.

'I've got a question,' said Margy, tersely. 'Didn't you do up these houses a few years ago? I mean, what's the bloody point if people are just gonna trash them?'

Nicola stood up to join her. They were a team when it came to slagging off the Council. 'It's not the houses, man, it's the people,' she said to assenting voices.

The voice of an old Scottish woman added to the growing mumbling. 'When there's scum livin' everywhere, you can't even go out without gettin' mugged for your fish and chips.'

'Hey!' another voice came from the other side of the room, a thickset woman with a shaggy, plum-coloured perm, white roots and a Borstal spot on her right cheekbone. She pointed at the old Scot. 'Who you calling scum? I've lived here forty years and I'm not scum.'

The floodgates were open.

'There's kids of five and six oot burnin' cars,' the old Glaswegian ranted.

The Director stepped in, his hands held up in appeasement. 'Let's not get into a bun fight, ladies.'

Lee winced and sunk lower in his seat as the Director continued, 'The reason we're here tonight is to get *your* views on the regeneration of the area. Involve *you* in what's going on. We can't do this without the community on board.'

Margy wasn't one for being patronised by paper-pushers. 'But you're not involving us,' she said, looking around for support, 'you're telling us what's gonna happen.'

Nicola felt the soapbox under her feet. 'And we're telling you,' she pointed at them, 'there's no point if you don't deal with the people who come in, wreck the place, then piss off. They're the ones who make the place crap, not the stupid houses.'

There was a ripple of applause from those present as she turned to sit down, noticing Lee at the back of the room as she did so. She dropped into her seat, her heart speeding up, her face red with embarrassment. Jesus, he'd think she was a right whiny old bag now.

'All you wanna do is bring in a load of yuppies,' yelled the plum-haired woman, turning to the consultant, Matt: 'No offence, bonny lad, but I bet they're paying you more in a day than we get in a month of benefits.'

And so it went on. The planners shifted in their seats uncomfortably, not used to being away from their computers and thrust out into the nasty world of actual people. None of them stood a chance.

***

When the meeting was finally over, the consultant and Council workers huddled around the projector and laptop, talking in hushed voices. Lee wandered over to the door of a windowless kitchen, battered and musty, the overhead fluorescent light buzzing and flickering annoyingly. Inside,

Nicola and Margy were pushing the tea urn back into its place.

'S'cuse me,' he said, and they turned their heads simultaneously. 'I was looking for the Gents.'

'Other side,' said Margy curtly, 'but the doors are locked.' Lee looked around him and hesitated.

Nicola slapped Margy on the arm. 'Here, he can use the office one.'

'The office is locked an' all,' said Margy, wiping her hands on a tea towel.

'Well then, I'll get the key,' replied Nicola, giving her a tight-lipped glare.

Margy looked from Lee to Nicola, sighed and pushed past them. 'I'll see you the morra,' she called, 'and don't be late!'

Nicola gave Lee a little shrug. 'I'll get the key,' she said.

'No, you're all right,' he said quickly, moving in front of her. 'I erm, I just wanted the chance to speak to you.' Nicola cleared her throat and waited. 'At the pub, the other night.' Lee fished around for the right words but they weren't coming. 'Were you okay, after …?'

She half-smiled. 'I'm fine, I know it was a bit mental but that's just how it is round here.'

'I know,' he said apologetically, then paused. 'I used to live here.'

'Nah,' she said, disbelieving. 'Where?'

'18 Elm Street.'

She smiled and looked at him curiously. 'That's near me,' she said. 'So why did you come to the meeting?'

'Well, partly because I've got a soft spot for the place, partly work.'

Nicola frowned cautiously. 'D'you work for the Council?'

He shook his head. 'Not directly but I have to work with them.' Nicola looked confused and Lee wasn't explaining further.

'Fair enough,' she shrugged, switching off the flickering light, 'but don't listen to them, they tell nowt but lies.' Lee laughed and followed her out of the kitchen, hovering awkwardly as she locked the door. 'Look, I'm really sorry but I've got to go,' she said.

'Yeah, sorry.'

For a moment their eyes met: there was chemistry. Nicola looked at his bruised, cut face and wanted to touch it, give him some comfort, then realised it was her fault he had it in the first place.

'Can I ... walk you home? Or something?' The words tumbled out of his mouth and tailed off as he realised the immaturity of what he was saying.

Nicola felt herself blush like a schoolkid. 'Have you got a car?'

'I left it on the West Road. In case it got pinched,' he joked and she laughed.

'Cheeky,' she said, 'But I wouldn't mind a hand with the shutters.'

As they walked out of the community centre, shoulder to shoulder, Lee couldn't help sizing her up. She was around five foot seven, strong-shouldered and straight-backed, the cute freckles on her nose softening the sharp edges of her features. Out in the damp evening air he pulled at the creaking, rusty shutters, wondering how she ever did this alone.

'Margy's usually here,' she said as if she'd read his mind, 'and she's a big lass.'

He laughed. 'Your huffy friend.'

Nicola was fiddling with the padlock now – it looked giant-sized in her hands. 'She's just looking out for me,' she said.

He took the lock from her, bent down and threaded it through the bolts, snapping it shut and offering a 'you're welcome' to her 'thank you.'

They started to walk along the road flanked by boarded-up properties. It was desolate apart from the dim light of a small supermarket in the distance.

Eventually she asked, 'When did you leave?'

'When I was sixteen. Had a fight with me dad and he chucked me out.'

'Lucky you.'

'Not really,' he said. 'Circumstances were horrible.'

'I bet you live somewhere nice now, though.'

'I'm homeless,' he said, and Nicola looked shocked: how could someone like him be homeless? 'Technically,' he explained, 'moved back for the job, need to find a place.'

'Well, don't let the Council put you back here, it's a dump and the police never leave you alone.' She shook her head. 'It's a wonder they weren't there tonight, blathering on, spouting rubbish. I hate them.'

Lee's stomach turned a little. 'Hate is a strong word,' he said.

'They've made my brother's life hell,' she said bitterly.

It was quiet for the next fifty yards until they reached the supermarket. She looked down the street at the crossroads while he looked up towards the West Road.

'I'll walk you down,' he said.

She wanted him to, but she knew it would be reckless. 'I'm okay,' she said confidently as she turned to him, his eyes resting on her face for just a moment too long. 'I'm Nicola, by the way.'

'Lee,' he said.

'Thanks for stepping in at the pub.'

He nodded. 'He took quite a beating.'

'The police would've just finished the job,' she said.

Lee cleared his throat. 'Well, my car's just up here,' he said.

'Yeah, I'm ...' She pointed over her shoulder, down the hill from the fortified shop.

'Bye then,' he said.

He watched as she walked down the hill, willing her to turn around. She didn't, and the world was suddenly empty, the only sound his own lungs pumping air in and out. He should have told her.

Next time, he thought. If he ever saw her again.

THREE

The nursery was buzzing with children, parents and smiling staff and volunteers, the smell of fresh paint and cement affirming its newness. It had taken years of petitions, letters, fighting – always fighting – to get their little ones out of the mouldy church hall and into the sort of nursery that children of more deserving areas enjoyed. Margy had led the campaign with the determination of a presidential candidate.

When Nicola walked into the brightness, flowers and bunting adorning the walls, she felt like she'd just stepped over the rainbow. It looked dazzling, and she felt something she hadn't felt in a long time: hope. It was a beautiful, crisp and sunny morning, a blessed change from the relentless showers of the last few days. The sun streamed through the high windows, slashing the light onto a sea of small faces. The children sat on the floor in rows, some of them yawning, some looking around for their mams, some sitting quietly in their too big cardigans, staring open-mouthed at the juice and biscuits, waiting to be consumed if they were good.

Nicola clung to Liam's hand and scoured the room for Mark and Kim, but she couldn't see them. Mark was in court later that afternoon but had promised to be there for his nephew's big moment.

She bent down to Liam. 'Now remember to smile, okay?' Liam nodded his reply and she let go of his hand, pointing to one of the nursery workers and giving him a gentle nudge. Liam stepped over the squirming legs of the other children, looking back at Nicola who gave him an encouraging wink.

The adults' chairs were at the back of the room where Nicola spotted Margy with her husband, Joe, his eyes red with tiredness after a long night shift on the road. Joe was a gentle soul, his heart as big as his beer gut. Their son, Jimmy, was the double of him, wide-set eyes behind thick glasses, a jutting jaw and a button nose.

Margy patted the seat next to her on the front row, right next to the window. Nicola was delighted – she'd be able to see it all from there. Margy was explaining to Joe the type of glass used in the windows, the cost of the whiteboard, the length of time it took to import the roof tiles from Belgium, the energy-efficiency measures that had been built into the cavity walls. Joe nodded the odd '*aye*' and shook the odd '*never!*' with his head. He knew how much this nursery meant to her. He knew all too well the amount of time she'd spent raising money, shouting at politicians and civil servants. Her commitment to Valley Park left little time for him and Jimmy, but he wouldn't have her any other way. The estate seemed to be her life's mission, and this nursery was her first big achievement. He'd never been prouder, and so he forced his eyes open and resigned himself to another hour of wakefulness.

The tiny mayor and his ridiculously tall wife entered the hall to lazy applause. Nicola could sense Margy stifling giggles, Joe nudging her in the ribs, covering his own dimpled grin with his hand. It was bizarre to Nicola to think of herself with a man smaller than her. Micky was heavy and strong, and with him she had, ironically, always felt protected. He'd been on his best behaviour lately –

wasn't spending so much time at the gym and had even taken Michael Jnr to school a couple of times, much to the delight of their eldest son who thought the sun shone out of his dad's arse. There was a time when she would have welcomed this change, but now it lay heavy on her shoulders as she dug deep inside herself to cuddle him back, kiss him back, enjoy the sex. She struggled to fit her arms around his bulk, his lips felt wet and spongy, and she'd taken to faking it just to get it over with.

She concentrated on the children singing a tuneless song, looking at Liam who sang the wrong words, her heart melting at the cuteness of it. After the song was finished everyone clapped and a few of the adults wiped their eyes, others yawning with boredom, needing a fag or to get back to bed.

While the mayor began to speak about schools being at the heart of communities, Nicola's mind wandered. Over the last few days she'd had to shake her head free of the image of Lee, the touch of his hand on her arm and the lines of his face rippling from the corners of his mouth to the corners of his eyes when he smiled. As she stared blankly out of the window, an image disturbed her thoughts: a woman with bleached blonde hair staggering along the street in fluffy mule slippers and a short skirt, holding her denim jacket close to her chest. Nicola turned away and shook her head: *surely it's a bit late for the walk of shame,* she thought. She felt a shudder run through her as the sun fell behind clouds and darkened the room.

Liam stood shyly, holding a small posy of flowers in one hand, and clinging to the skirt of the nursery worker with the other. He looked round for Nicola who gave him the thumbs-up. He grinned, his cheeks red like apples, and his eyes turned back to the floor in front of him.

As the speech came to an end, Nicola glanced out of the window again. The blonde woman was nearer now, her steps so quick she looked almost comical. Nicola raised an eyebrow as she noticed blood running down one of the woman's legs, and she sat up in her chair to get a better view. Then her stomach hit her mouth. It was Mark's wife, Kim.

She grabbed Margy's arm and Margy turned to look out of the window, too. Kim was limping towards the school, her left hand and left leg streaming with blood.

'Oh my God,' Nicola said under her breath.

She had no choice but to watch as Liam handed the posy of flowers to the mayor's wife, everyone clapping and smiling. Nicola clapped along, the fear rising in her lungs like a furnace. She looked outside again but Kim wasn't there.

'We'll watch him, you go,' said Margy quietly, sensing Nicola's panic.

Nicola got out of her seat and stumbled, stooping and apologising towards the exit. When she got there she glared with annoyance at the red ribbon across the doors, caging her in. She looked towards the other exit, but there were too many people in the way, and the room suddenly seemed huge and stifling.

As the mayor and his wife stopped a few feet away from her to have their photo taken with a pair of scissors by the ribbon, Nicola saw Kim's terrified, blood- and tear-stained face at the glass of the door, one side of her hair chopped off oddly. She lunged forward, tearing at the ribbon and pulling the door open while people gasped and stared, straining to see what was going on. The doors swung shut behind her and, with relief, Nicola heard the piano start up and the singing begin again.

In the lobby, Nicola took the distraught Kim by the elbow and guided her to the ladies' toilets next to the reception. She could see a middle-aged secretary with glasses strung around her neck talking animatedly on the telephone, looking with horror at the drops of blood on the new laminate floor.

In the toilets, Kim was sobbing, her body bent over. 'I just asked him ...'

Nicola ran Kim's hand under the tap, blood mixing with water. 'What's happened?' she asked, trying to stay calm. 'Kim. Tell me what happened.' The wound was deep, and Nicola thought she could see the white of bone.

'I just asked him ... if he was gonna get ready for court.' Kim stuttered. 'He just went off it.'

Nicola searched her pockets for a packet of cigarettes. 'Mark did this?'

Kim nodded and Nicola lit a cigarette with steady hands, handing it to Kim who dropped it straight onto the floor. Nicola picked it up and held the cigarette to Kim's mouth. She took several long, hard drags, neither of them noticing the secretary walk into the toilets in a flap.

'I've called the police,' the woman said, a little out of breath.

'What the hell for?' retorted Nicola angrily.

The secretary looked flabbergasted at being challenged.

'I'm going round there,' said Nicola, taking a long drag off the cigarette herself, then handing it back to Kim.

'I don't think it's wise to go anywhere,' said the secretary with authority.

'It's none of your bloody business,' Nicola pointed at her aggressively.

The secretary grabbed the cigarette from Kim's hand. 'You can't smoke in here,' she said, holding the cigarette away from her like a reeking sock.

Nicola pushed her aside and ran out of the toilets with orders to get Kim's wounds seen to.

She got to the house in under a minute, running as fast as her leaden legs would carry her. She banged loudly on the door and looked through the letterbox. She could see the edge of the sofa in the living room, the filling pouring out onto the floor where the fabric had been slashed.

'Mark!' she shouted through the letterbox. 'It's me. Open the door!'

She put her ear to the letterbox, her chest heaving from the effort of running, but all she could hear was the baby crying upstairs and sirens in the distance. She stood up to try to gauge how close they were, then bent back down to the letterbox.

'Mark! Let me in, *please.*'

Getting no response, she walked up the path to see if she could spot any movement upstairs. She shaded her eyes against the sun gleaming off the window, noticing the torn net curtains of the front bedroom.

The sirens were coming closer and she ran back to the front door, hammered on the glass.

'Come on, come on,' she muttered to herself. If she could just get to him, she could talk him out of it, just like she'd done a hundred times before. She heard the police cars screech around the corner.

'Shit!' she spat. '*Mark!*'

Her face was back at the letterbox and she peered in again, but could see nothing, hear nothing other than the baby's cries which were getting louder, more frantic. When she stood and turned around she watched with amazement as four or five police cars and an armoured van pulled up, armed officers pouring out of it.

'What the ...?'

An officer in charge ordered the swarm to take positions and then held a megaphone to his mouth. Nothing came out and he fiddled with it in frustration, giving it a couple of wallops before raising it to his mouth again.

Nicola continued to pound on the door. 'Mark, just open the door before there's any bother.'

'STEP AWAY FROM THE HOUSE!' boomed the officer in charge.

Startled, Nicola turned to face the officers, looking from one blank face to another, each staring through her as if she were a piece of the infrastructure. She pursed her lips and with a final hateful glare bent down to pick up a half-brick as more sirens announced the arrival of ambulances and another unmarked car.

'PUT THAT DOWN! STEP AWAY FROM THE HOUSE!'

Lee stepped out of the unmarked car just as Nicola turned to face the front door. She smashed the brick into the glass pane, swiftly putting her hand inside and releasing the lock. She barged in, the officer in charge shaking his head and dropping the megaphone to his side, looking around in disbelief that someone would disobey his orders.

'Bastards!' Nicola sputtered. *'Bastards! Bastards! Bastards!'*

She tumbled over the baby walker and hit the floor with a thud. Pain shot through her ankle and she cried out, tears of frustration spiking her eyes. Hopping into the living room, she surveyed the devastation, the walls hacked at, curtains and furniture in pieces. She made for the stairs, dragging herself up with her hands and on one leg, wondering why Mark wasn't comforting the baby whose wails filled the house.

When she turned the corner at the top of the stairs, her hand clasped her mouth in horror. There, hanging from the catch of the loft hatch was Mark, a belt around his neck, his face contorted, his eyes bulging blood red, his tongue black and fat. The samurai knife that once hung over the fireplace lay on the floor under his feet.

'Oh no ... no.' Her shaking hand went to her heart, and she held her breath, tidal waves of nausea rocking her body.

Outside, Lee heard a cry that came from the depths of the soul, primal and anguished. Looking up at the bedroom window, he saw a hand throw it open and Nicola's face appeared.

'Help! Can somebody help!' she screamed, then disappeared.

The officer in charge held up his arms. 'Wait! Nobody moves till I give the order.'

Ignoring him, Lee hurdled the garden wall and ran into the house, taking the stairs two at a time. At the top, Nicola stood with her head through Mark's legs trying to take his weight, her face scarlet with the effort, her teeth clenched and exposed like a wrestler.

Lee quickly picked up the toppled chair, stood on it and released the belt from Mark's neck, Nicola collapsing to the floor under her brother where she lay, still and exhausted.

Lee felt for a pulse. Nothing. He bent forward and listened for breath. Still nothing. He pulled Mark from Nicola and laid him on his back, pulled back his head and started to breathe into his mouth, but the airway was blocked by the swelling in his throat and his bloated tongue, and Lee felt his own breath escaping from the sides of his mouth. Placing his hands on Mark's chest, he started compressions. One, two, three, rest. One, two, three, rest. He looked at Nicola, his sweating brow crushed with regret.

Nicola stumbled to her knees and looked down at her brother, putting her hand on Lee's arm as blood started to trickle from the side of Mark's mouth. Lee stopped, and Nicola put her hands around Mark's face, almost touching it, but frightened to feel the lifeless skin. She swallowed a sob, took Mark as gently as she could in her arms and rocked him back and forth, holding his head to her cheek, her eyes tight shut, the tears streaming out.

With Lee sitting next to her, she looked up, eyes pleading, but his expression was one of defeat.

He pulled her head towards his chest. 'He's gone,' he said gently, and she clung to the sleeves of his jacket, sobbing. When his arms closed around her she felt herself melt, allowing the grief to envelop her.

'*DS Jamieson, please respond*.' The voice came from inside Lee's jacket, and Nicola lifted her head and wiped her face.

'*DS Jamieson, pick up*.' Nicola sat up sharply now, looking at Lee's chest, puzzlement turning to dismay as he released his radio from his inside pocket and raised it to his mouth.

'Send in the paramedics,' he said in a low voice, avoiding Nicola's eyes.

Nicola sprang back away from him, clinging to Mark, trying to get him free of Lee who reached out to her.

'Get off him!' she spat.

Lee backed off and looked away, ashamed, getting to his feet as the paramedics came up the stairs to prise Mark from Nicola's arms. Nicola screamed at them to leave him alone; she clawed at their hands and kicked out with her good foot, only relenting when the cries of the baby overpowered her own. Panting, defeated, she stood slowly, wiped her face with her arm, and hobbled into the bedroom, scooping the baby out of her cot.

'Shhhhh. It's all right, it's all right,' she cooed.

The baby gave little hiccup cries as Nicola searched the cot and found her dummy, popping it into the baby's mouth as she walked back to the landing and watched the paramedics strap Mark to a stretcher, his face covered with an orange blanket. She wiped her face again and, gathering all her dignity, followed Lee and the paramedics down the stairs.

As they filed past the crowd of police, the officer in charge grabbed Lee by the arm. 'I'll be speaking to your superiors,' he scowled.

Lee pulled his arm away and skipped up to Nicola's side. 'Hang on,' he said. But Nicola kept on walking. 'We'll need to talk to you.' Nicola ignored him and pushed past a line of police officers with the baby in her arms.

'One less smackhead to worry about,' one said to the other as the stretcher was carried past them.

Nicola turned, seething. 'What did you say?' She squared up to the officer and he looked at her vacantly. 'My brother was not a smackhead, right?'

'If you say so,' he shrugged. 'Come on.' He slapped his partner on the chest with the back of his hand. 'Shift over.'

They walked away and Lee touched Nicola on the shoulder. She sprang away as if she'd got an electric shock.

'I'm sorry,' he said.

She gave him a look that told him all he needed to know. He stepped back and she limped away, her head high, her heart broken.

FOUR

'It won't happen again,' said Lee, one hand in his trouser pocket, the other holding the back of the black leather chair.

'Dead right it won't,' affirmed Carole Meadows, perched on the edge of her desk. 'You might've had a reputation to live up to in London, but you don't here.'

'I thought that's what you employed me for,' replied Lee, stony-faced.

'What, disobeying an officer in charge?'

'Getting results.'

'You didn't get a result.' DI Meadows leaned forward as Lee's shoulders fell and he looked at his feet.

'Valley Park is unpredictable.' She pointed a finger at the window. 'Send a couple of uniforms in at the wrong time and it starts a riot—'

'I know Valley Park,' interrupted Lee defensively.

'You *knew* it,' snapped Meadows. 'From now on you stick to procedure. Police procedure, *not* your own.'

Lee waited, his retaliation sticking in his throat as DI Meadows rose from her desk, sighed heavily and strode to her chair.

'Close the door behind you,' she said, conversation over.

Lee left the DI's office feeling like a kid again. He could never do anything right then, and he felt the humiliation as hotly now as when his father would rant at him day and night about how useless he was. As he walked into the silent, open-plan office he felt the eyes of his colleagues looking anywhere but at him. He sat at his desk amidst the odd cough and rustle of paper. He called Jane Thompson over.

'Everything okay?' she asked cautiously.

Lee looked petulant and avoided her eyes. 'Could you get me Mark Redmond's files, please?'

'What, all of them?'

'Yes. And where's Gallagher? We're supposed to be handing over.'

'Sick, Sarge.'

'Sick? What do you mean, sick?'

Thompson shrugged and walked away apologetically while Lee's stomach groaned with hunger: he'd had nothing since breakfast and it was fast approaching four o'clock. He was logging onto his computer when six large files marked '*Mark Anthony Redmond*', a Twix and a can of Coke appeared in front of him. He turned to see DC Thompson walking back to her desk.

'Don't mention it,' she called.

***

A couple of hours later, Lee stretched his arms over his head and turned to look around the empty office. Only a noisy pedestal fan and DC Thompson, typing steadily, remained. Lee rubbed his eyes and sighed, fatigue washing over him like the tide.

Mark's file told a different story to the one he'd heard from Nicola. As far as he could see, the persecution and harassment had generally been on Mark's part, not the police's. His records stretched back years, the sort of kid who plagued the life out of the authorities, knowing exactly what he could get away with and how to play the system.

With a first offence of shoplifting at the age of five, his run-ins with the police had become a regular occurrence over the next decade and beyond. This lad liked cars, too, twocking from the age of nine, one brand new BMW, belonging to a local magistrate, driven to Swan Hunter Docks and launched into the Tyne to its watery end. Besides the shoplifting and the petty crime, Lee counted eleven serious offences by the time Mark was ten. A copy of a care order from 1981 reported that Mark and his eight-year-old sister had been found dirty and malnourished in their home by a truancy officer, abandoned by all accounts by their mother for weeks on end several times a year. The mother was never found, the father not even on the birth certificate. A series of foster parents had been unable to curb Mark's voracious appetite for criminal behaviour. In fact, it seemed the arrests increased in gravity whenever he was placed with a family – criminal damage, handling stolen goods, possession of drugs – until finally, on his sixteenth birthday, he left care only to be detained in a youth offenders' institution for six months. The last entry in the files was dated August 1995 when Mark was twenty-one, and he was given a four-year suspended sentence for burglary. From then on, one toe out of line and he'd be locked up for six years at least. Lee didn't see anything in the files on this last arrest, the one that would have had Mark in court that afternoon and, if found guilty, facing a long jail sentence.

'Jane?' he called, flicking backwards through the file, his back to DC Thompson who was putting on her coat. 'There must be another file?'

She looked at her watch, already twenty minutes late for her date. She sighed and walked back to the filing cabinet, searched for a minute then called over to Lee that there were no more files on Mark Redmond. She watched with unease as Lee walked over to DC Gallagher's desk and searched through the mess. He tried the drawers. All locked. He surveyed the office, hands on hips.

'Go home, Jane,' he said.

'Yes, Sarge.' She gathered her bag quickly before he could change his mind, but it was too late.

'Actually, there's one thing we need to do,' he said, 'but you can keep your coat on.'

***

Nicola put a chattering Liam on the living room floor next to Michael Jnr, their combed hair still wet from their bath, Power Ranger pyjamas rolled up at the sleeves and legs. She pressed play on *The Lion King* video for the hundredth time and sat on the sofa next to Mark's baby girl, Amy, propped up with cushions and playing with one of Nicola's hairbrushes. Her head was heavy from the waves of grief that racked her body every ten minutes or so, and her hand rubbed at the Tubigrip around her throbbing ankle. It squashed her foot, making her toes swollen and blue.

It was getting late – she'd been calling Micky all day, left him half a dozen voice messages. Most of the time she couldn't move for him, but now she needed him he was nowhere to be seen. She heard shuffling from the hallway and walked to the living room door, peering round the frame to see Kim making her way down the stairs. She guided Kim to the sofa, sat next to her and put her arm around her limp, frail shoulders.

Kim rested her head on Nicola's chest. 'They'll think he's guilty now,' she slurred through the Temazepam given to her by the hospital doctor.

'Who?' asked Nicola.

'Everyone.'

'They won't,' said Nicola, rubbing Kim's back.

'I don't know what I'm supposed to do,' said Kim, chewing on her thumbnail and staring into nothing.

'Shall we get Amy ready for bed?'

Kim shook her head and Nicola stroked her clumpy hair, still matted with dried blood.

'Okay, I'll do it for now, but she needs her mammy.' Kim nodded but didn't move.

Nicola couldn't help but feel the burden of taking care of others, when she desperately needed some comfort herself. But she had to make sure Kim was okay. Mark had loved her since they were teenagers. Kim was the younger and the weaker of the two and easily beaten by life's problems, often turning to drugs and alcohol. But Mark had become a man, shouldered his responsibilities and kept her straight for the last few years. They had been devoted to each other and blessed with this beautiful baby girl whom they'd both adored.

They both jumped as the front door slammed closed. Micky. With that little turd Mooney clinging onto his shirt tails like a limpet.

'Seen me trainers?' Micky asked, standing in the doorway.

'Where've you been, Micky?' asked Nicola, her voice shaking.

Mooney peered around him and immediately caught sight of Kim's chopped-off hair. He pointed at her. 'Fucking hell, who did that? The fucking apprentice?' He laughed loudly, self-consciously trying to cover his rotten teeth with his lips and the back of his hand as he pranced on hot coals and looked to Micky for acknowledgement.

Micky ignored him and walked into the living room, taking in Kim's bandaged hand. 'Taking up boxing or what?' he asked suspiciously.

Mooney laughed even louder, still glancing at Micky, yearning pathetically for a wink or a playful punch to his arm.

Nicola turned on Mooney. 'Shut up.'

'Hey!' Micky shouted at Nicola, making Liam jolt with fright and begin to cry. Micky picked Liam up and cuddled him to his massive chest, looking at the faces of his wife and sister-in-law and realising all wasn't right.

He turned to Mooney. 'Want a cup of tea?'

'Aye, cheers,' said Mooney, beaming behind his hand, lowering his watery eyes to the floor, then back up to Micky.

'Go on then, make me one while you're at it.'

Mooney's smile faded to a twitching grin and he left the room, scratching the back of his head and muttering to himself.

'So?' Micky asked.

Nicola pulled him towards the window. 'Mark's dead,' she said quietly, her chin quivering, her fingers pulling at her top lip.

'What?' He put a recovered Liam back onto the floor.

'This morning ...' She pressed her forehead into his chest and he put his arms around her. Nicola's hands went to her face as the comfort of the embrace brought fresh tears.

Mooney appeared back at the door. 'How many sug -?' He stopped dead, staring out of the window, Micky following his gaze and seeing a squad car pull up outside the gate.

'What's going on?' asked Micky, confused.

Nicola looked up, saw the car and stiffened. 'I'll tell you later.'

'Tell me now,' he ordered, his eyes darting between the window and Kim who cowered, her fingers in her mouth, staring out of the window at one uniformed and one plainclothes officer glancing around them as they locked the car. 'Why are they coming to my door?' demanded Micky. But Nicola was free of his grasp and heading for the hallway. '*You better tell me,*' Micky yelled after her. He turned to challenge Kim but changed his mind when he saw her trembling body wilting like a discarded doll in the corner of the sofa.

'They're here because Mark killed himself,' Kim whimpered.

'That's a bit drastic like,' said Mooney, fidgeting awkwardly.

Micky threw his head back and sighed, looking up at the ceiling, as if the news were just another irritation in his life.

Mooney hovered, agitated, his hands searching deep in his tracksuit pockets before he slumped down next to Liam and Michael on the floor and joined them in their love of Simba.

Outside, Nicola blocked Lee and Jane Thompson coming up the path. 'She's not saying anything till she's had some advice,' she said.

Lee stopped in front of her. 'We just want to see if you need any help with—'

'We'll go to the community centre for help,' said Nicola.

Thompson held out some leaflets. 'We've brought some information on funeral support and—'

'Are you here to arrest anyone?' Nicola looked directly at Lee.

'No, we—'

'Or maybe you've come to plant some drugs in my house. That why you're here?'

DC Thompson pulled at Lee's arm. 'Come on, this is pointless,' she said.

Lee nodded resignedly, took the leaflets from Thompson and put them on the pavement at Nicola's feet before following Thompson to the car.

Funeral. Nicola heard the word and it rested in her throat, choking her. Kicking at the leaflets, she headed back into the house, pushing past Micky who stood at the bottom of the stairs like Colossus. He grabbed Nicola's arm and pointed into the living room.

'She's not staying here,' he said.

'Let go of me.'

'I say who comes and goes in here.'

'Oh aye, like Mooney?'

'What about it?'

'He's a junkie.'

'So, who gives a fuck?' said Micky, raising his voice.

'Shhh! I do. I don't want him here. Can you not show a bit of respect?' She indicated Kim with her head.

'What's it got to do with me? I didn't even know Mark was dealing.'

'He wasn't!'

They turned to see Michael Jnr at the living room door, holding a football under his arm.

'Wanna game, Dad?'

'Not now,' said Nicola firmly. She watched Michael Jnr walk back into the living room, guilt and regret adding to

59

the raft of emotions. She turned back to find Micky's finger pointed at her.

'She'd just better be gone by tomorrow, that's all,' he said.

Nicola's bitter eyes burned into the back of her husband's head as she followed him into the living room, Kim, having heard every word, eying her sister-in-law with barely concealed hostility. Slumping down onto the sofa, she put her head in her hands as Micky and Mooney slammed out of the front door, leaving only the soaring music of *The Lion King* between her and Kim.

She gathered her energy. 'Right: bed, you two,' she said.

Michael Jnr dragged himself sulkily off the floor and out of the door, his face like thunder. Liam stayed where he was, oblivious, happily playing with the contents of Nicola's handbag.

'Come on, soldier boy,' she said, crouching behind him, and when Liam turned to her she noticed the sherbet on his mouth. 'What've you got? Show Mammy.'

Liam licked his finger and dipped it into the tinfoil wrap he had open between his chubby legs, putting his finger into his mouth just as Michael Jnr had shown him.

'Oh my God ...' Nicola whipped him up off the floor and into the kitchen where she held him over the sink, frantically splashing water over his face and into his mouth. As he struggled and whinged, Nicola shrieked, 'Kim! *Kim!*'

***

Micky had been bouncing around the ring at the boxing gym with his door mate, Stevie, for twenty minutes when Tiger pulled up outside the open double doors. Stevie was no match for Micky in sparring terms, but he'd let Micky pound the pads on his hands for as long as he wanted. And Micky was pounding today. Stevie's arms were ablaze, and he felt his forty-three years for the first time.

Micky was attempting to punch Nicola's fraught face from his mind. He didn't want to see her like that. She couldn't go to pieces, not now, not when he had opportunities to think about. Why did she have to be the grown-up all the time? Why was she always so busy looking after everyone else? Her and Margy, they just couldn't leave it alone. Why couldn't she just love him without question like before?

He punched at Stevie's pads with renewed vigour. He knew why. He wasn't good enough. He'd known that all along. Why she'd fancied him in the first place he had no idea: he'd never considered himself much to look at. She was a mischievous seventeen-year-old, working in Greggs in the Green Market in town. He'd eaten a lot of cheese pasties in 1989. He'd thought she was in her twenties. She had the broad shoulders of an athlete, a mature voice and even some lines across her forehead and around the eyes. The full lips, wide green eyes and freckled nose made him want to shag her and look after her at the same time. And she'd loved him. Loved his body and his soul. She couldn't get enough of him. She wasn't even pregnant when they got married, so it wasn't like she did it for any other reason than because she wanted to.

Stevie sighed with relief when the sound of Tiger's car diverted Micky's attention. They both lowered their arms as Tiger paraded into the gym. At sixty years old, he was wearing well. Still in good shape, he sleeked back his full head of white hair with utmost precision, his tiny, albino eyes behind dark glasses. His heavy brow and thick, white eyebrows gave him a look of something primeval. He was dressed formally – Tiger Reay wouldn't be seen dead without a shirt and tie, even at weekends.

'Stevie!' Tiger's face lit up as he approached the ring, hand outstretched.

Stevie pulled the pads off and climbed out of the ring. He was sweating profusely and Tiger, thinking better of it, put his hand back in his pocket.

'Is he giving you the runaround?' he asked warmly, nodding towards Micky.

'Nah, it's the weather, man,' said Stevie, 'just wait till there's thirty kids in, the walls'll be dripping.'

Tiger looked around the grubby gym, a Portakabin stuck in the middle of his old car lot. The Council had slapped a compulsory purchase order on it over a year ago. It blocked access to the site of a new supermarket, a B&Q and a bingo hall, but Tiger, realising he wasn't going to profit enough from this much needed progress, was keeping them on their toes. The judicial review would delay things for a couple of years until they were so desperate for the land they'd pay him what he deserved. It was all sorted now with a little help from the miniature pisshead of a mayor who'd sell his own mother for a box seat at Newcastle United.

He turned to Micky. 'Y'all right, son?'

'Aye, never better,' replied Micky. 'You?'

Tiger nodded and swivelled on his heels to face Stevie. 'Right, Stevie, got you some cash for the football strips. What did we decide – purple and gold?'

Stevie nodded approvingly. 'D'you want the logo on the front or the back?'

Tiger shrugged. 'Not bothered.'

Stevie opened his mouth to speak, but Micky got there first. 'You'll want it on the front for the photos when they win,' he said, 'publicity like.'

'Now that's fighting talk,' said Tiger, slapping Micky on the shoulder while Stevie inwardly curled his lip. Tiger took a fat roll of fifty-pound notes from his pocket and peeled off ten. 'Reay's Waste Management, then. No, Reay's Skip Hire, it'll fit better.'

Stevie took the money and tapped it to his temple. 'That's very kind of you, Tiger, I'll reserve the balcony for you and the lads.'

Stevie glanced sideways at Micky and headed to the office to put the money in the cash box while Tiger took Micky to one side.

'Make your mind up time,' he said.

'Never any doubt,' replied Micky confidently, undoing the Velcro of his boxing gloves.

'Put your money where your mouth is, then. Where is it?'

'What, now?'

'Here, I'm doing you a favour. If you haven't got it, Stevie'll take your place, no messing.'

'Nah, I've got it, I've got it.'

'Where?'

Micky threw his gloves into the ring. 'I'll run and get it now. Just wait, will you? I'll be twenty minutes. Max.'

Tiger sighed and gave Micky a nod – if he was quick.

Tania's house was only a ten-minute drive away in Gateshead. Tania wasn't home – she was due back tomorrow from the caravan in Seahouses where she'd been with her sisters and all the kids while it was cheaper during the school term. It meant Micky had been able to spend a bit more time with Nicola and the boys. It tired him out, juggling these two lives, but Tania filled a gap that

Nicola couldn't anymore. Nicola was the love of his life, he worshipped her, would never leave her, ever. But Tania was tough, independent, didn't let the sorry, sordid lives of other people get in the way. Some might call her rough, but to Micky she was a breath of fresh air, undemanding and uninhibited, just like it used to be with Nicola once upon a time. Now it was all about the kids, getting the house perfect, asking him where he was all the time, expecting responsibility, legitimacy, dependability. Tania asked for nothing, got on with life; she helped him with his work and took a cut of the profits. During sex, Nicola told him to slow down, to be gentle. But sometimes he just wanted to fuck. And Tania liked it rough. If it came down to it, though, Tania could take him or leave him. Nicola was his wife. She belonged to him. Tania belonged to no one and made it clear she never would.

Micky dug the shoebox out of the under-stairs cupboard where Tania kept the business proceeds. There should be just enough and, unlike Nicola, she wouldn't question his reasons or motives. She'd trust that the investment would be worth it, for all of them.

When he got back to the gym he found Tiger standing at the door in the dusk, shaking hands with the boxers as they arrived. Though small in stature, Tiger radiated an assurance that gave the impression he was towering above everyone else. While Stevie stood next to him, proud as Punch, Micky indicated to Tiger to meet him inside and Tiger followed, leaving Stevie to usher in the spectators alone.

'What do I have to do?' Micky asked, wiping the sweat from his forehead.

'Just pay your money and take your chance.'

'What'll I get?'

'Let's wait and see what's on the boat.'

'There's five grand.'

Tiger flicked through the money and raised a silvery eyebrow. 'Well, that'll do for starters, but if you want to be in the big league you've got to speculate to accumulate, Michael. Some of the lads are putting in twenty-five each.'

'I would if I could.'

'You can turn that five into twenty-five easy if it's a good turnout. Then maybe next time, you can take a bit more of a lead. Put it back in the pot and we'll see what comes up.'

Micky nodded, eager to be up there, flashing the cash and living the Tiger Reay lifestyle. 'I really appreciate the chance,' he said. 'I won't mess you around.'

'I know you won't, son. But this is big, and if you do, there's plenty out there ready to take your place. Understand?'

'Aye. Cheers, Tiger.'

Tiger slapped him on the back and squeezed his way out of the door, smiling at the punters as they paid their cash to Stevie for the fight. Stevie held his hand out to Tiger, but Tiger's hand was back in his pocket, so Stevie brushed his palm over his bald head instead, jealousy twitching in his biceps.

As Tiger's gleaming car pulled away, Micky wrung his hands. This was his chance to make something of himself at last. He'd always known it would happen. He'd bided his time, done the day job, earned the loyalty, kept his nose clean. He thought of his parents, scraping a living from the fruit and veg stall, working from dawn till dusk, the weather beating the redness into their aging faces. They'd worked and then they'd worked more, and for nothing but a few quid saved for a week in Scarborough once a year. A city-centre stall was always the ambition, but forever out of their reach. They were happy enough, they saw the humour in it, they were loved by their punters, they had a laugh, but Micky couldn't stand the pitiless counting of the pennies on a Saturday night. At first, at a young age, it was a novelty to help, but as time went on and the coins reduced in both number and value, the light-hearted Saturday night ritual became a dreaded portent of debt for him, despite his parents' unfailing positivity. The new Safeway supermarket was the inevitable final nail in the coffin of that God-awful stall. His mother and father took it with their usual 'what will be will be' attitude, but he had vowed then never to work hard for nothing. There had to be gain, there had to be advancement, and he would do it by knowing his marketplace, his customers, his suppliers and his enemies better than they knew themselves.

'Hoy, Micky!'

A piercing whistle brought Micky back to reality. Mooney stood greasily at the door to the gym and Micky's face fell. To achieve this dream he would have to deal with toe rags like Mooney, his stuttering but loyal foot soldier.

'Are ye gannin back to Valley Park?'

Micky nodded.

'Giz a lift, then.'

***

Lee sat in his car and grabbed the phone from the passenger seat. The number was burning a hole in his contacts list. He looked at the time, 11.15 p.m. He'd seen Louise close her curtains, the light going out just a few minutes later, but the living room was still brightly lit. He felt like a stalker, but he dialled the number anyway and waited, his finger and thumb holding his eyes closed. After three rings, a chirpy female voice answered.

'Hello?'

Her voice was still the same, slightly deeper.

Lee cleared his throat. 'Debbie, it's Lee.' He waited for some sort of acknowledgement, but none came. 'Lee Jamieson.' Silence. 'Is that you, Debbie?'

'Yes, it's Debbie.'

'I'm sorry, it's late but—'

'Lee, why are you ringing me?'

'You know why, I hoped we could talk – about us, about Louise.'

'Well ... no.'

'Debbie, please, just hang on.'

'What?'

'I have to tell you something. I'm here now. I need to sort things ...'

'Where are you?'

Lee hesitated. 'Outside your house.'

He saw the curtain being pulled to one side and her face appear at the window. He waved to her and she quickly snapped the curtains shut.

'Go away,' she said, and hung up.

FIVE

Another early morning in Lee Jamieson's life. He couldn't remember the last time he'd been able to lie snoozing in bed until the sun was high in the sky. Either work, insomnia or necessary occasions like this all too often dragged him from his pit before the dew had dried on the grass. He stood now at the red front door, the knuckle of his middle finger poised and ready to knock when it was flung open and Debbie stood there, frozen, coat half on with a slice of toast in her mouth.

'Can I come in?' he asked, nervously.

It was a big, old Victorian living room, with high ceilings, picture rails and an ornate ceiling rose, tastefully decorated in grey and taupe shades. The mirror over the marble fireplace threw his sleepless night right back at him.

'Mind if I sit down?' he asked, forcing a half-smile at her stony stare.

Debbie nodded and he sat on the sofa, plumped with huge cushions. Debbie crossed her arms over her chest.

'Well, what do you want? I need to get to work.'

'Debbie, I haven't seen you for sixteen years.'

'Exactly.'

'I'm sorry for just ... turning up.'

'Like a bad penny.'

Lee sighed. 'Wait a minute, I tried ...'

'Shame you didn't turn up when you were supposed to,' she butted in, 'at the doctors to talk about our 'options', remember that?'

'Of course I remember. I remember my dad tearing me to shreds, ending up in the hospital. I couldn't come, I just couldn't, and I couldn't get a message to you either.' Debbie rolled her eyes as if she'd heard it all before, but he carried on with his defence. 'Nobody would speak to me, Debbie, how was I supposed to get word to you? You didn't want anyone to know.' He rubbed his forehead. 'I've told you all this before. I wrote to you. I tried to explain it after Hoots told me about Louise.'

Debbie scoffed. 'I don't believe you. I stood there waiting and waiting. You left me completely alone. You just pissed off.'

'I didn't ...'

'You never even checked to see if I was all right.'

'I tried. Your mates told me you'd got rid of it, that I wasn't allowed to see you. That your dad would have my legs broken. Or words to that effect.'

'Shirking your responsibilities, more like.'

'No. I had nowhere to go, I had to leave. You told them to lie to me, Debbie. If I'd known you'd gone through with it, I would've come back. Legs or no legs. You didn't want me to be involved, so whose fault is it?'

Noticing a framed photograph of Louise and her mother on the nest of tables, Lee picked it up and looked straight into his own brown eyes. Debbie looked down at her feet.

'You'd let me down once, that was enough,' she said, 'and my dad would've broken your legs for sure.'

'But even later, when I found out, even then you didn't want me to come. I was going to come.'

'I was with somebody else, it was complicated.' she said. 'I sent you a photo ...' She stopped herself, knowing how inadequate it sounded.

'I shouldn't have listened to you,' said Lee, regretfully. 'I should've been stronger. Well, now I am.' He put the picture down and picked up another of Louise as a toddler, blowing out birthday candles. 'You're not married, then?' He looked up into Debbie's troubled face, but she looked away, not sure if it was a question or a criticism. 'She doesn't have a stepdad?'

Debbie shook her head, annoyed at his personal intrusion. Her voice became suspicious. 'Have you lost your job or something?'

'No, no. Just got a new one.'

'Where?'

'Here.'

There was a long, gaping silence. Debbie let her bag slip from her shoulder and she sat down in the armchair opposite him. 'Shit,' she said under her breath.

'She knows I exist, doesn't she?'

Debbie stared at the floor. 'Of course she does.'

'Any chance I could see her?'

'Why?'

'Well, what if we bump into each other? I mean, isn't she curious? Does she ask about me? What do you tell her?'

Debbie bit at her fingers. What did she tell her? Childhood sweethearts, lost touch, probably for the best, one day they might meet again ...

Lee sensed her hesitation. 'Debbie, we were kids. I was stupid, scared.'

'Not as scared as me.'

'I'm sorry.'

'I've got to go.' Debbie stood and put her bag over her shoulder.

'It's her birthday soon, isn't it?'

'If you're trying to score Brownie points, forget it.' She hunted in her bag for her car keys as Lee stood up.

'Please, Debbie, don't be bitter. Let me see her.'

Debbie flinched. Bitter? It was something she'd always told herself she'd never become. She'd made the choice. She had no one to blame, yet blame and bitterness overwhelmed her right now.

She dropped her shoulders and looked at this man, the ghost of the teenager she'd fallen for all those years ago still there in the eyes and around the mouth. His jaw was set in stress as he looked away from her, the hope in his eyes turning to sadness. She'd imagined the father-daughter scenario many times before. Not just for Louise, but for herself. What if her own real father had looked for her? What if her adopted mother and father had kept him from her? She blinked the memories away and gathered her thoughts. Not now. She'd have to think.

She headed for the hallway and Lee followed closely behind. As she opened the front door, he held out his business card to her, but she held the door open, waiting for him to pass. Lee left the card on a small table and walked reluctantly out of the house. He stopped and turned at the bottom of the steps.

'Just ask her, will you?'

But Debbie was closing the door and he had no choice but to walk back down the path towards his car.

***

It was gone 10.00 a.m. and Lee waited impatiently for DC Gallagher to arrive. He surveyed the grey office, the stained suspended ceiling, the battered old desks and overflowing paper trays. It was a far cry from the modern, chrome and tempered-glass station in Islington with its flat-screen computers and ergonomic chairs.

The ticking off from Meadows yesterday still stuck in his throat as he sat at his desk and polished off his second murky coffee of the morning. He missed his old colleagues. The people here seemed apathetic at best and downright rude at worst. Whatever happened to the warm, friendly Geordies this town was famous for? There was nothing warm about this place, nor the sterile hotel room that was costing him a fortune. He was putting off looking for a flat to rent, wondering during the long night if he really wanted to commit to the place even for six months. Debbie hated him. He'd messed up and she wasn't going to forgive him. He'd thought he saw her soften for a moment, and he held onto the hope that she would see his side of the story, given a little time.

At 10.05 Gallagher walked in as cocky as hell, joking with his ginger partner, DC Clark, who was carrying a cardboard box marked *'Evidence'*. Lee waved him over.

'How're you feeling?'

Gallagher feigned a poorly look. 'Bad belly: sorry, boss. Came on all of a sudden.'

'Let's get this handover done, then.'

'Can you give us a minute to sort the files?'

'You haven't prepared anything?'

'I've done the stats.'

'I can get the stats off the computer.'

'Aye well, computers aren't my forte, Sarge. Can hardly switch the bastard on.'

Lee could well believe it. The man was antiquated. 'I want real cases,' he said. 'Start with Valley Park.' He headed for the kettle and brewed up again while Gallagher rifled moodily through an overstuffed filing cabinet. A few minutes later, a dozen spring files were hurled onto Lee's desk.

Gallagher pulled a chair up and slumped onto it. 'Right, last twelve months I've got two murders, one was a stabbing, the other a domestic. Six arson—'

'Six arson?'

'Oh aye, they love arsin' about on Valley Park, favourite pastime.' Lee wasn't laughing, so Gallagher raised an eyebrow and returned to the files. 'One GBH, fella broke both his wife's legs with a baseball bat – allegedly – but he says she fell down the stairs. We're still looking for the bat. One robbery.'

'Where?'

'Post office-cum-supermarket, it's the only shop left open.' Lee remembered the fortified shop he and Nicola had stood opposite. 'Then there's a couple of rapes.'

'I expect the burglary rate's high.'

'See Uniform,' Gallagher stretched his arms above his head, revealing stale and fresh sweat stains. 'To be honest, you get nowt reported. They'd rather put up and shut up.'

'What about drugs?'

'You'll have to see Drug Squad. They're the hippies down the hall.'

'So how come you were the arresting officer in Mark Redmond's case?'

'Just happened to be there.' Gallagher put his hands behind his head.

'Just happened to stick your hand up a drainpipe and find a bag of cocaine? That's a stroke of luck.'

73

'Got a tip-off.'

'Shouldn't you have passed it on to the Drug Squad?'

'Seemed an opportunity too good to miss, Sarge.'

'Didn't you think it through? You got a small-time dealer, DS might've got the supplier.'

'Water under the bridge. CPS were happy with it going to court.'

'Good for them. I want everything you've got on Mark Redmond.'

Gallagher heaved a pissed-off sigh. 'Can I sort it later? I need the toilet.'

'No. Get me the latest file, it's not with the others.'

Gallagher hauled himself out of his chair and took some keys from his pocket as Lee picked up the pile of files from his desk, balancing them under his chin. Gallagher unlocked his drawers and pulled out a fat file, slapping it on top of Lee's armful.

'Want me to go through the details?' he asked with a fake smile.

'I can read, thanks,' Lee replied.

He took himself into a private room, sat down at the table and took the first folder from the pile, eager to complete Mark's story. He opened it at the first page, September 1995, when Mark was on remand at Deerbolt in County Durham. Lee was well aware of its reputation as a ruthless and unforgiving place, raging at the seams with temper and testosterone. With three to a cell, it took little more than a fart taken the wrong way to turn a bit of bad humour into cold-blooded brutality. Mark didn't come out unscathed. There were reports of two hospital stays, one for superficial knife wounds to the neck, and another stating only '*recuperation*'.

Lee was about to launch into the next long court report when he was interrupted by DC Thompson. Nicola Kelly's kid was in hospital, suspected overdose.

'Kid?' he asked.

'Two of them.'

***

In the brightly coloured hospital ward, Nicola was stroking Liam's dimpled hand while Margy hummed 'Circle of Life' to him, wiping his wet fringe from his sleeping forehead. He'd been unconscious by the time they'd scrambled him into the hospital the night before, Margy calmly doing all the explaining as Nicola pleaded with the nurses to help him. The doctors had laboured behind closed doors, and a couple of hours later her baby was wheeled out of the trauma room, his eyes spookily dilated, but open.

Nicola had stayed all night by his bed, hoping and praying that Kim and Michael would be taking care of each other and Amy at home. She felt a surge of guilt and her stomach churned at the thought of Kim all alone. Even though the current crisis seemed to have snapped her out of her stupor, she knew that Kim's emotional state was brittle. Margy was the one Nicola needed right now. Someone strong and composed, and, as usual, Margy had been at Nicola's door just seconds after she'd made the call.

'Thanks, Margy.' Nicola grabbed her friend's hand over the bed.

Micky had disappeared off the face of the earth. Words could not describe the shame and confusion that engulfed her as she looked into the innocent face of her baby. Never in her life had she wanted to physically harm a living being, but now, as her guilt turned to anger, she understood the urge to lash out and punish.

Margy looked at her watch. 'You better go and sort out Michael and Kim, eh?' she said gently. 'Then come back and we'll talk about what you need to do, okay? And then you're going to get some sleep. I'll get them to put a bed in here for you.'

Nicola nodded, too tired to argue. 'I'll not be long,' she said, stroking Liam's head.

'Take your time, he'll be under for hours, they said.' Margy squeezed Nicola's hand and watched her leave. She knew it would only be a matter of time before social services were there, and files would be submitted to places where decisions were made behind closed doors and lives were either saved or ruined. Knowing Nicola's thorny relationship with the authorities, Margy knew she would fight tooth and nail to keep her kids out of care. But a person could crumble under this sort of pressure, and Micky wasn't exactly being the supportive husband. She thanked her lucky stars for Joe, the man who would be glued to her side if it had been little Jimmy in this hospital bed. All this talk of changing – Margy didn't believe it for one minute. Micky Kelly wouldn't change a damn thing unless it was for his own benefit.

She was tucking in the sheets around Liam when she saw a pair of black shoes standing at the curtain.

'Knock, knock,' she heard a man's voice.

'It's open,' she said sarcastically.

Lee pulled back the curtain and walked in, standing behind Margy and looking over her shoulder as she adjusted the oxygen mask on Liam's face.

'Hello again,' he said.

Margy turned to face Lee.

'How is he?'

'All right. Under observation.' Margy's brow creased into a puzzled frown and Lee held up his ID. 'Detective Sergeant Lee Jamieson.'

'Oh Christ,' said Margy, laughing cynically.

Lee took out his notebook. 'The hospital are obliged to report cases like this. The social worker's outside.'

That got Margy's hackles up. 'She doesn't know where he got it,' she said.

'Is she a user?'

'No way.'

'What about the father?'

***

Nicola closed the door behind her, walked into the living room, and threw her keys onto the coffee table. She surveyed her house, empty, messy and confused. She felt dirty. She needed a shower. She needed to wash her hair and change her clothes. If anything made her feel out of control it was being unclean.

She sat for a moment, shell-shocked by the events of the last twenty-four hours. She tried to piece it all together: Kim, Mark, Lee, Micky, Liam. She would get through it, she just needed a plan, then she'd be able to cope. She looked for a pad and paper so she could start writing down everything she needed to do. Then she heard it – a big, fat snore creeping down the stairs and through the living room door. Her breath became shallow and she blinked at the pen in her hand. Putting it on the coffee table, she stood, robotically walking through the door and up the stairs, pausing at the bedroom door which stood a little ajar. As she entered, the mound under the white quilt moved up and down steadily.

She snapped the curtains open, the light streaming onto Micky's face. He woke, bleary-eyed, shielding his eyes from the sunlight as her silhouette stood over him.

'You couldn't even come and see if your own son was all right?'

'I'm knackered, man.'

'It was him, wasn't it?'

'Who?'

'Mooney!' Nicola's voice was reaching the kind of level that would get her into trouble, but sod it, it was out of her control. 'You couldn't give a shit, could you?'

'Who's supposed to see to Michael?'

'Well, where is Michael?'

'At school.' Micky burrowed back into the bed.

'Exactly. And you're in bed. And Liam's in hospital. And Mooney's walking the bloody streets.'

Micky pulled the quilt over his head.

'And where's Kim?'

'Don't fucking know,' Micky mumbled.

'You never let her go home?'

'Nicola, just piss off, will you?'

Nicola stared down at her husband. There was nothing to love about him when he was like this. She opened drawers and started flinging his clothes onto the bed, walking to the rank, old wardrobe, so ancient it still locked with a key, Micky's only possession from his mother and father's house. She opened it and pulled boxes of trainers from the top shelf.

'You're the one who can piss off,' she hissed.

Micky flung the quilt from his head and sat up. 'Put them back,' he said calmly.

'I will not. You're a bastard. You don't even care about—'

'I said, *put them back.*'

Her glare was vicious, and she threw a box at him hard, hitting the hands that came up to shield his face.

'Right. Get out.' Micky, fully naked, was out of the bed and pulling her forcefully by her arm.

'No.' She heaved her arm out of his grasp with as much strength as she could muster, but he'd spun her round and was pushing her towards the bedroom door. She resisted, turning and hitting out, kicking at his shins.

His hand came from nowhere and slapped her across one side of her face then the other with the force of a hammer. She stumbled backwards, one hand to her cheek, her other outstretched arm useless as he pushed her to the floor before she could get her balance. He stood over her, and she got to her feet shakily. *You bastard* ... She fought down the words but couldn't stop the furious tears.

Gathering her last bit of nerve, she walked up to him and pummelled his chest with her fists. It was like hitting a lump of iron, dead and unyielding, and he moved forward, pushing her, his mouth snarling, his eyes cold and detached, giving her no choice but to retreat backwards out of the door. She turned and ran down the stairs as fast as her throbbing ankle would allow her and, hearing him following, pulled a knife from the draining board in the kitchen and held it up in defence. Micky, still naked, stopped just inches away from the blade, grinning, goading her.

'Go on, then.'

'It's Mooney who needs a hiding,' said Nicola, her voice starting to crack.

'I haven't had time to give anyone a hiding.'

'Oh yeah, what's this, then?'

'Nicola, if I gave you a hiding, you'd know about it.'

'I hate him. You'd better not be dealing again. I mean it, Micky. You swore on the kids' lives.'

'I never touch the stuff.'

'You're lying.' Micky grabbed the knife from her effortlessly, leaving her utterly vulnerable. 'I know you're lying. If that was your stuff—'

Micky pushed her towards the back door. 'Out.'

'No.'

He put his hand to her throat. Immobilised, Nicola looked down her nose at his wrist, fear creeping into her eyes, her hands flailing behind her helplessly. She knew what could come after this and she braced herself. But there was no further beating. Instead, he opened the back door and shoved her roughly outside. She fell backwards onto the concrete paving and the door slammed before she could get to her feet again. Her chest burning with renewed loathing, she threw herself at the back door, rattling the handle and pounding on the wood panelling.

'You better open it!' she yelled.

The door opened and Micky's fist came at her like a bullet, hitting her squarely in the face. As the door slammed closed again, Nicola stooped over, stunned, her hand over her nose. She could hear Micky's feet stomping up the stairs and the bedroom door slamming so hard that birds fluttered from the TV aerial. She looked up, her eye catching the washing line and a procession of clothes that had been out since yesterday morning. She took a tea towel and put it under her nose, which had started to bleed. Fighting back tears, gathered herself, some jeans, a top and some underwear and bundled them up under her arm, then hurried down the side of the house and through the side gate into the front garden.

As she turned into the street Lee and DC Thompson pulled up outside the house, Lee stepping out of the car and following behind her.

'Mrs Kelly?'

Nicola half-turned to look at him, but carried on walking.

'Nicola Kelly? Are you okay?' Nicola ignored him and quickened her pace.

He soon caught up. 'I need to talk to you about Liam.'

'I don't want to talk about Liam.'

'We need to know where the drugs came from.'

Nicola stopped in her tracks and walked up to him defiantly. 'Just look around you.'

Lee surveyed the boarded-up houses, the junk-filled front gardens, the fortified railings and barbed wire surrounding a sheltered housing block to his right.

'How about there?' Nicola pointed. 'Or there? or even there? They're giving them away. Sale of the fucking century.'

'You're bleeding,' he said, getting closer to her. But Nicola backed off, put the tea towel to her nose and kept walking.

'I'm sorry about your brother,' he said, catching her up again and walking by her side.

'The smackhead?'

'I didn't say that.' Nicola gave him a look that said, *You're all the same*. But Lee stepped in front of her and started walking backwards. 'I need to talk to you. We can do it here or back at the station.'

Nicola avoided his eyes and held the bundle of clothes across her chest, half of her embarrassed that he was seeing her in this state, the other wanting him and all his scum friends dead.

Lee continued. 'So did Liam pick the drugs up in the house?'

'No.' She stopped and stared past him blankly.

'Could he have got it from your brother's?'

'Look, either arrest me or piss off.' When he didn't move, she shoved past him and strode on.

Lee caught up with her again, could hear Thompson kerb-crawling behind him as he pulled out his card. 'Here's my number.'

'I know your number by heart.'

'Well, at least take this, then.'

Nicola shoved his arm away.

'Nicola, I'm trying to *help*,' he pleaded, exasperated.

Nicola stopped, the sincerity of his voice colliding with the turmoil in her head. Taking the card from him, she looked down at it. 'Women's Aid.' She laughed to herself under her breath.

'They've put an emergency care order in place.' Lee stood where he was as she walked away from him again. 'It could be classed as neglect!' he called after her.

Nicola bowed her head, ploughing on to the bus stop at the end of the estate. His words cut her to the quick, and as soon as she was around the corner and out of his sight, she sat on a garden wall, lit a cigarette with shaking hands, and quietly began to cry.

***

Later that evening, Lee sat at the window of the hotel bar. He knew it was wrong, keeping the Mark Redmond file instead of handing it back for closure. But he felt a deep unease at the way it was being handled – or not, as the case may be. And besides, the more he found out about Mark, the more insight he had into the life and background of Nicola.

DI Meadows had already ordered him to let it go, it wasn't a live case, it wasn't their concern, they had to focus on the bigger regeneration picture for the estate. That was, after all, why they had employed him. Her demeanour was sharp and touchy, the Chief Constable was on her back – targets, targets, targets. Half of the department was either off sick or on maternity leave, and her spend forecast was going through the roof. Suddenly he wasn't the best thing since sliced bread anymore, more of a RoboCop with a rep who'd never had her vote in the first place. She'd thrown the Valley Park Community Strategy at him across the desk that afternoon. This is what they wanted, she'd said, this is how it's done now. Crime reduction by committee, and he would work to whatever approach she deemed appropriate.

It was a strategy he'd seen and read a hundred times before, the same trite, politically correct garbage endorsing CCTV, parenting classes and intergenerational projects, but no commitment to who would do it, when, how it would be paid for, and what effect it would have. Nobody took it seriously. When Lee had tried to brief the team on it, Gallagher and Clark were on their knees playing with half a dozen clockwork penises, winding them up and racing them across the floor, the box marked '*evidence*' lying empty on its side. He'd held up the Community Strategy and asked who'd read it. Three pairs of eyes stared blankly at him. He asked who attended the steering group meetings.

'Uniform – community plod,' they all agreed.

'And who does community plod feed back to?' Lee asked.

'Me, Sarge,' said Gallagher, his hands deep in his pockets, 'but thankfully that responsibility is no longer mine.'

'Right, well I'd like to see the last six months' feedback reports.'

'It's more of a verbal arrangement,' sniffed Gallagher.

Lee noted a private smirk between Gallagher and Clark as Gallagher picked up his clockwork toys and put them back in the cardboard box. *Fucking shower*, thought Lee, his conversation with DI Meadows earlier that afternoon still fresh in his mind. She hadn't taken kindly to being told that the detection rate was abysmal, not because the criminals were descended from Einstein, but because she had a kindergarten for a team.

He'd unlocked his drawer and taken out Mark's last file to take back to the hotel. As he locked the drawer, he heard an incensed *Jesus Christ!* from the other side of the office. DC Gallagher was holding his payslip in his hands, his eyes scouring the information.

'Have you seen the tax I'm paying?' he said, eyes wide and mouth open. 'I reckon I'm keeping a couple of single parents with this. I should have shagging rights.'

Lee had had enough. He grabbed his jacket from the back of his chair and put it over the file he held in his hand. As he left, he threw a pile of Women's Aid cards onto each desk.

'We don't do domestics,' lisped DC Clark.

'You do now.' He'd strode across the office and out of the door while Gallagher picked up his Women's Aid cards and threw them in the bin by his desk, sat back in his chair, and belched loudly.

Lee ordered another beer from the waiter and took Mark's file from his bag. He opened the file at Mark's mugshot. A tired, emaciated young man, and something in the melancholic eyes reminded Lee of who he could have been. What he could have become. What some of his friends from Valley Park had no doubt become many years ago. Hoots, Clarkey and Simon 'Dinger' Bell, mates he drank cans of Diamond White with in Darkie's Cave, the hollow of the big oak tree on the Rec where a black man was rumoured to have been hanged in 1963. Lee had had to work hard to become one of the crowd. No one had any sympathy for a family striving to be middle-class hitting hard times. You either fitted in or you kept yourself to yourself. He'd had to let his grades drop, not too much, but enough to be just above average, rather than unacceptably ahead. He started smoking, took on the role of lookout whilst cans were lifted from the delivery vans. The crime was petty, but the punishment severe from the community, parents and teachers if caught. These days, crime was destructive, yet either ignored or accepted by the neighbourhood. People were battle-worn, the authorities no longer able to deliver a clip around the ear or a truncheon to the kidneys.

He turned the page, and there, staring out at him, was the wiry, red-haired youth from the Nags Head. The same eyes, turned down at the edges, a pincushion of tiny pimples swamping his freckled forehead. Lee removed the photograph and turned it over – *Tyrone Woods, 23.06.82*. Behind it was a typed statement with Tyrone's rickety signature at the bottom. For the prosecution's key witnesses, the statement was basic. It stated that Mark had sold cocaine and cannabis to Tyrone on at least three occasions, and that he'd attempted to sell him heroin. He looked back at the signatures and saw clearly, *Paul Gallagher, Detective Constable*, scrawled across the bottom of the page. He flicked back to Mark's photograph again. It was Nicola's face, too, the sorrowful eyes that had pleaded with him as she'd held her dead brother in her arms.

He closed his eyes, and he was back in the house in Kenton, watching his father stride down the path on his way to work that blustery morning. He wondered if he'd romanticised his family life before the move to Valley Park. Who's to say his mother wouldn't have found solace in booze anyway, her expectations of Victorian houses with stripped floors in leafy suburbs always destined to be out of her reach, the disillusionment staring at her from the bottom of a glass of gin? Had his dad been quiet and strong, or just surly and morose, the blight of a disappointed woman hanging around his neck like an albatross?

The many paths Lee's life could have taken lay before him in Mark Redmond's desolate eyes, each route determined by some insignificant decision, like a trip to Eldon Square to watch the girls in their drainpipe jeans, or a pint in the pub at lunchtime on your birthday. These could have been his eyes, had Frank not bullied him out of the house. But instead they belonged to the brother of a woman who intrigued him. She was unbefitting of that estate. She had real beauty, dignity, strength and an intelligence that would normally have been wrenched from you had you shown it, growing up in a place like that. He found himself thinking about her a lot when he should have been thinking of Debbie, who was, after all, the mother of the child he ached to know. He knew it was out of the question, any kind of relationship with Nicola. But the least he could do was find some answers.

Lee looked out of the window at the river and the people streaming onto the quayside, dressed up to the nines for their night out. Every night was Friday night in Newcastle. The women, some teenagers, some old enough to know better, swung their white handbags as they linked arms in groups of four or five, heckling the red-faced men in their short-sleeved shirts, ironed to perfection by their mams. They shouted, they sang, they laughed raucous laughter. Some of the girls were just bairns, slaughtered already, smoking and tipping along in their heels and their boob tubes. One of them pulled her top down and shook her chest at him while her orange-faced mates screeched and howled silently at him through the thick glass of the hotel window, crossing their legs in case they pissed themselves. Christ, they hardly even had breasts yet, he thought.

Then it dawned on him and his heart lurched. He hoped like hell Debbie didn't let Louise come into town for a night out.

His phone buzzed on the table in front of him, and he looked at the flashing blue screen.

Debbie.

SIX

Nicola let the breeze of the open window of the taxi slide over her face. It felt good on her pounding skin. She kept her purple, swollen cheek buried behind her hand, hidden as much as possible from the judging eyes of the taxi driver who glanced at her frequently in the rear-view mirror.

She'd slept fitfully on the hospital fold-out bed over the last couple of nights. The social worker had been in and out, a skinny runt of a menopausal woman with a weak handshake and a sweaty top lip. As long as Nicola stayed away from the house and Micky, she could keep the children with her until the emergency case conference had been held, but any sniff of Micky and his associates, and the kids would be in a home without delay. She riled against it inside, but knew that any outburst of anger on her part would do nothing to help her case.

Last night was even worse, with Michael joining them, happily snuggling next to her in little Jimmy's Spider-Man pyjamas, pleased to be wrapped up in his mother's silence again.

Poor Michael. He'd had to endure two days at Margy's house, her phone clanging every five minutes, her door a constant haven for shouty women waving letters in the air – letters from the school or the Social, from the courts or the debt collectors. That was the trouble being a community worker on the estate where she lived. The job had become twenty-four-seven. The dog barked, the TV blared so Joe and little Jimmy could hear it over the noise of the unremitting raised voices, then they, too, had to shout over the TV to make themselves heard. Clothes, boxes and files littered the dark living room, piled high in pyramids in all corners. Michael had pined for a quiet hour on his dad's lap in front of *The Simpsons*, feeling the ripples of a laughing belly in his back. So when no one heard his unhappy whimpering, he howled and banged his fists on the arm of the sofa until the dog was hoarse and Margy gave up and drove him to his mother at the hospital.

When Nicola stepped out of the taxi, Liam on her hip clinging onto a plastic carrier bag, she expected to see an ugly fortress, barbed wire, barred doors and windows. Instead, she faced an ordinary house, just like every other one on the street. Michael sat sulkily in the back seat of the taxi, the school's sports day going ahead without their star egg-and-spooner.

'Michael, get out, the man's got to go.' Nicola smiled *Sorry* at the driver who nodded at her politely and fiddled with his radio. In the end she reached into the taxi and dragged the rigid Michael by his arm until he was out of the car and on the pavement. *Ow, ow, OW,* he accused her furiously until she let go of his arm, apologising, stroking his face and kissing his forehead.

As the cab pulled off, Nicola hiked Liam up onto her hip, took Michael's surly hand and, with a deep breath, walked with purpose up to the house and rang the bell.

She could hear laughter approaching the door, a laugh that suddenly bellowed when the door was thrust open and the owner of the voice, a massive, barefooted woman of about thirty, stood wiping her hands on a tea towel and staring down at them. The woman called behind her, 'Here's some more, lasses!' and a sea of hollow faces ambled out into the long corridor from hidden doorways, women in leggings and slippers, some eating, some smoking, some doing both at the same time.

The enormous woman ushered her in. She had the blondest hair Nicola had ever seen, shorn into a lopsided bob which she flicked constantly out of her eyes, a round, pink face and the sunken mouth of a woman who'd lost too many teeth. Self-inflicted tattoos littered her hands, and her forearm spelled out her name in lavish script: *Brenda.*

In the kitchen Nicola sat Liam on the table, and stroked Michael's head. He clung to her leg, trying not to look like he was interested in the huddle of women gathering around them. Tracey, 'a right scrubber', was vigorously wiping down the kitchen sink while Lisa, a stooped woman of nearly six foot with lank, salt-and-pepper hair, emptied the contents of a huge teapot into the clean sink, causing Tracey to kick up a cursing fuss. A good-humoured outpouring of expletives was exchanged between the two until Brenda raised her hands and shouted over them, reminding them of the rule of no swearing in front of the fucking kids, right? They backed down. Brenda was in charge.

While Tracey took Liam and Michael to the playroom, Brenda did the honours and showed Nicola the bedroom they would be occupying, three lonely, single beds hugging each corner of the room. She demonstrated the panic alarms scattered secretly under tables or high on the walls out of the reach of the kids, just in case the perps managed to find their way in. She boomed questions at her in quick succession. What had he done to her, the cunt? How long had he been thrashing her? How often? What with? What about the bairns? Did he wallop them an' all? She showed little interest in Nicola's mumbled responses, but had few misgivings about making known the niceties of her own circumstances. She boasted of a husband in jail, convicted of murdering her unborn twins with his booted foot, almost killing her in the process. Brenda laughed forcefully, recalling the fact that her fanny had bled so much they'd had to strap her up by the legs to stop her insides pouring onto the ambulance floor. Nicola noticed that the toothless, bragging mouth laughed hard, *HA HA HA*, but that the eyes remained empty.

She accepted the strong, orange tea thrust at her at the bottom of the stairs and entered the playroom. She looked at Michael Jnr and Liam, playing happily together with a Scalextric, making the noises of the cars, the skids and the horns.

Michael smiled up at her. 'Mam, can we get one when we go home?'

Brenda had asked about the bairns, and the thought made Nicola feel sick to her stomach. She'd withstood the fists, the feet, the pulled hair and punched arms, but the kids were fine. They didn't know anything. Micky would never hurt their children.

Nicola swallowed her guilt and felt Brenda's heavy arm go round her shoulder in consolation. But she felt no comfort, just the heavy heart of a woman between a rock and a hard place.

***

Lee and DC Gallagher dunked Jammie Dodgers into strong tea in stained mugs bearing the logos of stationery companies. They sat in an upstairs room at the Neighbourhood Housing Office, a converted house on the edge of Valley Park, the barred windows and heavy metal door testament to the fearful and suspicious personnel inside. The staff sat behind scratched perspex, handing out forms, stamping benefit books and rebounding off the angry voices of people whose boilers and windows had been left unfixed for weeks or months.

Gallagher was grouchy, wondering why there had to be pre-meetings for meetings that needed to be followed up with meetings. Lee tapped his fingers on the table while they waited. Joyce Oduwu, the Director of Housing, had requested an audience with the person taking responsibility for crime reduction on the estate. That would be Lee. She wanted him to meet the team, more ineffectual people with badges round their necks, no doubt.

When she arrived, apologising for her lateness with the air of someone who loved to be late, she smiled and threw her heavily pregnant bulk onto the chair opposite Lee. She held Lee's gaze for longer than a few seconds, a curious look that suggested she'd been waiting to meet him for some time. She was attractive, beautiful even, with flawless, olive skin, a shock of tiny brown ringlets framing her face and striking, hazel eyes. She threw a glance at Gallagher before looking pleased with herself then struggling to bend to her bag to pull out a battered copy of the Community Strategy. She held it up like a trophy and asked Lee if he had seen it.

'Absolutely,' he replied.

She was very pleased with it, she said, very pleased indeed. She'd spent a two-day residential at a country hotel in Northumberland with twenty other senior managers, planning and discussing the content of it. And oh! She'd had the best carrot cake she'd ever tasted in her life with her afternoon tea on day two. Lee smiled and nodded, while Gallagher helped himself to a custard cream, examining it before soaking it in hot tea and putting it whole into his mouth.

When Lee asked *how* she saw the strategy helping residents, she smiled a self-gratified smile. She knew the answer to this one all right. Her housing managers held regular meetings at the community centre, of course. Very popular with the residents. That's where they were going next, so she could introduce him to some very committed tenants and her wonderful staff team. Lee's thoughts turned to the miserable employees sitting downstairs, their eyes almost bleeding with scorn for the people they were paid to support.

He looked at the papers for the meeting they were about to attend. Margy Allen had been at the last one, he noticed, accompanied by two other residents, followed by a long list of housing officers. Popular indeed.

Lee asked what issues concerned residents most, at which point Joyce sucked in her breath and shook her head with woe. Dog muck. Broken taps. The lack of shops, she said sadly. Drugs? Crime? Harassment? No, no, they didn't want to discuss any of that. Not much point reporting burglaries when you can't get insurance. Besides, most people didn't hang around for long. She leaned forward and spoke furtively as if about to give away a national secret. Did he know that the average length of tenancy on Valley Park was twelve weeks? She sat back in her seat and threw her hands up helplessly.

Lee raised his eyebrows and tapped his pen on the table. 'So, doesn't it strike you that there's something seriously wrong here?' he asked.

'Aye, it's a dump,' said Gallagher.

Lee turned in his chair to glare at him. 'Do you mind?'

'Sorry, boss, forgot you were a native,' he said, the faintest of smiles flickering across his face.

'Of course there's something wrong,' she breathed, shaking her head at Gallagher like a disappointed parent, rubbing one hand around her protruding belly and stretching her neck from side to side. 'But you know, the crime and lawlessness ...' She pursed her lips and looked at Lee expectantly.

Lee smiled his acknowledgement. Of course. It was the police's problem and their solution to find. So much for partnership.

Outside, while Gallagher smoked and arranged his life on his mobile phone, Lee stood on the pavement and looked around him. The streets were empty bar a couple of dogs sniffing at bins, and a brown, leathery woman with a can of beer and a cigarette, sitting on her front step taking in the sunshine and swearing at her kids who were playing amidst the rubble of what had once been a garden wall. He wondered how you saved a place that was already over the edge. How did you rescue an entire generation growing up knowing no different?

Ten minutes later, he sat around a table in a small meeting room at the community centre with five local women, Joyce, Gallagher and four housing managers. Lee recognised Margy and the ranting Scot with the headscarf from the public meeting. Margy's face puckered into a frown when she saw him take a seat opposite her.

Once the tedium of the matters arising was done with, Joyce, radiant with pride, introduced Lee and DC Gallagher, who'd come to get the residents' views on reducing crime. Margy's eyes looked heavenward while Lee passed his business cards around the table and gave them some glaring statistics on crime levels, antisocial behaviour, conviction rates and the ages of offenders. Some tutted and shook their heads while others listened intently, giving nothing away.

'It's the small minority, though,' he explained, 'just eight per cent of the estate's population who are causing the problems, constantly on the lookout for cars to pinch, people to mug, houses to burgle. While the majority, the decent people like you, just want to get on with their lives and keep themselves to themselves.'

A dozen hooded eyes gazed at him: *tell us something we don't know.* He willed someone to speak, and was finally saved by the headscarfed Scottish woman, her handbag held tightly to her chest, her lined mouth pursed in cynicism like a cat's arse.

'It's the drugs, they'll pinch anything for the drugs,' she said with the trembling voice and shaking head of a woman who suffered from her nerves.

Relief spread over him. At least someone was speaking. 'And I'll do everything in my power to clean the place up, but I need your help.' Lee looked directly at her, but she turned to her neighbour.

What?

He tried again. 'Good people need to be more active, weed out the bad people, stop them spoiling it for everyone else.'

The old woman's mouth was hanging open and her clawed hands began to tear at the fastening on her handbag. 'What do you want us to do? Grass on drug dealers? Hey, we might be poor but we're not stupid.'

'I didn't say you were.'

Another woman laughed. 'I wouldn't tell the police nowt, me. I like living.' A couple of her friends sniggered with her.

Lee was determined to fight his corner. 'If people don't report crime, what sort of message does that give out? The kids see people getting away with murder while you're trying to teach them right from wrong.'

'He's right about the kids,' said Margy.

The Scottish woman pointed a knobbly finger at Margy. 'Here. It's all right for you, you and your man have got jobs, you can get out, we can't.'

'Why should anyone have to get out?' asked Margy.

'You know why,' the woman continued to point shakily from one person to another, 'because your life wouldn't be worth living if you started shopping people left right and centre—'

Lee interrupted. 'Nobody needs to find out.'

Gallagher sat up slowly: *what's he got up his sleeve?*

'They will, though,' another woman whined, 'and what if you're on your own like me? I haven't even got a phone, none of the phone boxes work.'

'If you're frightened we can give you panic alarms. Works like a radio, straight through to the station.' Lee waited in the stunned silence and heard Gallagher stifle a snort.

The Scottish woman threw her arms in the air. 'Jesus Christ, I've heard it all now. You might as well write *'Grass'* on your forehead and walk around the place with walkie-talkies. I've had enough of this.' She stood up and shuffled to the door.

'Dot, man, howay.' Margy's words were lost to the woman's enraged ears. As the door closed behind her, the other residents stood up one by one, muttering to each other and walking out of the room, leaving Lee, Gallagher, Joyce and Margy stewing in the silence.

'So ... that went well,' said Gallagher after an awkward moment. 'I'm away for a smoke,' he said, his delight evident at seeing Lee's cards strewn untouched around the table.

Gallagher and Joyce stood up together to leave the room. Lee watched them. There was something odd about their relationship. Their eye contact, though brief, made him suspect they'd known each other some time, and yet they didn't greet each other, or in fact speak to each other at all. He could see why Gallagher would want to keep this estate at heel. It was his pension. Cut the crime and what would he do? But the housing director? Surely it was in her best interests to keep people in their homes for as long as possible. It must have been costing her a fortune boarding up houses and getting them ready for the next lot of problem families.

He turned to Margy, but before he could open his mouth to ask about Nicola and Liam, she was on her feet.

'Got the lunch club,' she said sternly, and headed out of the room.

Getting to his feet quickly, he followed her into the lobby but was hindered by a series of shrivelled old people with sticks and Zimmer frames heading for the toilets with their carers. He zig-zagged into the main hall where his eyes met a sea of white hair but no Margy.

A blue-veined, wiry hand caught his sleeve and pulled him down onto a chair with surprising strength. He found himself at the end of a long trestle table between an ancient woman with a hearing aid and an even more prehistoric man with white hair pouring from his nose and ears. The woman kept her hand on Lee's arm, and sat so hunched that she could only talk to his chest.

'Nearly a year since he died,' she said. 'Went through agony after he got shot. Wouldn't heal, you know, just an open hole. Oh I do miss him.'

Lee stopped searching for Margy and turned his attention to the tiny woman who picked at his sleeve with her long nails, her eyes rimmed with the redness of severe old age. He put his hand on hers.

'Who?' he asked kindly.

'My bairn.' Her head shook slightly as she glanced up at Lee.

'Did the police get the person who shot him?' he asked.

'Why no. What's the point of telling the polis? They do nowt.' She pulled her hand away angrily.

Lee frowned and lowered his head down to her level. 'You didn't tell the police?' He felt another quaking hand on his other arm and turned to the liver-spotted face of the old man.

'Border terrier,' the old man said in a high-pitched, almost nonexistent voice.

'Ahhh,' said Lee, relaxing and turning to the old woman. 'Ever thought of replacing him?'

'Eeeh, I couldn't go through that again, son, you get too attached.'

Margy was at his shoulder, and she thrust a plate of food in front of the old man, rubbery mince with mashed potato and tinned, processed peas. Lee shared a glance with him, reading his mind.

'Aah knaa – shite, isn't it?' rasped the old man, staring at his plate.

'All right, Norman?' Margy asked him.

'Aye, pet. Smells lovely,' he beamed up at her.

Easing himself out of his seat, Lee followed Margy into the same windowless kitchen they'd stood in after the public meeting that seemed an age ago, the light still flickering tiresomely.

'I know what you're doing,' she said before he could speak. Lee looked puzzled and opened his mouth. 'With Nicola. I know what you want,' she went on. Lee held his hands up in defence but again couldn't get a word in. 'My advice to you is to stay well away,' she said.

Lee looked her in the eye. 'I can help—'

'Help how? Whole lot of help you've been so far.'

'She needs to get away from him if he's dealing. I can do what I can with social services, but if there's drugs in the house, she doesn't stand a chance.' Margy fiddled with her apron. 'Who else was in the house that day?'

Nothing.

He raised his hands in exasperation. 'Jesus, you people!'

'Micky doesn't deal,' said Margy, 'so he says.'

'So who else was in the house?'

Margy puffed up her chest. 'Kevin Moone,' she said, then pointed a finger at him. 'If you hurt her, or put her in danger, I will tear your eyes out,' and with one final glare she took two more plates of mush and left.

***

As darkness fell, Liam lay with Nicola, bottle in his mouth, his fingers twirling her hair while Michael Jnr sat sullenly at the bottom of the bed, refusing any interaction with her or anyone else. Margy had just left the refuge with news that Kim was exhausted, but managing to get things sorted with the help of one of the volunteers from the centre. Nicola felt reassured, the fear that Kim wouldn't cope lying heavily on her conscience. Micky was also looking for her, she'd said. He'd been to Margy's house three times that day, each time more persistent, each time more threatening. No doubt Kim had also had the pleasure of a visit.

When Margy saw the despondent look on Nicola's face, she'd leant in and grinned at her. 'Your policeman came to the residents' meeting today. All sorts of shite about zero tolerance, grassing on people, direct lines to the station ...' Her smile faded, though, when she saw Nicola turn her distressed face to the wall, and she'd left without mentioning him again.

Her policeman. Nicola touched her bruised face. She'd done her best to hide the discolouration, the other girls having a good laugh as they plastered their make-up onto her face that afternoon. Brenda told tales of how she'd used toothpaste mixed with foundation to cover up her black eyes, but that she'd ended up looking like something off that Michael Jackson video. They'd howled, and Nicola couldn't help but smile, wondering at their ability to find humour in such viciousness.

She felt Liam's head getting heavy on her arm. She had to think of them now, her children. Not some bloke she'd taken a fancy to. Not Micky. But Micky would never let her go. She'd have to find a way to either live without him, or live with him. Was it really that bad? It wasn't as if he'd broken any bones. Most of the time it was a thump in the arm, a twist of the finger, a foot in the kidneys. She'd lost great clumps of hair to his fingers, but she still had all her teeth. She closed her eyes. *Still*. The inevitability of what was to come was written all over the faces of the women in this place.

She fought against the image of Lee, sitting at the bar; his smile. Despite her revulsion for everything he stood for, she couldn't help but feel a flush in her cheeks when he tiptoed into her thoughts. She shook him from her mind. Her children. They were her top priority now. She would not turn into her mother. She wouldn't bring an inventory of men into their lives every few months. She wouldn't leave them to fend for themselves. Her mother's illness had driven their father away when they were barely out of nappies. The ridiculous highs, the shattering lows. She didn't know it was an illness then. Only now, when she watched TV programmes about mental illness, did she recognise the symptoms, symptoms she had recognised in Mark on his release from Deerbolt. One day he was climbing the walls, the next rolled up in a quilt on the sofa like a cocoon. The men came and went in her mother's life, most of them lowlifes, she desperate for adult love and the comfort of a pair of arms around her at night, them after what they could get. Nicola and Mark were still babies really when she'd started to disappear; four and three years old. First the odd night, then a weekend, then a week, then ...

She didn't dare think about it and she cuddled Liam to her. No. She would do for her children what her mother never did for her and Mark. She would put them first.

Liam had started to snore gently and she opened her free arm out to Michael Jnr, but he shook his head vigorously.

Michael had cried his face crimson earlier that evening. He didn't like this place that smelled of tobacco and air freshener. He'd refused to play with the other kids. She couldn't blame him. They were scary – either wild or moody, screeching or whinging at their mams for juice, biscuits, telly, toys, attention.

Nicola had found Brenda's nine-year-old, Damon, sitting on the stairs by himself while his mother smoked and drank tea in the kitchen with the other girls, her blackened, bare feet resting on the table, her sham laugh pervading the whole house above the noise. *Ha ha ha. HA HA HA!* Damon was kicking at the spindles, ignoring Nicola's requests to stop. She'd tried to entice him down, but it seemed the more she cajoled him, the harder he kicked, until the spindle shot out, clattering onto the hallway floor. Nicola had shouted at him, and Brenda had immediately swayed into the hall, her grey leggings showing every lump of fat wobbling around her thighs, her legs splaying out below the knee. Her eyes bore into Nicola, who felt the floor quake with the power of Brenda's feet. When Brenda picked up the spindle, Nicola held her breath and was about to apologise – never cross the line – never tell off other people's kids in front of their parents – but Brenda pushed past her and up the stairs, laying into Damon with the spindle.

'How man, I'll *fucking kill you*,' she'd bellowed at him.

Damon had wailed, *Gerroff!* But when his hands were at his face, Brenda aimed for the legs, and when his hands came down to his legs, she aimed for the arms.

Nicola had looked on, horrified, as Tracey, Lisa and one of the refuge workers prised Brenda off him, her raging face spitting at the world. Brenda breathed deeply, staring down at her crying child with the same expression of both satisfaction and fear she saw on Micky's face after she'd taken a hiding.

'Fucking little prick,' Brenda muttered as she tossed her white fringe from her eyes and calmly walked back down the stairs and into the kitchen with her lackeys, discarding the spindle on the floor as she went.

Michael had been sitting at the top of the stairs, his face stricken. Then the crying started.

Liam was still snoring lightly as Nicola put him under the covers and went to sit next to Michael at the end of the bed. 'You tired, too?' she asked, stroking the hair from his forehead. Michael nodded and finally gave in to his need for a cuddle. He snuggled up to Nicola's breast, thumb in his mouth, and she rocked him to and fro, vowing never to allow herself to become like Brenda. Hardened, pitiless and vicious.

***

Micky studied the queue of people filing down the hill into the club. Between him and Stevie, they created a human barrier to the good time to be had inside. Thursday was student night and usually one of his most lucrative, but the queue was only a fraction of what it usually was at this time of night. Most had exams or had gone home to their mammies and daddies to get fed and lounge around their bedrooms for the summer.

Micky hated students. Vermin. They talked from their stomachs, loud and cavernous. They dressed well and looked healthy, paying a tenner or more to get into their clubs – not like ten or fifteen years ago when he worked Rockshots and they were all scruffy and half-starved, scraping the two-pound entrance fee together, making sure they had enough left over for their poppers. Now everything was designer, even the drugs. Even the vermin.

He looked at his phone. He knew Nicola had his number by heart, he'd made her repeat it often enough so she could never say she didn't know it. That fat slut, Margy, had refused to take Nicola's mobile phone and give it to her. She'd stood at her front door, hating him with her pokey black eyes, denying she knew where his wife was.

'Honestly, Micky, she's not here,' she'd said in her flabby drawl of a voice, 'the social services won't let you near them, anyhow.'

Fuck that, he'd spat, did she think he was born yesterday? Where the hell else did she have to go?

'Exactly,' Margy said flatly, 'you've made damn sure she's got no one left, you prick.'

Micky was in two minds whether to admire her or slap her face. Not many people stood up to him, but there she was, standing at her door like the fucking Sphinx and he wasn't getting past. He'd held Nicola's phone out to her, but her hands had remained folded over the beachballs she had for tits. He'd put it on the ground next to her feet and she'd kicked it onto the pavement. Then she'd closed the door in his face, the fucking fat fuck.

Micky seethed. He should have gone after Nicola that day he'd locked her out, but his pride and shame had nailed him to the mattress. He hadn't slept after she'd gone, too much adrenalin. He'd stewed in his own guilt and rage instead. She'd come back to him, though. She loved him.

He concentrated on his hands in his pockets, wondering how it would feel if they were tender and gentle instead of savage and rough. The effort it took to control them was overwhelming, and often he had no choice but to let them rip. It was the only thing that relieved the build-up of frustration and self-loathing that ate him from the inside.

He took his hands from his pockets, examined them, opening and closing the palms, turning them over as if looking for clues. They'd been his bread and butter at one time when he was in the ring every week. He'd thought they would make him a champion, the best, his big achievement. Now they shackled him. Put paid to him being the good husband he'd never really wanted to be.

The ring was where he'd met Tiger. Tiger could see his potential, not as a boxer, but as a man people could both admire and fear. Just the sort of man Tiger needed on his team. But even after working for him for all these years, Micky still hadn't been able to earn enough to take the leap out of Valley Park to the decent life that Nicola wanted. He'd promised to give it to her, but he hadn't, and now she was slipping away. Slowly but surely, inch by inch, he could sense it. And the more he felt her cutting loose, the more repulsed he felt about his own sickening failure. He wished she would be patient. His time was coming, he could feel it.

As a couple of pissed teenagers stumbled into the club, he asked himself what would happen if she didn't come back this time. He would have to persuade her to stay, no question, he'd done it before and he'd do it again. His anxiety diminished as he reassured himself and he put his methods of persuasion back into the deep pockets of his jacket.

'Here, Micky!' Micky looked over his shoulder at Mooney who was smoking the remnants of a cigarette between his finger and thumb, two enormous, yellow welts crusting on his lips. 'Tania won't give us owt. What's the matter like?'

'You're off the team.' Micky turned back to face the queue.

'Eh? You're joking!' Not getting any response, Mooney stood in front of Micky, hopping anxiously as if the temperature had plummeted to twenty below zero.

'You're too careless,' said Micky.

'Me? What you on about?'

'My bairn, you stupid twat.' Micky turned to him, gritting his teeth. 'You're lucky I haven't taken your legs off.'

'Aaah, howay, that was nowt to do with me.'

'Nah, it was the fairies, was it? You've been replaced.'

Mooney's voice shook with alarm, it became high-pitched and urgent. 'What do you mean replaced?'

'I've brought on a substitute.'

'You can't, there's nowt the matter with me.'

'Nah, nowt brain surgery wouldn't put right.' Micky pushed him out of the way to let a couple of suited young men in high white collars through the red VIP rope. Mooney was cramping his style, getting on his tits.

Mooney danced, agitated, compulsively wiping his hands down his hips. 'Where am I supposed to get gear? I'm gonna see Tiger about this. Yer gonna be sorry, Micky.'

Bending forward, Micky took him by the collar and put his forehead on his. 'Fuck off and die.' He let him go roughly and turned away from him.

'I'm telling you,' cried Mooney, straightening his jacket and pointing at Micky. Micky turned, and with one threatening step towards Mooney, off he ran like a frightened cat.

Micky sneered at him, the creeping coward. Nobody, but nobody, hurt his kids.

SEVEN

The sun beat down as Nicola stood at the graveside. At least it wasn't raining, was all she could think. The weather she could fathom, but this she just couldn't. Micky stood to her left, head bowed, leaving an acceptable distance between them as she'd requested. Margy had brought her the message. Micky was running out of patience. He'd given her the space she wanted for two weeks, but now he was at Margy's door every five minutes asking where she was. He was at the school, the community centre, demanding, demanding. Eventually, the note landed on Margy's doormat. He'd be at the funeral, whether Nicola liked it or not. Tell her. He knew the date, wasn't hard to get it out of the priest.

As the day of the funeral grew closer, waves of emotion swelled and tumbled, threatening to take her under as they receded. She didn't have the energy to fight him. She'd given Margy a note to put through Micky's door. He could come to the funeral, but he could stand well back from her so she could grieve without being smothered.

She listened now to the lament of the priest as he swung the censer of incense over the coffin. She didn't take in what he was saying, just stared at the top of the wooden box being lowered into the ground, the gold plaque reading simply 'Mark Anthony Redmond. 1974-1999. RIP'. His body was in that coffin. Mark's body, once alive, getting his life back on track, now gone forever.

Kim, pale and thin, clung to Nicola's elbow, shivering despite the heat. They stepped forward together on the gentle nod of the priest, feeling every pitying eye on them as Nicola picked up some earth and threw it onto the coffin. It made a hollow sound, like the coffin was empty.

'Tara, Mark,' she said, quietly.

Kim, too unsteady on her feet, fell to her knees on the fake grass that protected their shoes from the soil. Nicola bent down and held her under her arm, but her strength had deserted her. A hand took Kim under her other armpit, and Nicola looked up into the freckled face of Tyrone Woods. She gasped and held her breath, panicking, looking behind her and extending her hand to Margy in alarm, but Micky was there first. Tyrone stepped back, repelled by Micky's stare, and he watched through shamed eyes as Kim was pulled back to her feet, only to slump back to the ground, groaning, her arms wrapped around her waist. Micky bent down and gently picked Kim up, holding her in his arms like a sleeping child, Kim turning her crumpled face to his chest as he returned to his allocated spot, eyes on the priest. Sorrow tore at Nicola's throat and she felt Margy's hand grasp hers when the priest said his final Amen.

It was over. She raised her head to look around her. As well as friends from the estate, half a dozen young lads surrounded the grave, lads Mark had worked with down at the youth project, standing in borrowed suits, gelled heads bowed, hands clasped in front of them. Tyrone stood back, a few yards behind her, and she wondered how long he'd been there. She had no time for anger, not today, but she couldn't help but question the audacity.

As people crossed themselves and started to walk away, she glanced into the distance, and, beyond the big oak tree, she spotted Lee with a woman beside him. His colleague, his girlfriend. She didn't care.

Nicola felt in her pocket and closed her hand around a set of keys. The keys to her own house, secured within just a matter of weeks with the help of the refuge manager. She couldn't bear to live in that loveless place any longer than she had to. A few bin bags of her things lay upstairs in the empty front bedroom of the new house. So desperate were the Council to let out properties on Valley Park, she'd had her pick of the crop. The refuge manager had wanted to send her to County Durham or North Tyneside, but Nicola was adamant. She needed to be near Kim and that was that. Micky would just have to live with it, she'd have to be strong and he'd have to get the message. If the only empty houses near Valley Park were in Valley Park, then Valley Park it was. But this was *her* house now, *her* life, and she would call the shots.

Waiting for the coroner to complete their inquest and allow the funeral to go ahead had been torture. Time had stood still as she tried to live her life without her brother and her husband in a place that had 'temporary' written all over it. The refuge made her nerves scream. The kids ran wild, the refuge workers trying their best to keep them occupied with paints and Lego, but there weren't enough naughty steps and the mothers seemed happy enough for others to be dealing with the spillages and the fights while they gossiped, drank tea and smoked countless fags. Nicola had found herself joining them out of boredom and the need to clear her head of the worry that dogged her mind. But on Monday, she'd got the good news. The house she'd wanted, just a few doors from Margy, was ready for her to move into. The refuge manager had held the envelope out to her with a wan smile that asked questions Nicola didn't want to be asked. Margy had worked relentlessly with the housing office, bugged them several times a day to the point where they nearly threw the keys at her to be rid of the constant harassment. Nicola had stared at the envelope for twenty minutes or more – a set of keys and a rehousing furniture package from the Council. The Holy Grail for homeless, battered wives.

Brenda had joined her at the table, stirring sugar into her tea with a critical spoon. 'Valley Park? Worse than mad,' she'd said. 'You'll be back here before the month's out, you watch.' Of course, Brenda had done it already. She'd made the break, got away. But Nicola could see through the bullshit. Brenda was boastful enough now that the husband was safely behind bars and she had no choice in the matter. Nicola had changed the subject, wondering instead how she could get her belongings out of the house that Micky now occupied alone. She'd been wearing borrowed clothes for weeks. She missed her make-up, bras that fit, her fluffy white dressing gown and slippers, her handbag containing her keys to the front door that was no longer hers.

'Well, just break in, man, Tracey did,' Brenda said, munching her way through a packet of Bourbons. 'Then run like the fucking clappers if he catches you. *HA HA HA.*' She belted out her signature laugh, and Nicola had to smile at this grotesque woman who filled her simultaneously with both fear and hope. Break in? She might just have to. The house wasn't exactly secure – who would break into Micky Kelly's house?

Nicola turned away from the grave, her arm linked through Margy's. She sensed Micky behind her, watching, waiting for an opportunity to get near her and offer her some false comfort. She had, indeed, taken Brenda's advice the day before, only it hadn't quite worked out as planned.

***

Lee stood watching Mark's funeral from the shadow of the oak tree, observing Nicola from a safe distance. Despite her obvious grief, she looked poised and composed in black jeans and the same black top she'd been wearing the night he first saw her. DC Thompson stood next to him. She'd done a sterling job getting information out of the pregnant housing director and her fabulous staff, badgering her for weeks to get details on current tenancies – who was moving in and who was moving out of the estate. He knew they couldn't guarantee they were all who they said they were, but it was a good start. The list had arrived by fax that morning.

'Think the kids must be from the youth club,' observed Lee.

'Maybe they've forgiven him.'

'There was no evidence other than possession.'

'You could hardly say a kilo of coke was for personal use.'

Lee didn't answer. He was staring at the familiar face of a spotty teenager, the red hair parted at the side in deference of the situation. The face from the pub, and the photograph in Mark's file. The kid looked haunted, his bent shoulders adding fifty years to him, his eyes darting warily around him.

Lee watched Nicola bend down to pick up some soil.

'There's his sister,' said Thompson. 'Housing says she's just taken up a tenancy of her own. Must've left her husband.'

Lee nodded. 'Got anything on him?'

'Pretends to be a bouncer. More likely he runs a protection racket.'

'Where?'

'Pubs and clubs in town. I've heard it's carved up between a handful of hard cases.'

Lee huffed and smiled knowingly. Landlords and club owners paying local hard men to keep the worky-tickets and the drugs out, but letting their own dealers in.

'That's him there,' said Thompson. Lee watched Micky pick up Mark's crumpled wife and carry her back into the small group of mourners.

'D'you think he's supplying on Valley Park?' he asked.

'Don't think he'd be stupid enough to do it on his own turf.'

'If his wife's left him, she might grass.'

Thompson snorted. 'Doubt it. Who to?'

Lee looked at her and raised his eyebrows. 'Me.'

Thompson laughed quietly behind her hand. 'No way.'

'You never know, she might want to turn over a new leaf.'

Thompson shook her head. 'She'd be *lynched*.'

Lee watched the mourners file away one by one, nodding at the funeral director and shaking hands with the priest, saw Nicola look at him for a moment before throwing her hair over her shoulders and walking away.

She'd left her husband. He'd known that yesterday when he got the heads-up from DC Gallagher who'd sighed in boredom at the report of a domestic at 10 Elm Street. Lee had gone straight to the address, walked into the living room to find a couple of uniformed officers standing between Micky and Nicola. Mrs Kelly had broken into the house to get some things, one of them said. There'd been a bit of a row. A few things broken.

Lee turned to Nicola. 'You got what you came for?'

'She's taking nothing,' Micky said, narrowing his eyes at Lee. He never forgot a face.

Nicola stood guarding a couple of black bin bags. 'Are these your property?' Lee asked her, and when she nodded he told her to take them and go.

'She's going nowhere.' Micky was held back by the outstretched arm of one of the officers and he didn't resist. He wasn't daft. With Tiger's deal on the party boat coming up, the last thing he needed was to be in trouble with the law.

'Would you like to press charges?' Lee asked him calmly.

The sarcastic 'No thank you' was the end of the conversation, and as Micky slumped onto the sofa, Lee picked up the black bags and left the house, Nicola following behind.

Outside and away from the house he'd put the bags on the pavement and shook out his hands. 'You all right?' Nicola nodded. 'No blood this time?' He'd smiled and she'd half-smiled back, declining his offer of a lift, but gracefully and with a hint of gratitude.

As Lee and DC Thompson watched the cemetery empty of the last few mourners, they turned and walked towards the north entrance. His grandfather's burnt-out house greeted them on their exit, and Lee remembered the quiet, monosyllabic old man, hunched, frail and bossed about relentlessly by his mother for his inclination to live in squalor and his love of all things feline. More than once he'd witnessed his mother kicking one of the squawking animals up the arse and into the backyard 'where they belonged'. The poor man must have been more than thankful when they left him in peace with his mounds of *Evening Chronicles* and his friends swirling happily around his ankles.

They headed for Lee's car, a brand new police-issue, in exactly the colour he'd ordered – electric blue. He winked at Thompson over the roof of the car as the central locking chirped open.

She grinned. Men and their toys.

***

The station was buzzing when they arrived back, uniforms everywhere. The weather forecast was for several days of scorching heat, and that could only spell trouble as people threw pints of sunshine down their throats in double quantities at double speed. They were all ready for a couple of evenings of cracked heads and overtime.

Lee headed straight for DI Meadows's office and knocked on the door. He heard a '*Yes,*' and entered, walking up to her and taking a document from his work bag. He put it on her empty desk, and, when she didn't acknowledge it, bent forward and moved it under her nose. She put her pen down and looked at the document entitled *Feel the Force*.

'New strategy,' said Lee.

Meadows laughed. 'Just like that? Who said I wanted one?'

'The other one doesn't work.'

Meadows removed her glasses. 'You can't just sit down and write a strategy for an area command.'

'Why not?'

'Firstly – it's not your job.'

'I don't mind if you want to take the credit.'

'And secondly – there's been absolutely no consultation. It took two years to set up the Community Strategy for Valley Park.'

'With all due respect, ma'am, it's shite.'

DI Meadows stared, speechless at the arrogance of the man, but he sensed his advantage and continued.

'I mean literally, people sit around in meetings talking about dog shit – social workers, housing officers, pensioners. The criminals must be pissing themselves.'

'I don't think the Chief Constable would appreciate you rubbishing—'

'I'm not rubbishing it, I'm sure there's a place. But it's as much use as a chocolate teapot when it comes to crime. That estate is ruined—'

'You've only been here five minutes.' Meadows's eyes flashed with vexation.

'I grew up there. I know what it's supposed to be like.'

'This is not your personal crusade.' She pushed the strategy towards him.

'But you're getting literally nowhere.' Lee's patience was running thin, too.

'Well, that depends on what criteria you measure it by.' Lee rubbed his eyes with frustration, but Meadows kept on. 'The community beat officer—'

'—is useless,' he said. 'Let me go to the meetings.'

'No.' Meadows picked up her pen once more, the air vibrating with her displeasure.

Lee swallowed his pride, picked up his strategy and marched out of her office.

Sitting at his desk, he drilled the front page of the document with his fingers, staring at DC Gallagher who was looking at his computer screen, his face scrunched in confusion. He punched the keys slowly with one finger, grimacing at the screen and shaking his head.

Thompson brought Lee a cup of tea and he smiled up at her in thanks.

'I thought it was good, Sarge. You should go for it,' she said, indicating the strategy on his desk.

'No point,' he replied. 'Got to stick to pussyfooting around.' He sighed and threw the strategy resentfully into the bin. Fuck 'em, he thought. He had more important things to think about. The social services case conference for one, scheduled for nine o'clock the next morning. He'd got his facts straight. There was no evidence that the children were in any danger, neither Nicola nor Micky had any convictions for drug offences, but Kevin Moone had a record as long as his arm. He had a witness who would testify that Mr Moone was in the house that day. Nicola had her own place now: the husband and his cronies were out of the picture. She'd done the right thing, and they needed to back off. He could almost see their suspicious glances already: they would challenge him about Micky having access to the children, what with him living so close. Visits would have to be supervised if she were to avoid a longer-term care order. The process would be long and drawn out, but he could help them with an injunction. He just needed Kevin Moone to admit to dropping the wrap into Nicola's bag.

***

'Here, I've got sommat for you,' said Margy as they stood outside the gate, looking at the grey, pebble-dashed walls. She opened the boot of the car and took out a small, portable TV, Nicola smiling widely at it. 'You should get a dog,' said Margy.

'It'd have to be a bloody big one to frighten off Micky.'

Margy tutted. 'I meant for company.'

'God, you make me sound like a pensioner.' Nicola grinned, giving Margy a hug.

'Watch it. Top of the range, this, you know.' Margy hoisted the telly up and followed Nicola into the house.

Inside, Margy tried to hide her distaste at the sad state of the place. An armchair, a bookshelf and a small console table furnished the sparse living room. Putting the TV on top of the built-in cupboard in one of the alcoves, she gazed around her. The gas fire was covered in splashes of paint, the middle heat panel black and burned out. It was dark and gloomy, and the bare bulb made little difference to the presence of light when Margy switched it on. *At least there's curtains,* she thought, purple yes, but they would offer some privacy.

She walked into the kitchen and started unpacking the refuge's box of essentials while Nicola got changed upstairs and Liam slept in his buggy. A kettle, a toaster, some cutlery, cups and plates. Four of everything. When Nicola joined her, Margy could see she'd been crying again.

'You need vodka,' said Margy firmly, but Nicola shook her head.

'Wine? Methylated spirits?'

Nicola laughed. 'I need to get Michael.'

Margy nodded and told Nicola what she needed to hear. Everything was going to be fine. New start. New life. New curtains for sure.

***

Later that night, with Michael and Liam asleep in bed, Nicola settled down into the armchair with a cup of steaming tea, quilt wrapped around her, the Ten O'Clock News chiming out of her little television. It had been one of the worst days of her life and she hoped sleep would envelop her soon.

Outside, the silver car slipped silently through the blackened streets of Valley Park. They'd followed him onto the estate. He was thoroughly plastered after six hours or more of drinking. Twelve pints, maybe fifteen. He staggered along the street, looking for Micky's house, muttering to lampposts. Flies open, mouth dribbling, eyes streaming. Micky Kelly could fuck off. *Fuck off*! He toppled over as he shouted it, rolling off the pavement and into the gutter. He'd told Micky straight earlier on – thought he'd give him another chance. Game on, Micky, he'd said, how long did they go back? Wouldn't even have a team if it wasn't for him. Who would he get to do all the shit jobs now, eh?

'Mooney,' Micky had said, 'I can find any number of dickheads to sell gear for me. People who don't shit in their own nest.'

He'd tried not to stutter, but stuttered all the same. Said he'd heard where Micky's missus was even though he didn't have a clue. He'd have one up on him, the greedy get. But Micky had taken him by the throat, asking where she was, walking him backwards and up against the wall. He didn't tell him. He couldn't tell him, but he'd said he *would* tell him when he got some gear.

Mooney got to his feet now, sniggering, slobbering, trying to hold his head up, squinting at the car headlights approaching and wondering where he was, what street he was on. When he heard the shots, his legs gave way under him, and he felt pain. Agonising pain. His legs. *His fucking legs!* He heard himself screaming, tasted the vomit in his mouth. Then someone was there at his side, the fat one, the one that was always knocking around with Micky's missus, and then another woman was shouting at her, *What's happened?* The fat one's husband was there an' all, telling Micky's slut wife to get inside, watch the kids, and he heard the door close. The husband was telling the wife, *Howay inside, Margy man, it's not worth it. Leave it, will you?* But she wouldn't leave it, and she took off her cardie and tied it round his thigh telling the husband to get an ambulance before he bled to death. No one else came. The streets stayed deathly silent apart from his own heaving groans.

EIGHT

Liam was a few steps in front of her, pushing his own buggy, his hands high above his head. For the first time in weeks Nicola felt brave. It had been six days since the funeral, and she'd dressed herself properly, donning a pair of high-heeled ankle boots and her favourite red jacket. A little lipstick had made her feel she could leave the house and not be stared at as the latest Valley Park victim. She glanced down at Michael who skipped along beside her, excited about prizegiving day and receiving his trophy for his reading.

At the school gates, the other mothers huddled in small groups, smoking and gossiping, pushing their little ones harshly back and forth in their buggies to stop them screaming. Chinese whispers about the regeneration of the estate were rife. Some said a billion pounds was coming, jobs for their men and grown-up sons. Some were cynical that anything would happen at all. Nicola waved at Margy's husband, Joe, dropping little Jimmy at the school door before heading off to his bed after another long night shift. Some of the women offered their condolences. Just a young lad an' all, terrible thing. And him helping keep the other young 'uns off the street. Others looked at her nice clothes briefly then turned back to the topic of the day.

She bent down and tucked Michael's shirt into his shorts. 'Ready?' she asked. He nodded maturely, and she turned to her left to pull Liam back to her side so they could go into the school together. But Liam wasn't there. She spun round to her right and took a startled step backwards. She faced Micky, Liam hanging from his neck.

'Want Daddy to take you home?' he asked Liam, who nodded shyly, his shoulders around his ears.

'We're going to the post office after assembly,' said Nicola, holding her arms out to Liam. But he slid away from her, grinning and snuggling into his dad's neck while Michael jumped gleefully on the spot. *'Dad! Dad!'*

'Joining the giro queue, are you?' said Micky, rubbing Liam's back but ignoring Michael pulling on his sweatshirt.

Nicola didn't take her eyes off Liam. 'It's clean money,' she said.

'All money's dirty.'

'At least I know where it's coming from.'

Micky sneered. 'Don't come on all Mother Teresa with me while you're breaking up our family. These bairns love me.' He pulled Michael's head to his leg, and when Nicola didn't answer, moved his face closer to hers. 'Why? Why are you doing it?'

'It's not me, Micky,' she hissed at him under her breath. 'They won't let you see them without someone there.'

Micky pulled her away from the gates and the gossiping women, leaving Michael standing a few feet away, glancing impatiently at the school entrance as the bell rang.

'Come here,' Micky said. 'Stand here and tell me you don't love me.'

'What did you have to go and get involved in drugs again for?' she demanded.

'Nicola, I work the clubs. It's part of the scene. People drink, they do drugs. It doesn't mean I'm dealing.'

'Where did Liam get it from then?'

'Look,' he said, 'there's no way you're standing in a giro queue. Come home.'

Nicola stood her ground. 'I don't want to.'

'Who's gonna look after you?' he asked.

'Mammy!' Michael called, the pavement clearing of people.

But Nicola still held Micky's glare, astonished. 'I can look after myself.'

Micky's mouth started to twitch. 'I'll tell you this for nowt,' he said through gritted teeth. 'It's a shitty world and you'll not survive it without me.'

'If I survived you, I can survive anything.'

Micky stood up straight slowly. 'Where you staying?' Nicola set her jaw firmly. 'Tell me, Nicola, you're not keeping me from my bairns.' She took her cigarettes from her bag and pulled one out of the packet.

'Come on, it's starting!' Michael's anxious voice shrieked.

'Fine,' said Micky. 'Get on with it. I'll take the kids.'

Nicola pushed the cigarette back in the box. 'You can't ...'

'Say bye-bye to Mammy. Come on, Michael.'

Liam obliged and waved, smiling to Nicola over Micky's shoulder as he walked away, but Michael stayed rooted to the spot, his desperate cries turning Nicola's head. He held his hand out to her, tears starting to brim in his eyes. *My prize!* they said.

'*Michael!*' Micky's voice roared from the corner of the street.

Michael sobbed as Nicola hunched down to his level. He wanted his daddy; he wanted his prize. She took him by the shoulders.

'Go on, darlin'. Get your seat and Mammy'll be there in a minute, okay?'

She watched him run hell for leather into the school, his bag dragging on the pavement, but when she stood up and looked around her, Micky was gone.

***

Margy answered her door bleary-eyed, just out of one side of the bed as Joe climbed into the other. She pulled her friend inside and put the kettle on while Nicola paced, thinking.

'You'll have to get the police,' said Margy.

But Nicola shook her head vehemently.

Margy was searching in her handbag, digging deeper and deeper. *Where the hell is it?* She tipped the contents onto the kitchen top and there it was. She wiped the crumbs from it.

'Here,' she said, handing Nicola a business card. *Detective Sergeant Lee Jamieson*, it read. 'I don't think you've got much choice, do you?'

An hour later, her baby was delivered back to her at Margy's house, carried up the path by a tall officer who bounced a giggling Liam on his broad shoulders. She thanked him as he passed Liam into her outstretched arms, and she glanced past him to see Lee standing at the gate, his sunglasses reflecting the windows of the house. She shielded her eyes against the glare of the sun as he walked down the path, shaking hands with the officer as they passed each other.

Lee expected the door to be firmly closed in his face, but it wasn't. Instead, she stood motionless, waiting for him. When he reached her, he raised a hand before she could speak and fished in the breast pocket of his shirt, pulling out a black keyring. A panic alarm, he told her. Just press the red button and the alarm will sound in the police station. He'd got it all sorted, so she wasn't to worry. He was on personal standby.

Nicola looked around her anxiously. 'I can't take it.'

'It works just like—'

'Listen, I'm sorry for giving you a hard time,' she said, 'but he wasn't a dealer, my brother, he wasn't.'

'A kilo of cocaine and a bunch of kids at the funeral?'

'I know how it looks, but there's no way he would have given drugs to those kids. He worked with them, they loved him. Lost his job, lost everything.' Her sincerity pulled him in. 'It was horrible, seeing him. Hanging there. I tried …'

'I know, I know.' He slid the alarm back into his shirt pocket. He wanted to take her in his arms but knew what the consequences might be for both of them if he caved.

'I'm sorry,' she said, looking around her. Anyone could be watching.

'So you said.'

'No, I mean for not thanking you, for trying to save him.'

'It's okay. I think you'll find the care order's been dropped, too.'

Nicola put her hand to her mouth. 'Why are you doing all this for me? You must think I'm a right ungrateful cow.'

Lee raised his eyebrows. *Well, now you come to mention it.*

She tried not to smile. 'It's just …'

'I know, we're all bastards.'

She frowned at him apologetically.

'Let's start again,' he said. 'I'm Lee Francis Jamieson.'

While she laughed through her drying tears, not daring to shake his hand in public, Micky Kelly's neighbours at 12 Elm Street wondered if they should call back the cops who had just left. There was a hell of a racket coming from next door – growling and snarling, shouting and bawling, things breaking, doors coming off their hinges. Instead they locked their doors and turned up their TV until the neighbour they knew wouldn't appreciate their concern left his house like a tornado.

***

Two cups of sweet tea and a packet of chocolate biscuits later, Margy peeked through the closed curtains of her living room window and looked cautiously up and down the street. Nicola was desperate to get to school for the lunch break so she could see Michael. Poor Michael, her heart ached with guilt, but she was terrified to leave the house with Liam. Micky would be livid. He'd lost the battle, and now he would be all out for war.

'Nah, he's not coming,' Margy said, but Nicola's alarmed face opposed any permanent opening of the curtains, so she pulled them to again.

'What's that noise?' Nicola asked, her ears straining towards scratching and whimpering coming from the kitchen.

Margy's hands flew to her cheeks and she gasped, 'Eeeeh, the dog!'

Nicola looked puzzled.

'The bliddy dog, man!' Margy rushed to the kitchen, tripping over Liam and upsetting his jigsaw, much to his vexation. Nicola followed her, still baffled, and Liam, wailing, got to his feet and toddled after her. Margy opened the door to the small utility room and out bounded a little Jack Russell, white with a couple of brown patches and a short beard that made him look like a sweet old man. He ran straight to Liam who stopped crying immediately and began shrieking with delight. *Is it ours? Is it ours?* He sank down onto his backside, tickling its ears and belly, the dog snorting happily, wagging its tailless behind and wriggling from side to side like a worm. *Am I yours? Am I yours?*

Nicola looked at Margy open-mouthed, crossed her hands over her heart as Margy nodded at her. 'Ah he's lovely, thanks, Margy.'

'They're lethal, these things, when they sink their teeth in.'

'What's his name?'

The dog barked. *'Woof! Woof!'* Liam echoed, clapping his hands.

'Rufus,' said Margy. 'He says he's called Rufus.'

'Doggies not talk,' giggled Liam.

'Yes, he can,' said Margy defensively, giving Liam a tennis ball and opening the back door. Rufus dashed outside ready to play and Liam was more than willing.

As they stood watching Liam throw the ball about three inches from his feet, there was a loud rap on the front door. Nicola ducked instinctively onto her hunkers.

Shit!

Her heart was in her mouth and she felt her breathing become shallow, her head spin. She knew he would come eventually and she had the female independence speech all worked out. But now the moment was here, she felt paralysed.

Margy shuffled to the living room window. 'It's all right, it's just Kim,' she said.

Heaving a sigh of relief, Nicola made her way unsteadily to the sofa, thinking back to the days when she lived without fear. Before that night out in the new Russian vodka bar in town where the big NatWest used to be. The fella was just some kid, some young professional type who'd looked at her breasts, still swollen from having Michael Jnr a couple of months earlier. He'd stared right at them, smiling drunkenly to himself, imagining his head between them, her hands behind his head pulling him closer into her cleavage. Micky, too, watched the scene unfold in the bleary mind's eye of the young man. His fist propelled the kid backwards like a skittle into the drinks and gaping mouths of the other punters. It was the night that same fist came at her face for the first time. She'd seen stars. Literally, like Tom and Jerry, she'd reeled and fallen over, her head hitting the corner of the vegetable rack. There was blood and she was stunned, his face hovering over hers within seconds, not angry, but satisfied. That's when it started, the fear.

Kim came in holding out a piece of paper. The bill for the funeral. Her face was lined and puckered as Margy took the bill and read it, her hand springing to her forehead.

'Kim, you should've got the basic one,' she said.

'Well, I didn't know, did I?' Kim's hands trembled as she lit a rolled-up cigarette.

'Did you get your grant?' asked Margy, a little impatiently.

'Yes, but only, like, a thousand.'

Nicola took the bill from Margy and her jaw dropped. Three thousand, five hundred pounds, and a quote for seven hundred for the headstone.

Kim picked tobacco from her tongue. 'What about Micky? Ask him for us,' she ordered.

Nicola shook her head and swallowed, 'I can't—'

'He was your *brother*.'

The accusation hit Nicola in the face as brutally as any fist of Micky's. She stammered, 'Look, as soon as I'm straight, I'll see if I can get a job or I'll give you something each week out my giro,' she said.

'It's got to be settled in fourteen days,' said Kim sullenly.

'I'll put them off,' offered Margy, holding her hand out to Nicola for the bill.

'No, giz it.' Kim snatched it out of Nicola's hands, and Margy pursed her lips. She'd never had much time for Kim, always thought her a bit of a whiny leech, but tolerated her because of Nicola.

'What about a collection?' suggested Margy, trying to lift the mood with solutions.

'Hey, man, I'm not a friggin' charity case.' Kim headed for the door, Nicola reaching out to her.

'Kim, hang on ...'

'Don't bother,' she snapped, 'and don't bother coming round either.'

Reeling again from the blame, Nicola sank onto the sofa as Kim walked out the front door, leaving it wide open. Liam skipped into the room with Rufus at his heels and she picked him up, cuddling him into her lap, thinking of Michael, hoping the dog would make up for the disappointment of this morning. Liam's thumb went in his mouth and he curled his fingers around her hair. *Michael Kelly!* She imagined the teacher calling his name, and Michael taking his trophy amidst applause, his head bent to the floor as he headed back to his seat to put the trophy on the empty chair next to him.

Margy watched Kim scurry down the path as she closed the door, but she stopped short when she saw little Jimmy come plodding down the path, home for his lunch and holding out a piece of paper. When her son looked at people he had a habit of scrunching up his nose and baring his teeth as he tried to focus through his thick glasses. He did just that as he looked up at Margy and said, 'This is for you, Mam.'

Margy took the note and unfolded it.

'YOU'RE DEAD,' it read.

***

The hanging baskets either side of Debbie's front door dripped water onto his shoes as Lee stood on the step and took a deep breath. He was finally taking Louise out for the evening, maybe to the pictures so they'd have something other than each other to concentrate on for a couple of hours before she hurled the accusations at him, pointing the finger, blaming him for the neglect and the missed Christmases and birthdays.

He rang the bell.

Debbie opened the door with an 'I'm not impressed' look. He was late.

'Louise!' she called, not taking her eyes off Lee.

Louise thudded down the stairs, her hair blonde now, tucked behind her ears with a sweeping fringe framing her flushed face.

'Louise, this is your dad.'

'I know, stupid.' Louise pushed past Debbie and smiled at him, apprehensive but excited. 'Where're we going?'

Lee exchanged a look with Debbie, not expecting it to be this easy. 'Erm, I don't know. Anywhere you like.'

'Metrocentre? Is that your car?' She bounded down the front steps and towards the gate.

'Yeah,' said Lee following her with his eyes, then turning back to Debbie. 'What time do I have to—'

'Nine-thirty. She's got a key. Good luck,' and Debbie stepped back into the house.

'Thanks...' But the door was closed, and Lee turned and faced his car, Louise in the passenger seat, making herself comfortable and checking out the dashboard.

She gestured to him and shouted through the open window, 'Hurry up, Dad, the shops shut at eight.'

***

The Metrocentre was Lee's idea of hell. The biggest shopping centre in Europe – or on the planet: he didn't know – but he generally avoided these places like head lice. It was heaving with people dragging their screaming children around Topshop and Dorothy Perkins, placating them with candyfloss and popcorn.

It had been two hours and they were finally on their way to Pizza Hut, Lee carrying two bags full of Jane Norman stretch nylon and Miss Sixty jeans. He'd drawn the line at what she'd termed 'slut shoes', deciding it would be better to be an old-fashioned parent than a downright bad one. Louise skipped along, her arm through his, her new Playboy handbag laden down with gold belly bars, Hi Beam highlighter and Juicy Tubes lip gloss. Her smile shimmered, and she tried her best to catch people's eyes as they walked past. *My dad. He's fabulous!*

They sat by the window, looking out onto the emptying car park, Lee ordering a double pepperoni which was met with a whoop of delight. That was *her* favourite pizza, too. He laughed back, revelling in her pleasure, answering her never-ending questions. What else did he like? Whopper or Big Mac? Blur or Oasis? Christina or Britney? They agreed on everything. It was so exciting she thought she might *burst*. They yakked and yakked like brand new best friends, about school and exams, her best friend Becky, music and clothes, *The Simpsons* and *South Park*, what would happen in the millennium. Would the world stop?

She hardly came up for breath.

After their plates were cleared and they sat holding their full stomachs, he stared at her, searching her face until she blushed and looked away embarrassed.

'*Da-ad.*' She loved saying the word.

'Your mum's done you proud.'

'Thanks,' she said. 'She's a bit tight, though, not like you.'

Lee surveyed the bags around him and imagined Debbie's face, angry and hurt that he could just turn up out of the blue and buy Louise's affection. He felt bad. She didn't deserve that, and he resolved not to spoil Louise too much, though he was utterly enjoying doing so.

On the way home, they sang along to the car radio, Shania Twain and Ricky Martin, clicking their fingers in unison. Louise sang to the advert jingles, making faces and mimicking the voices. She pointed out her school and the houses of friends, bitches and bullies. As they passed the Freeman Hospital, however, she became quieter, looking out of the window pensively, her hands clasped between her knees. The silence became uncomfortable as they neared her house in the darkness.

Lee struggled for something to say, so said nothing, turning the radio down as he pulled up alongside the front gate, the rasp of the handbrake punctuating the end of the evening. Louise looked out of the window and Lee loosened his seat belt and turned his body towards her.

'Want to come flat hunting with me?'

She turned and smiled. 'God, yes. You'll have to call me, though, I'm not allowed to ring mobiles.' When he leant forward to give her a hug, she rested her head on his shoulder, not wanting the embrace to stop. 'Will you come to my birthday dinner?' she asked, tentatively.

'Wouldn't miss it for the world.'

With a kiss to his cheek, she climbed out of the car and waved at him as she headed up the path with her bags. He waved back, and once she was inside, he sat back in his seat and heaved a glad sigh. It was perfect. She was perfect. He was at her university graduation, walking her proudly down the aisle, his grandchildren played happily at his feet in a family photograph. But he soon realised he was in the picture alone, a single man. He tried to pull Debbie back into the frame, but it made his heart lose its optimism.

He turned on the ignition and headed back to the crisply made bed in his soulless hotel.

NINE

Nicola clutched the edges of the bench under the Gothic arch of a cemetery gateway, wearing a summer dress she'd regretted putting on the minute she stepped out of the house. She wasn't sure why, but she'd felt the need to look nice, feminine. But her athletic build often meant feminine was out of reach and now she felt conspicuous, like a footballer in a frock.

She didn't know this place, but she found it more peaceful than eerie considering recent events. She'd taken two buses and a Metro up to the north of the city where no one would know her. She felt a million miles from Valley Park. Big houses with netless windows, their curtains wide open, confidently showing the world their contents. Sloping gardens with trees, and gates with numbers on them. Each house had a different front door, some with porches and some with names like 'Sunnymead' and 'The Lodge'.

She wouldn't ever want to live in a place like this, though Micky seemed to have ambitions to move them all to Gosforth or somewhere like it. She would feel as fake as her D&G sunglasses – like she didn't belong, like people were judging her for her accent and her crap handbags. Once upon a time she'd shared Micky's dreams of what they thought would be a better life. She'd dreamt of living somewhere affluent like this, away from the broken glass and graffiti. But wanting it and living it were two different things. Now she was happy to be amongst her own, with people who understood her, didn't question her motives and just let her be who she was.

Margy was gone. At six that morning, she'd heard the van pull up amidst the dawn chorus of blackbirds, robins and wrens. Margy had been round the night before, her eyes swollen, her nose blown into a red mush. Joe was angry, a rare occurrence. She should have stayed in the house that night, he'd said, let Mooney bleed to death on the street: who would have cared about the little shit anyway? But that would have gone against her very soul, and Margy never compromised her character. Surely that's what he loved and respected about her? He'd taken her upstairs and they'd looked down at little Jimmy, already asleep, his glasses still on his nose, always a good boy, sweet-tempered, geeky and shy. Then he'd shown her the note. 'YOU'RE DEAD.' And she knew.

As Nicola sat in her armchair in the early hours she could almost hear the twitching of the neighbours' curtains as the van pulled up. She should get up to say goodbye, but they'd agreed not to. So she stayed where she was, awake and completely alone, tears slipping silently down her cheeks, listening to the scraping of furniture being loaded into the van. Her touchstone was leaving, and she would have to cope on her own.

She knew now it was only a matter of time before Micky came to her door. She was surprised – she'd been in her house more than a week and no sign of him. Each day she waited, flinching at every sound. She kept the children tight by her side when they were out, looking round at every car engine she heard behind her. But Micky Kelly was nowhere to be seen. Her bed was unslept in. She preferred the armchair, a kitchen knife on the floor within easy reach. Joe had fitted the bolts to her doors, but now that Margy was gone, she felt like a sitting duck. The anxiety ate at her fingernails until they bled. Food stuck in her throat and she retched at its dryness. She'd told Micky she could take care of herself, but now she wasn't so sure.

***

Lee's phone had rung the minute he sat at his desk. Nicola wanted to meet him: she sounded anxious, upset. So when he heard her voice he was out of his seat like a jack-in-the-box. He was happy to get out of the office, already bollocked by Meadows again for setting up panic alarms without her permission. Was he controlling the budget now?

They'd ranted at each other for ten minutes: Meadows accusing him of undermining the team, him questioning whether she would know a team approach if it kicked her in the face. He'd told her straight – it wasn't a job to that lot, it was a pension. They avoided training like the plague, half of them didn't know how to turn on a computer, and you couldn't get a higher degree of prejudice if you advertised for it. Take DC Gallagher ...

But she'd stopped him there. Gallagher was qualified well beyond his current post; he was acting up before Lee got there. Oh yes, Lee had said, he could act up a treat. There was only one decent officer in the place and he bet Carol Meadows fifty quid that she was the last in line for any promotion.

With no defence, Meadows had reverted to what she was comfortable with and blethered on about the Community Strategy, how committed everyone was to it, how it was the bedrock of change. Lee challenged what it was about the brass and the politicians that was so shortsighted. No idea could be any good if it hadn't taken three years to think about. Panic alarms: simple, cheap, bags of information for very little cost. There's more than one way to get a result, he'd told her.

'You don't know this city!' she'd shouted, her face fracturing at the seams.

'And you don't know the people who live in it,' he'd responded bitterly.

He'd walked past Gallagher on his way back to his desk, throwing his ID at him. 'If you want the fucking job you can have it.' And when his phone rang, he wasn't seen for dust.

***

Lee arrived at the cemetery bang on time, eleven o'clock. She was waving furtively to him from a concrete bench, sitting awkwardly under a Gothic arch. He felt self-conscious as he walked up the uneven steps, conveniently created by the roots of the trees, and he saw her looking at him with an intensity that almost matched his own.

'This is very clandestine,' he said. Nicola looked puzzled and pulled her denim jacket together at her chest. 'Secretive,' he smiled.

'Have you got the panic thing?' she asked nervously.

He took it out of his pocket. 'At great expense,' he said.

'Do I have to pay for it?' Nicola looked alarmed.

'No, no, of course not,' he reassured her. 'What's frightened you?'

Nicola looked at her hands. 'Margy's gone.' Then she looked up at him earnestly. 'You don't know where she is, do you?'

'I can't tell you.'

'Is she all right?'

'Yes, she's fine. Here.' He held up the panic alarm. 'Better show you how to work this.' He showed her the on/off switch, the red panic button, the green to reset. It didn't make a noise but it connected straight to the station and they could even trace where she was. He'd even had it programmed to go straight to his mobile. There would be someone there in minutes.

She sighed and nodded gratefully, but her mind was still on Margy. 'Who sent her the death threat?'

'Probably the same people who shot Kevin Moone. Somebody's upset. Any ideas?'

Nicola shook her head.

'Even if you knew, you wouldn't tell me, would you?' He pressed her, but she remained silent. 'See, this is the bit I don't understand,' he said. 'People would rather live in fear than grass on anyone.'

'It's like that everywhere, it's not just us.'

'Even when it's your own child? What about Liam? You could have lost him.'

She looked away.

'You know how he got that cocaine, don't you?'

Nicola sighed. 'How is Mooney, by the way?' she asked.

'He won't be playing for Newcastle any time soon,' he said.

'Might scrape into Sunderland, though,' said Nicola, turning to him and grinning.

Lee laughed loudly until Nicola shushed him, indicating the graves all around them. 'He's signed a statement for social services, saying he left the drugs in your house, though he swears to me he didn't. He'll get a rap on the knuckles for possession.'

Nicola thought about it. No more care order, but that meant Micky could come by at any time.

'Why do you want to save the world?' she asked.

Lee chuckled again. 'The world? I don't.'

'Valley Park then.'

'Because I went away, and when I came back somebody had ripped the shit out of the place.'

As they searched each other's eyes, Lee's phone rang in his pocket. He ignored it.

'That might be an emergency,' she said, their eyes hooked on each other.

'They can leave a message.'

'I thought you were the Caped Crusader.' Their faces were getting closer.

'I was, but I think I just put myself on the transfer list.'

'Oh,' she said.

'Oh what?'

'I was just getting used to you.'

'But all coppers are bastards.' Their lips were almost touching, and Nicola's eyes started to close.

'You're different,' she murmured.

'So are you.'

He put his lips onto hers then brought his hand to the side of her face. He felt her body thaw, her shoulders drop as he put his arm around her waist and pulled her closer to him. She relented and kissed him back, breathing out deeply through her nose, her hand moving up his arm and to his neck. *This is it*, she thought, her ears buzzing, her pulse racing. *This is what it's supposed to be like.*

***

Lee felt everyone's eyes on him as he walked into the office. Conversations stopped. Mugs were held halfway to mouths. Eyes followed him, blinking, accusing. He felt his palms begin to sweat. Did they know? Had somebody seen them?

He straightened his tie, sat at his desk and started opening his mail – a wad of papers an inch thick for the next Valley Park regeneration meeting, held together with a bulldog clip, the agenda stretching to three pages. A memo from HQ in Ponteland about new procedures for strip-searching, and a colourful invitation to an equalities seminar. *Valuing Diversity: Your role as a public sector servant in ensuring equal access to grass roots services.* He looked around him. Aside from Thompson, the room was full of white, red-blooded men. It was a far cry from his office in London where people of all colours and cultures rubbed shoulders. These white men were keeping their eyes down today, though, and a noiseless atmosphere continued to shroud the office. Damn it, they knew something.

Gallagher started to sing to himself, '*Ooh ooh ooo-oooh. Can you feel the force.*' Another officer stifled a giggle, and even Thompson grinned behind her hand. Lee looked up, more irritated than puzzled, and Thompson mouthed to him: *Where've you been?*

Lee sat back in his chair as DI Meadows entered the room, grim-faced as ever.

'We've been trying to get you all morning,' she said to Lee sternly.

'Sorry, ma'am, detective stuff, Valley Park,' he smiled up at her, dropping his post into his in-tray.

'Well. Good. Okay, then.' She stood in a way that clearly indicated she was about to address the room. Everyone stopped what they were doing and paid attention. She held up the Community Strategy and Lee groaned inside. 'The strategy that we've been using for the last year with our partners at the local authority has been a major initiative in bringing people together to tackle problems.' People shuffled, and DC Clark yawned loudly. 'However,' she took a deep breath, 'we need to move on to a new phase.' She paused, and Lee started to pay attention. 'As some of you already know, I've spoken to the other services today and told them we're about to embark on a more proactive approach. We need a presence, we need information, and above all, we need the criminals to know that we're going to be there to knock them back every time they rear their ugly heads.'

'Can we use physical violence?' asked Gallagher.

'Is that in the Code of Practice?' she asked, her voice dripping with sarcasm.

'I think we should get light sabres as standard issue,' Gallagher said, buzzing and mimicking the actions.

'As well as the duty of care that is expected of *all* officers,' she continued, glaring at Gallagher, 'you will now be working towards *this* strategy for Valley Park.' She held up Lee's document. 'You've got copies on your desks, read them please and any questions, see DS Jamieson.'

'You really think people are going to tell us stuff when someone just got their legs blown off?' asked Gallagher sourly.

'I want a summary of everything we've got so far,' she said, ignoring Gallagher. 'I believe Housing were helpful?'

Lee nodded – he still had a job, then.

'Good,' she said. And with that she passed Lee his ID and marched back up the corridor to her office.

Lee's self-satisfied grin filled the room. At last, a good day. He watched Gallagher scratch at his head like Stan

Laurel as he picked up Lee's strategy, no doubt peeved at the prospect of having to do some real police work.

As Thompson smiled at him like a proud sister, Lee reached down to his bag and took out Mark's file. He'd had it for several weeks and had been over every detail many times. It seemed like a straightforward case. The drugs were found in money bags, the ones you get from the bank to put your copper in. Just over a kilogram up a drainpipe at the back of Mark and Kim Redmond's house. Partial fingerprints on the bags matched Mark's, and there was residue from the same cut of cocaine found in the fine grain of Mark's kitchen table. Kim, with no previous convictions, was soon released, but Mark had remained in custody while forensics did their work.

Tyrone Woods was the one key witness. He had a clean record and good GCSEs, unlike his brothers who'd been in and out of prison for violent offences. His father, Sean, was a known IRA man, released under the Good Friday Agreement the year before and now living with his wife and six sons on Valley Park. If Nicola was right, and Mark wasn't dealing, then why would Tyrone Woods lie? He seemed like a decent enough kid, despite being surrounded by violent men all his life. Lee looked at Tyrone's photograph for the hundredth time. His eyes were gentle, but adrift and forlorn.

What puzzled him most about this case was that Mark's last offence before this more recent arrest for dealing had been four years earlier for aggravated burglary. This was a long gap for someone intent on law breaking. He'd avoided prison for that last burglary offence by the skin of his teeth. After three months on remand in Durham Jail, he'd had time to get dry, grow up and think. In the file was a letter Mark had written to the judge. The handwriting was like that of a ten-year-old, written on a ruler to keep it straight, the words slowly and carefully formed and corrected at various intervals. The letter told the judge how sorry he was for frightening the people who had disturbed his crime: he never would have hurt them. He'd never hurt anyone in his life, just things. He acknowledged his difficult past, his drug habit and his disregard for other people's possessions that they'd worked hard to get. What touched Lee was his seemingly total commitment to change:

I have made a promise, on my sister's life, and she is the most precious thing to me, that I will never reoffend or take drugs again. The choice is now up to you, whether to keep me locked up or to let me go, and I will respect your decision because it is your job to protect the innocent. But I promise to you that if you give me a chance, I will turn my life around and give something back to the world.

Lee was pretty sure that Mark would not swear on Nicola's life without one hundred per cent meaning what he said. And, by all accounts, he *had* turned his life around. He'd kept his nose clean, got married, had a baby. He was volunteering and training as a youth worker. He'd shown no signs of addiction, his boss and colleagues had all given positive character statements to the court, saying he was their best worker and that the kids respected and admired him.

The judge who had presided over the aggravated burglary case had read the letter in the peace and quiet of his own home over a glass of port. Something in it was authentic enough for him to actually give Mark the benefit of the doubt. He released him into Nicola's care on a four-year suspended sentence. Alas, for Mark, he was released on licence which hadn't quite expired when he was arrested this time for drugs offences. There was no question he would have faced a long prison sentence if convicted – four years for the burglary and probably longer for dealing. How convenient, though, that he was arrested just before the licence expired. Maybe someone wanted him out of the way. He'd made the police's life hell for years and they wanted retribution. Or maybe he'd had enough of bringing up his family in poverty and wanted a way out. Maybe he was just guilty.

***

It kept happening, all afternoon, every ten minutes or so. Nicola would stop what she was doing, blush and smile uncontrollably. She put herself on the bench again, feeling the warmth shroud her like a snug winter duvet. She could have stayed there all day, just kissing like kids at a bus stop. She'd smiled *Hiya!* at everyone on the way home from school, skipping with Michael who was delighted to see her happy again.

A sharp rapping on the front door wrenched her from her dreams.

Micky stood, his hands clenched together at his chin, his tongue feeling his top teeth as if he'd just eaten something pippy. He didn't give her time to speak.

'Thought I'd give you the benefit of doing it voluntarily,' he said.

'Doing what?' she asked warily.

'Coming home, to me.'

'Dad! Dad!' Michael came running to the door. 'Are we coming home?'

'This is your home,' said Nicola, but Michael wasn't listening and continued to smile widely from one ear to the other while Micky stared at her questioningly. *Well?*

'I'll get the ball,' called Michael, already in the kitchen.

Nicola held up her hands. 'Micky ...'

He was having none of it and pushed past her into the house.

What a dump.

Rufus growled and snapped at his feet and Micky kicked him harshly away in disgust, bringing a yelp from the dog and sending him scuttling behind the armchair to lick his back leg. Michael, now standing at the kitchen door with the ball under his arm, looked uneasily at Micky's foot. Micky ignored Michael's hurt look as his elder son put the ball down cautiously on the floor and sat next to the dog, stroking his head and telling him he was a good boy. Liam was soon at his side, and they both petted their beloved friend, avoiding Micky's eyes as he sat on the frayed armchair, his elbows on his knees, his hands joined as if in prayer.

'Get your things, you're coming home,' he said to the children.

Nobody moved, and Nicola stood frozen by the window, watching Michael Jnr's eyes flitting now and then in Micky's direction, Liam continuing to chunter in a language only he and Rufus could understand.

She kept her voice calm. 'I said, this is our home.'

The blood vessels in Micky's temples pounded and Nicola moved to the little table by the door where her bag was, the panic alarm next to it on full display. She stood by the table as casually as she could. As Micky rose from the chair and walked towards her, she stiffened and put her hand over the alarm. He took hold of her arm and squeezed tightly, but feeling Michael and Liam's eyes on him, spoke affectionately while he dug his fingers deeper in.

'Come on, sweetheart, hurry up. Michael wants to watch the big telly, don't you, son?'

Michael wasn't so sure. He bent down to Rufus, covering the dog's whole body with his own in a big hug, more for his own comfort than Rufus's.

There was a knock on the front door, making everyone but Micky start.

'*Milk!*'

Rufus was at the door like a shot, barking incessantly.

'Get it,' said Micky sharply.

Nicola closed her hand around the alarm and pushed it up her sleeve, hanging onto the cuff with her fingertips as she walked into the hallway to open the door, pulling the barking dog back by his collar.

'Can I give it to you next week? My giro hasn't come,' shouted Nicola over the din. The milkman shook his head and Micky rolled his eyes, *fucking hell*. In just a couple of strides he was at the front door, taking a wad of money from his pocket. He peeled off a ten pound note and gave it to the milkman while Nicola slipped back into the living room and put the alarm into the back pocket of her jeans. When the milkman was gone, Micky closed the front door and came back into the living room.

'Look, Micky,' said Nicola, 'can we just calm down and talk about this?'

'I'm not talking anymore. I'm going out for a couple of hours, and when I come back, if you and the kids aren't home, you've had it. Do you understand?'

Nicola stared at him defiantly.

'There's your keys. You left them.' He held out a set of keys to her, but she didn't move. He put them on the table, then put a small plastic carrier bag down next to the keys before making his way to the front door, looking at each one of them individually with a touch of menace and no goodbye.

Giving Michael Jnr's confused face a reassuring smile, she took the bag from the table and tipped out the contents. Her mobile phone and charger. The phone rang and she sprang away from it, the display blinking 'MICKY' at her. She picked it up and switched it off, dropping it back on the table like a hot coal. She wouldn't let him intimidate her. This place might be damp and musty and sparse of furniture, but it was hers, and she wasn't going to let it go that easily.

While Michael hugged the football to his chest in front of the TV later, she pushed the bolts firmly across the front door.

***

That evening, Lee sat opposite Debbie at the restaurant table, the red wine going straight to his head via an empty stomach. She looked nice with a little make-up and a red dress that showed off her toned arms and slim waist. Next to him sat Louise, lording it over the table, the centre of attention and loving every minute of it. Around the table sat twenty-odd teenagers, a bumbling mixture of braces, pimples and shiny foreheads. Like Louise, many were as thin as sticks, wearing tiny, grown-up clothes that left little to the imagination. Lee wondered when this happened. His memory of being a teenager was to be surrounded by girls wearing anything but clothes that would cling to their bodies – big, baggy, batwing jumpers, sweatshirts and leg warmers. These girls looked like pageantry, pouting and constantly pushing straightened hair from their eyes with perfect nails.

By the end of the main course most of them seemed to have settled into small groups of three or four, leaning over each other to bitch about some poor sod on the other side of the table. They made no attempt to hide who they were talking about, often turning quite deliberately to throw an evil glance at someone before swirling their hair back to the witches' coven to drag up some more filth. A couple of boys sat together next to Louise, playing on their Game Boys and generally ignoring the oestrogen-sodden air.

The flat hunting had been stressful. Louise had made her feelings quite clear. They'd seen four flats – one in Byker, 'full of charvers', she'd stated. The second, a Victorian property with amazing fireplaces: 'Studentville', and the third, a cute, one-bedroom place on the Quayside. As he stood at the window he could see downriver to the cranes and half-structure of a bridge being built for the new millennium. The deserted Baltic Flour Mills, a dilapidated fortress and home to countless pigeons and their grey shit, grimly faced the living room window. Clothed in scaffolding, it prepared itself for its new life. He'd liked it, until Louise flounced out of the bathroom, 'Well, where am I going to sleep?' she said.

Finally, at the very top end of his price range, was a two-bedroom mezzanine apartment in the old cigarette factory building on the Coast Road, an Art Deco monster that had lain in ruins for years, now a monument to housing redevelopment for the professional classes.

'We'll take it,' she'd said to the estate agent, her head turned upwards towards the twenty-foot, spotlit ceiling. Lee could only blink at her.

'What,' she'd declared. 'You can afford it.'

They'd sat in the car afterwards with their McDonald's milkshakes from the drive through, Louise reeling off the list of friends coming to her birthday pizza. Twenty or more. Lee waited patiently, sucking hard to get any ice cream through his straw and shaking his head. He'd been planning to pay for the birthday meal, but it was starting to sound expensive.

'What's wrong with being popular?' she'd said. She had a lot of friends. Surely he'd prefer that to her being some kind of weird loner with ringworm and fungi toes. He'd choked on his drink, and she'd grinned a gappy, imperfect grin at him over the straw of her milkshake. He was hooked. And she knew it.

The waiters brought out dessert menus and there was much shaking of heads and sharing of spare tyres between the skinny ones, and round-eyed delight from those of a more robust stature as their mouths drooled in anticipation of chocolate fudge cake and squirty cream. There was a hush around the table as girls conferred with each other on the menu, some leaving their chairs, pulling their skirts down and wobbling on heels to their pals further down the table to help them decipher what a crème brûlée was.

With the puddings devoured and the second bottle of red wine going down well between Lee and Debbie, the waiter brought out a birthday cake with candles, another waiter by his side with a ukulele hanging from his neck. Everyone turned to face Louise and she squealed excitedly.

The music began and everyone sang 'Happy Birthday', the other diners in the restaurant joining in good-humouredly. When Louise took the knife from the waiter, Debbie stood up to take pictures, Louise cutting the cake to applause. She looked around her sincerely and thanked everyone for coming, for her cards and presents, and for her mam, *and* dad, for making it a lovely birthday. She was sixteen and couldn't believe it! Everyone laughed and Lee looked up at her proudly. She was beautiful.

Louise glanced at her mum, looking really pretty for a woman of her age, and caught her staring at her dad over her glass of wine. She smiled dreamily and plonked herself back down next to Lee, asking if she could have a bit of wine just for the toast.

'No,' said Debbie firmly. Then she pointed at Lee. 'Don't you let her have any,' she said, 'I mean it.' Debbie scowled tipsily, then stood up and made her way to the Ladies while Louise slumped back in her seat, her bottom lip hanging out. Lee realised that he saw none of his own characteristics in Louise, only Debbie's – the non-stop talking, the wonder and optimism at the world around her, demanding, bossy, bold and impulsive. And funny as hell. When he left her he felt like he'd run a marathon, exhausted but a little thrilled.

'Can I come and live with you?' she asked.

'Erm, no.'

'Why?'

'Coz your mam would go mad,' he said matter-of-factly.

'It's not up to her.'

'Louise,' he warned, 'she's brought you up, sacrificed—'

'Is it because you don't like me?'

'Of course I like you.' Lee put an arm around her shoulders, and she relented a little.

'But you don't love me enough to want me all the time,' she said.

Lee was lost for words.

'Did you love my mam?' Lee looked away embarrassed and Louise threw her arms up in the air. 'Why won't anybody *talk* about it!'

Lee fiddled with his serviette as Louise charged at him, keeping her eye on the ladies' toilet room door, trying to cram it all in before her mother ended the conversation with a look that would cut steak. 'If you never got married, how long were you together? Were you, like, childhood sweethearts? She was only my age when she had me. How old were you?'

Lee shook his head, but she persisted.

'*Please* tell me, why did you go?'

'Because I was a coward. Leave it at that, Louise.'

To his relief Debbie returned to her seat, fresh lipstick applied, trying to stay composed after drinking the majority of the wine on top of a glass for Dutch courage before she left the house.

Louise stared at them both crossly. 'I wasn't a one-night stand, was I?'

Eyebrows raised, neither parent gave anything away and Lee hid a smile behind his hand as Louise huffed out of her seat and strode off to give big, teary hugs to a couple of her friends who were putting their coats on. Lee stole a glance at Debbie who pursed her lips and scratched at her forehead while he raised his hand to the waiter and indicated, *the bill please.*

'Sixteen,' said Debbie, looking straight at him. The age rang in both their heads. How young they had been, how grown-up they'd thought they were, how stupid and naive. How much would Lee want to murder any cocky adolescent who touched his daughter.

Debbie remembered her mother and father, the lack of shock on her mother's face when she told them she was pregnant, as if she'd expected it all along from one of 'her kind'. She wondered sometimes why they'd adopted her in the first place. Her father was fun and showed her off to his friends, but they'd shown her little love, and she'd never bonded with them. She'd concluded some time ago that people are people and she supposed she was better off with them than in a children's home. Still, she would always live with the rejection, from both her mothers. The adoption of her own baby was, therefore, never a possibility, despite her mother trying to make arrangements with agencies behind her back. Debbie had had to be resilient in the extreme. She'd stood her ground, she'd fought back to the point where her mother gave up and her father bought her a little flat in Jesmond. Anything to bury the disgrace and shame.

Lee's voice interrupted her thoughts. 'There's something else I wanted to talk to you about,' he said, sitting forward and bracing himself.

'Yeah?' Her smile was cautious.

'About money. I'd like to help out.'

Her smile was gone. 'We can manage.'

'Well, I've worked out how much—'

'Why, Lee? Why bring this up now?'

As the waiter put the never-ending bill in front of Lee, he leant in towards Debbie. 'Because I realise how daft I've been. If I'd tried harder, if I'd been braver, I could have had you, her—'

'Don't flatter yourself.' She saw him wince and she regretted it the minute it came out of her mouth. But she was no victim. Old habits die hard, and he couldn't just bat his eyelids at her and expect her to fall at his feet.

'I just want to help,' he said, all eye contact gone. 'If there's anything I can do, just ask.'

He handed the waiter his credit card and Debbie drained her glass, feeling guilt creep up her throat. Maybe he didn't deserve her spite, maybe he could be a good dad to Louise. Maybe she could trust him.

'Well,' she said, thoughtfully, 'she really needs to go shopping for more new clothes.' She grinned wickedly and Lee swallowed, narrowing his eyes at her cheeky smile.

Touché.

Debbie sat back, seeming more relaxed. 'What shall we do now?' she asked. 'Eighth party city in the world, Newcastle.'

He looked amused. 'Who's seventh?'

'Rio de Janeiro,' she said, grinning.

As he signed away nearly three hundred pounds, his phone rang, and, as he recognised the panic button number, he grabbed at it more quickly and with more anticipation than Debbie would have liked.

'Work,' he said, and went outside to take the call.

***

The house was quiet, the children asleep, the little television keeping Nicola company. She lay curled up on the armchair under a blanket, watching a romantic comedy. As she watched the couple on screen kissing, she sank into her sadness. Micky's visit earlier had put paid to any stupid romantic notions of seeing Lee again anytime soon. But she remained in her house, the alarm in her pocket and the phone by her side, the knife at her feet; the bolts across the door. But she was still frightened, and she braced herself for another fitful night.

She closed her eyes and saw Kim's colourless face. Despite instructions to stay away, she'd been to the house that afternoon. When Kim eventually opened the door to her, she knew immediately. The stench of dope pervaded the house, Kim's eyes, red-ringed and watery, staring into nothing for several long moments before she stood aside to let Nicola in. Seeing the state of the house, Nicola barked at her angrily, asking if the baby had been fed and changed, and when was the last time she'd washed herself and Amy? What the hell would Mark think of all this?

'Shut up about Mark,' Kim had said. Why should she pull herself together? What the hell for, eh?

Nicola could hear the baby crying in the bedroom, but Kim blocked her attempts to get up the stairs, her eyes trying to be bitter, but failing to register any emotion at all.

'Kim, we need to talk,' said Nicola desperately.

'There's nothing to talk about. Go home to your *husband*.'

Now, as the TV lights flickered around the room, Nicola pulled the blanket tighter to her and considered her options. Social services would be such a betrayal, she just couldn't do it. Kim and the baby would just have to come and live with them, and they'd all get through it together, like a family. Safety in numbers. It was a good plan, she liked it, and as the worry eased its way out of her muscles she felt her body relax a little. She rested her head on the chair and watched the film credits roll up the screen. She'd missed the end, but she was certain it was a happy one.

An hour later, she awoke to Rufus whining and scratching at the living room door. She thought she heard running water and wondered if she'd left a tap on upstairs. Pulling herself off the chair, she checked the time on her watch: just after 10.00p.m.

Yawning, she walked wearily to the living room door, but when she opened it the stench caught her throat and she coughed as the fumes burned her nose and windpipe.

Petrol.

As if in slow motion, she turned, ran back into the living room, grabbing the phone from the chair and reaching the bottom of the stairs just as a gloved hand dropped a lit match through the letterbox. She lunged for the bannister, blue tongues of fire clambering up the walls and licking at the back of her heels as she hurled herself upstairs.

In the boys' bedroom she shut the door and tried with trembling fingers to unlock the phone, but the buttons seemed miniscule and her fingers fat and swollen. *Come on, come on!*

As smoke inched in under the door, she gave up on the phone and shouted, '*Michael! Liam!*' pulling Michael's quilt back but falling to the floor when a window exploded downstairs. She scrambled around the carpet on her hands and knees, searching for the phone, found it and held it as steadily as she could, swearing through frightened tears as she tried dialling 999 without unlocking the phone. With relief she heard the connection and the ringing on the other end. She hauled Liam out of bed by his arm, not caring if she hurt him, screaming at Michael Jnr to get up. The line connected and before anyone could speak she was screeching, '*Fire! There's a fire!*' She panicked, her mind blank: she couldn't remember the number of the house. They asked her to stay calm. What street was it? '*Oak Grove, Valley Park,*' she cried.

She threw the phone onto the floor. Liam was crying, the room was filling with smoke, and she could feel the heat of the fire on the other side of the flimsy door, the paint bubbling and melting. She took the panic alarm from her back pocket and pushed the red button, twice, three times, she didn't care how many, then dragged Michael's quilt to the door and shoved it against the gap at the bottom. But it seemed as if twice as much smoke came in over the top and she found she couldn't breathe let alone scream. She racked her brains. If she opened a window would that feed the flames?

She pulled Liam and Michael to her, hanging onto them for dear life. They coughed and cried, clung to her with their little hands. She'd never prayed before in her life, but she prayed now. *Dear God, have mercy.*

She sat under the window, held her hands over the mouths of her children, not knowing if it would kill them or save them, and as her head began to spin, she heard the sirens, could see the fire clawing its way over the door. It crackled, it roared like the Devil coming for his dues.

When she felt Liam going limp in her arms, she gasped for air, the panic subsiding and a strange sense of relief taking over. She could just stay where she was, let it take them, then it would all be over. She almost succumbed to the temptation but one last drop of survival instinct surged through her. She scrambled to her feet and opened the window, heard the roar and watched the quilt go up in flames. She tried to scream but there was no air. All she felt was her own heart thudding in her belly, her ears, her bones. She could see flashing lights, blue and red.

Then she saw his face at the window, an angel in a yellow helmet. He gestured to her to come to him and she grasped at what little life she had in her, picked up Liam and passed him into open arms. She wondered if she was giving her children up to Heaven as she heaved Michael off the floor and, just as her eyes were about to burst like balloons, she fell into a blazing blackness.

***

Lee's taxi screeched to a halt outside the burning house as the stretcher was wheeled into the back of the ambulance, the paramedics ducking the missiles being thrown by a handful of laughing, scruffy kids. There were no other people out on the street. Neighbours had quietly shut themselves in their houses, waiting for the police to leave so they could get a gander at the damage and gossip about the Kellys. Micky was a good lad, kept the real criminals out, didn't deserve to lose his family.

Two uniformed officers stood at their car. Without any protective gear against the bricks and stones, they were useless. Or cowards. Lee got out of his car, raging, and picked up an armful of broken bricks lying in the road, hurling them back at the baying youths. He kept on, one after the other, defending himself with his arm, throwing whatever he could find powerfully towards them. As Lee's missiles hit their mark, the kids ran off laughing and giving him the finger while the two officers looked on in astonishment. Lee approached them hastily, held out his ID and asked them what happened. The heat was immense, and the roar of the fire meant he had to strain his ears to hear what they were saying.

'Well, there's been a fire, Sarge,' one of them said sarcastically.

Lee turned away from them angrily, marched to one of the ambulances and leapt into the back where he leant over two small, blackened faces, their eyes blurred and bewildered.

'Where's the mother?' he asked. The paramedic indicated the other ambulance, and Lee bounded down the ramp towards the other vehicle just as they were closing the doors.

'Wait!' He showed his ID and they bundled him in before locking the doors, jumping into the front seat and sounding the siren.

As the ambulance pulled off, Lee sat by Nicola's lifeless side while a paramedic strapped an oxygen mask over her face. He willed her to breathe, he stroked her hair, his face next to hers. She didn't open her eyes, but a tear slid down her temple, leaving a gulley of white along her charred skin. He leant closer, kissed her singed hair and reached for her hand as the ambulance sped its way off the estate.

Nicola tried to clasp Lee's hand, to give him some sign that she didn't want him to leave, but there was no consciousness of the world around her. Just the muffled and distant sound of her choking babies ringing in her ears.

TEN

As the taxi pulled off, the refuge loomed large before the three of them once again in the fading light of the day. They had nothing with them but wheezy chests and the borrowed clothes Lee had brought to the hospital from the refuge's basement wardrobe. The clothes smelt damp and stale, and Nicola felt like an orphan once again, without home or possessions. It wasn't a new feeling to her. She'd spent her childhood being passed from pillar to post, Mark trailing behind her, his swollen eyes in his pale skin making him look like something out of a Dicken's novel.

From family to family they'd travelled. Up to Northumberland, down to Yorkshire. Each time she'd hoped this would be it. They could finally get a mam and dad to love, a room of their own, toys, clothes, a cup of hot chocolate and a cuddle before bed. She'd yearned for it, the warmth of a bosom to lie against, the smell of toast in the morning. Fresh towels and a hand to hold as she crossed the road. But Mark's hatred of the world would end it all after a few months, weeks or days. We'd love to keep Nicola, they'd say, so much potential, but him? He's out of control. She'd cry, the temporary mother, as she held her husband's hand and watched them walk down the path with their bags and into the social worker's car once more, the guilt of their failure tinged with relief as calmness entered their home once again.

At the hospital, Lee had been precious, stayed with her all that terrible night, and spent as much time as he could with her in the days after that. He'd sat by her bed after dark and talked when she couldn't, her throat closed up and her breath rasping. He'd stroked her head, told her about Louise, about Debbie, about his father and mother and cat-mad grandfather who'd given him three hundred quid in cash from a tin under his bed to get him started down in London. How the bus journey south had made him sick and he'd puked all over the stinking egg and salad cream sandwiches of some old fishwife sitting next to him.

Nicola listened, finding some peace as his smooth voice washed over her and filled her head with silk. She cuddled into Liam, her chin on his head, lapping up Lee's stories about life on Hackney construction sites, the squats, the navvies and the loneliness.

He'd turned off the light as she drifted off, stretched his arm around the back of her head and laid his own head down on the pillow, his nose only a finger width from hers, and he told her of the murder in the corner shop that changed his life. An Asian man, beaten about his stubborn head with the butt of a gun for the hundred quid that lay in the till in tens and fives. The man's wife and child watching helplessly as he died on the floor behind the counter. Lee had done nothing to help. He didn't know how to, and six months later he was sitting the police exam.

Lee felt the touch of her hand on his cheek, and, as her sleepy eyes searched his face, he felt all the barriers between them wash away. He smiled at her, kissed her parched lips and told her to sleep. She nodded, and he watched a calm slumber overtaking her. Their breathing synchronised and they'd both slept, hands entwined.

Inside the refuge there were familiar faces and some new ones. Tracey and Lisa were gone – rehoused – though Brenda curled her lip as she told Nicola under her breath that Tracey, the stupid bitch, had let the fucking twat back into the house. He was practically living there under the pretence of finding God and becoming a better person. Brenda flicked her nearly-white hair from her eyes and snarled at Tracey's weakness. She'd get nowt more off her. If she wanted to put herself in the battering line again, that was her problem. She was done with her. She should have been stronger, put an end to it like she did with her man. It's not as hard as you think.

Not if he's behind bars, thought Nicola, cynically at first, but then it made her stop and think again as she listened to Brenda's bare feet slapping out of the kitchen in search of someone more willing to talk to about the failures of other people.

Behind bars.

If Micky was behind Margy's death threat, perhaps she'd be able to come home. Brenda's hypocrisy and unforgiving charm made Nicola miss her friend more than ever. She felt like she'd lost a vital organ and, as she gave the boys milk and biscuits before bedtime, she remembered her girlfriends from her teenage days, before Valley Park, before Micky.

There were four of them who used to hang out together - Sharon, Catherine and Mary. She'd lost touch with them all. Micky had become her everything and she'd stopped going out, stopped messing around with them in town and nicking stuff from Boots. She'd moved into his flat – played house, kept it clean and tidy, did his washing, cooked meals, made cushions and curtains. The perfect wife, the perfect mother to a grown man. And she'd loved it, loved taking care of him, running his bath, lighting candles, massaging his shoulders, putting on the underwear he bought her, dancing for him, satisfying him. She'd needed no one but him and slowly her friends stopped calling round, stopped phoning, and grew up into their own lives. She hadn't missed them at all. She had everything she needed, and when Micky Kelly asked her to marry him she felt like her heart would burst.

The wedding was a riot. Micky was boxing then and had stacks of muscle-clad friends with rough wives. The Dolphin in Benwell had jumped to Flipper's Disco. She'd made her own dress, full, flouncy and frilly, her permed hair topped with a great structure made of white satin and lace. She'd lifted her skirts and danced to Vic Reeves. She spun round with the women, *Dizzy!* until she fell over, howling, and had to be hauled back to her feet. She was smashed – everyone was smashed – singing, swaying, spilling beer and hanging onto each other while they laughed their faces scarlet. Even the fight didn't last long – with a room full of boxers and bouncers, it was swiftly taken outside and a few arses kicked for good measure.

They didn't have the money for a hotel or a honeymoon, but Nicola Kelly was happy as Larry. She'd sprinkled confetti on their bed when they got in at three a.m., and, even though they both passed out immediately, they made up for it the next morning – and for the next six months until she fell pregnant with Michael. It was then that she felt like she'd arrived. Wherever it was she was going with her life, she'd got there the minute the doctor told her she was having a baby.

With a child on the way, they'd got their house on Valley Park. She knew it was rough, she'd lived there till she and Mark had been plucked from their musty house into the loving arms of the state. But no one messed with Micky Kelly, so she feared nothing for herself or her house. Kim and Mark quickly followed when Mark was released from Deerbolt with a supported housing package. They, too, enjoyed the protection Micky had to offer. He was hard as nails, well respected and knew the right people in the right places. There was violence, there were guns, she knew this, it was part of the package, and she liked that people were frightened of her husband, little realising that she'd end up the one living in fear. But it was only when she held Michael Jnr in her arms for the first time, kissed his hot, downy head and smelt his baby sweat, that she started to question the influence Micky would have on her tiny, innocent one.

Brenda dragged herself back into the kitchen, sighing, bored as hell. She looked grimy, her pink T-shirt stained with slobbered food, dirt collecting between her toes. She seemed to be even bigger, and walking just a few steps was a huge effort. She sat at the table, spilling out over the chair. Her keys were coming, she said. This week. A nice, little two-bedroom flat for her and Damon out in Westerhope. She'd done well to hold out for nine months to get what she wanted. See what you can do when you put your mind to it? No need to be letting bastards back into your house, and she looked at Nicola with what seemed like a warning. Nicola gave Brenda a congratulatory smile and croaked that she'd better get the kids bathed and into bed.

Brenda followed Nicola with her eyes as she left the kitchen and headed up the stairs with Liam and Michael. She'd seen girls like her in and out of this place three or four times over the last nine months. Didn't stand a chance in hell unless she had him put away – or killed him.

Their room was right at the top of the house, in the attic this time. It was lovely, brightly coloured, with skylight windows that pulled in the star-carpeted sky when the lights were off. Like before, on one of the single beds was a welcome box containing toothbrushes, toothpaste, soap, flannels and towels. It was a lovely gesture and it made her feel cared for in a small way.

In the bathroom she stripped the children of their smelly clothes and sat on the small stool by the bath while they played in the water, Liam giggling uncontrollably at a wind-up turtle that wagged its flippers in the water but didn't move anywhere. As she washed their faces with the flannel, Michael coughed, and the grinding sound filled Nicola with a horrible guilt. Michael had suffered the most. He'd vomited for two days in the hospital and had just come off the oxygen forty-eight hours ago.

Michael and Liam were asleep by nine o'clock, their bellies full of cornflakes and their heads full of *The Cat in the Hat.* Nicola lay in her bed and thought of Lee. She felt like she had when she first met Micky – the whole relationship an unknown, all of it in the future rather than the past. And yet, the last few days they'd spent together seemed to spread back down her entire lifetime. But it was different this time. There was less need involved. Lee seemed to care for her. Why, she had yet to fathom, but it was almost impossible for her to resist, impossible to rein in the impulse to reach out her arms to him when he walked in the room in the hope that it would get him to her side quicker.

Blenheim Street, Lee had told her. That's where the petrol had come from. A garage on Blenheim Street. The dread stuck in her voiceless throat. Tiger's gym sat like a sweating slab of peeling white steel on Blenheim Street.

Her eyes closed and Lee's face faded from view. If Micky couldn't have her, nobody could. He'd destroy all of them before he let her go.

She hugged herself and drew her knees to her chest, lying on her side and burying her head in the pillow. Her life felt void. Great holes had appeared where once there were people she loved. Kim, Margy, Mark, her darling Mark. She missed Lee now, too, but she could never have him. Not while Micky confined her in his life like a vice.

Behind bars.

At least she was safe here for tonight. At least he wouldn't find her here.

ELEVEN

'You shouldn't have,' Nicola croaked, grinning from ear to ear at the beautiful bouquet of flowers in Lee's hand.

'Who said they're for you?' he replied as he pushed past her into the hallway.

'Hey, wait,' she said, 'no men, remember?'

He stopped, turned and headed back contritely, handing her the flowers as he passed her and stood again at the front door. He held out his other hand containing a bag full of new clothes.

'Oh, it's like Christmas,' she said, holding her hands to her mouth then taking the bags gratefully.

Lee leant against the door frame. 'Come out with me. Let's go for something to eat,' he said.

'I can't, the kids are off school ...'

Lee couldn't hide his disappointment. 'When will I see you?' he asked, taking her fingers in his hand.

'I need to think,' she replied. 'It's just too dangerous.'

He nodded. Micky Kelly knew everyone, and everyone knew Micky Kelly. He took a pen from his pocket and lifted up her hand. On her palm he wrote: *Flat 8, Wallace Building, Coast Road.*

'My address for the last twenty-four hours,' he said, 'I'll be in all night. Billy No Mates.'

Nicola looked behind her down the hall, heard the laughter seeping from the TV room. Maybe she could leave the kids for a couple of hours after they'd gone to sleep, just this once. The others did it all the time after all, out at bingo or down the karaoke on a Friday night, babysitting for each other so they could get pissed and have a laugh before the drudge of refuge life kicked in again on a Saturday morning.

'Please?' Lee said, sensing her hesitation.

Nicola felt herself tear in two and bit at her bottom lip, unsure. 'I'll see,' she said. 'I have to go.'

Lee stood for a moment and stared at the green door closing on him. His head was all over the place. Up to his neck in meetings about the Valley Park regeneration scheme and his new policing strategy, everyone wanting to know when they would see results. He could sense their cynicism. Some people looked dazed, some confused, some nodded sagely, but most shook their heads and spoke to their colleagues behind their hands, sharing their bad breath and declarations of seeing it when they believed it. He was trying to fit it all into his head, but the truth was, all he could think about was how to nail something – anything – on Micky Kelly. But Micky was like Teflon and Lee didn't have the evidence to make anything stick. GBH, drug dealing, arson, not even pissing in public.

He'd wanted to talk to Nicola about Mark. Get a bit more of a feel for the man – who he was, who he'd become, what had frightened him so much that he would take such drastic measures to stay out of prison. He'd been through the files again, reams of information but nothing that gave him a hunch to follow up. The only lead was Tyrone Woods, the flaming-haired kid who'd ignited the fight in the Nags Head and who'd shown up at Mark's funeral. There was nothing on him in particular, but his family were tyrants. It was common knowledge at the station that brother Gerry once ran a money laundering racket out of

Jarrow, that someone else had served time for it, another IRA man who was shot in the head three days after his release. This wasn't the kind of family you messed with, so why would Mark give Tyrone drugs? Pick any other kid on the estate, any other nobody put on this earth to make the numbers up, but not the baby of a family with the ability to unleash the dogs of hell on you.

Walking back to his car, he considered trying the youth centre again, but the manager had hardly welcomed him with open arms that morning. Lee's zero tolerance strategy wasn't going down well, stop and search tactics being the least favourite policy on the youth and community workers' agenda. It spelled riots. It set back their confidence building and self-esteem workshops by years. They'd made it clear to Lee that morning that he had no friends there, and he'd pushed it too far when he'd cornered Tyrone Woods in the games room. After a meeting with the youth workers that was no meeting, he'd spotted Tyrone, playing pool, smoking and picking at his fingernails. Lee had sauntered in and picked up a pool cue, the other lads looking at each other and then back at him. With second thoughts, he'd put the cue back up against the wall and leaned against it next to Tyrone, his hands in his pockets. He asked the lads about Mark and they were suitably coy, but none more so than Tyrone whose eyes stayed firmly on his bleeding fingertips, his nails gnawed to the quick.

'The meeting's over,' the youth centre manager stood in the doorway, his face like a smacked arse, his warning tone spurring the lads back to their pool game. All except Tyrone.

'I know,' Lee said, turning towards him.

'Members only,' said the manager.

'I'm having a conversation,' Lee said, taking in the lads' embarrassed faces – they'd crossed the line, talking to a copper. They knew where their allegiances should lie. The youth workers at the centre were always on their side.

'Sounds like Mark Redmond was popular here,' said Lee, fishing.

A muffled voice said, 'pure gold.'

But the manager had had enough and entered the room. 'You'll have to do your talking off the premises. Are you leaving, lads?'

The boys shook their heads and began chalking their cues. With all eyes on the next break, Lee knew he'd been frozen out, and with one last glance at Tyrone, he'd left the youth club with one thing clear at least. These lads were the key to the truth about Mark Redmond.

***

For several hours Nicola battled with herself. Every time she decided she would go she felt a sense of relief. But, soon after, reality crept back in and her heart sank back again. The swings turned to roundabouts until she decided there was only one thing for it. She'd flip a coin. Heads she went to see Lee, tails she stayed where she was. She fished her purse from her bag, opened it and looked with some resentment at the pathetic coins inside – all she had left until her next cheque arrived from the Social. She took out a twopence piece, threw it in the air, caught it and slapped it onto the back of her hand. She lifted her palm, her lips tight, her eyes closed. She opened them. Tails.

Best of three.

As she stepped off the bus on the outskirts of Valley Park, Nicola pulled on her hooded top and headed towards

Kim's house. As she'd dried her hair and put on the new jeans and pretty pink top Lee had bought her, her mind had wandered to Kim. Here she was getting ready to go and meet a man for God knows what, and there was Kim, her friend, her brother's soulmate, alone and sad, trying to cope without the man she'd loved all her adult life. She couldn't shake Kim's face from her mind. The hope, the guilt, the fear, whatever it was, she didn't feel she could go through with something so selfish without making sure Kim was all right first.

Her heart racing, she pulled up her hood and looked around her cautiously in the fading light, her walk turning into a slow run as she sensed cars slowing as they passed her, faces looking at her through windows.

Kim's house was only a couple of minutes from the bus stop, and it was a good ten minutes further to Micky's house. Nevertheless, she was suddenly gripped with fear, only her conscience driving her on. She kept her head down, her hood pulled over her face, and counted each step – about sixty until she reached the corner of Kim's street.

When she got there she stopped dead at the corner. Outside Kim's house was Micky's car, and she had to blink to make sure she was seeing right. Jesus, could he not just leave them all be? He'd be in there, hounding her for information, Kim sitting on the sofa wishing them all dead. Then the front door opened, and she spun around, her heart in her mouth. She ducked behind an overgrowing hedge, heard footsteps, then the car door open and close. She waited for the engine to start. Waited, listening to the blood storm through her ears. But the car engine lay silent.

After a few seconds she peeked her head around the corner and saw the car, but Micky wasn't in it, and when she heard Kim's laughter and the front door to the house closing again, she bit into her knuckles, pulled herself together and ran back to the bus stop.

**

Lee's ear was red-hot, so he moved the phone to the other one as he drained his mug of tea and tried to take in the sports news.

'But, Dad, I haven't seen you since my birthday.'

'Louise, it was only a few days ago. Come round tomorrow, I've said.'

'It's been nearly a week, actually, and if I come tonight I can get a lift straight from Becky's.'

'Becky's?'

'Erm, my best friend?'

'Becky, yes.'

'Then I've got all tomorrow and Saturday at your really nice flat instead of this dinosaur of a place, please, please, please ...' She finally took a breath, but not for long. 'Hang on, Mam's here.' Her voice became muffled as she put her hand over the receiver, then he heard her clear her throat. 'She says to say thank you for the birthday dinner.'

'Tell her she's very welcome.'

Louise laughed. 'No, you muppet. Thank you from *me*, not her.'

'Okay, well you're very welcome, then.'

'She's blowing you a kiss.' Louise giggled and gave a loud *OW!* as Debbie gave her a whack.

Lee sighed. 'Haven't you got school or revision or something?'

'Exams are finished. But that's a brilliant idea. I'll bring my end-of-year project. Can you sew?'

'No, I can't sew.'

'Well, you can't be worse than her, she's useless.' Another *OW!*

Lee rubbed his eyes. 'Okay, okay, what time are you leaving Becky's?'

'About ten, her dad'll give me a lift.'

'Ten? I'll be in bed by then.'

'You're so old,' said Louise. 'And you said you had the day off tomorrow.'

'Just the morning. Can't your mam drop you earlier?'

'She's drinking wine. Got the other oldies coming round for a "girls' night". It's horrible, Dad, they always end up singing till, like, after midnight. With *wooden spoons*. It's embarrassing.'

'Oldies? We're thirty-two ...'

'Please, Dad, *please* don't make me listen to "Chiquitita" again. I might have to ring ChildLine or something.'

Lee smiled, looking at his watch. It was 8.30. If Nicola was coming, she would have been here by now.

'Okay,' he relented, 'but straight to bed when you get here, yes?'

'Yes.'

'No sewing.'

'Promise.'

'We can do something tomorrow morning. Help me unpack.'

'Definitely.'

Grinning, he hung up the phone shaking his head, then headed to the kitchen to get a beer from the fridge. As he closed the fridge door, his door buzzer rang brazenly. He answered it with a bright hello.

'Lee?'

'Yes.'

'It's me, Nicola.'

His grin became a wide smile. 'Come on up, second floor.' He pushed the key button and ran quickly into the bathroom to check himself in the mirror. He sniffed at his armpits, opened the cupboard above the sink, and gargled with some mouthwash. He skipped up the spiral staircase into the bedroom and just managed to spray some deodorant, kick off his old Homer Simpson slippers, and pull a clean T-shirt over his head before he heard the knock on the door. *'Just a minute!'* he called, running back down the stairs, picking up the washing from the dining table and throwing it into the spare room. He got to the door, took a deep breath and opened it.

'Sorry, I was on the phone,' he said. 'Come in, come in.'

'I need to talk to you.'

'Of course, sit down, can I get you anything?'

With a shake of her head, Nicola sat on the sofa. He could see she was agitated so he sat next to her and took her hand. 'What's up? What's happened?'

Her voice cracked with distress. 'He always uses that petrol station. It's next to the gym.'

Lee thought for a moment then raised her chin so she had to look at him. 'If you think he's capable, then you've got to make a statement.'

'But I can't.'

'Why?'

'Because I'm frightened, Lee. I thought you'd understand.'

'I do, I do.' He pulled her to him.

After a few moments, Nicola pulled back from him and straightened her back. Just for a few hours she wanted to forget about everything, just be normal for a while. She looked at him, frowned and stifled a laugh.

'What?' he asked.

'Your T-shirt's on back to front and inside out.'

He looked down and smiled. 'Oh yeah.'

He leant into her, putting his hands to her ears.

'Mmmm, minty,' she said.

They kissed forever, lips locked and hands wandering. At last her fingers gripped the bottom of his back-to-front T-shirt and it was over his head a second later. He pulled his head back to look at her, just to make sure, but she brought his face back to hers before he could even take a breath. He unzipped the pink top that had looked so *her* on the hanger in the shop the day before, and he followed her as she lay back, their lips never parting.

After that, everything was perfect. His chest pressing against her breasts, her hips moulding into his. As he looked down at her naked body, he felt like he already knew every curve, every blemish and shadow, every groan and intake of breath. He slid into her and they both held their breath for a moment.

Perfect.

He buried his face in her neck and she closed her arms and legs around him. *This is it,* he thought. *This is what it's supposed to be like.*

***

They lay on the wide sofa, just the flickering light from the TV illuminating the room, their feet entwined, her head resting comfortably in the nook between his shoulder and his chest. He stroked the back of her arm as her fingers combed the dark hairs on his chest, a blanket loosely covering their nakedness. She pulled it up to cover her upper body, but he pulled it back down, not wanting to lose sight of the white silky skin of her shoulders, or that gorgeous shape women make with their hips when lying on their sides. He ran his hand down the line of it now, lit up blue then red by the flashing lights of the television. He ran his fingers over the yellowing bruises at the top of her arm, the perfect imprint of Micky's fingers.

Lee tried not to think of Micky hurting her. He thought he might kill him if he touched her again – he wondered if he would be able to stop himself. He felt her breath against the side of his neck, her chest rising and falling, her toes teasing his. He told her he wished they could stay where they were all night. For a week, a month. Order pizza and watch Sky Sports. She punched his chest playfully and he laughed, cuddling her to him.

The door buzzer made them both jump. Nicola pulled herself up on her elbow and looked backwards towards the door.

'Ah no, she's bloody early,' said Lee looking at his watch. 'Louise,' he explained to Nicola, sitting up and pulling his trousers on. 'She's coming for the weekend.'

The door buzzed again once, then continually until he picked up the entry phone.

'Yes?' he said in an irritated voice.

Louise sounded annoyed. 'Dad? It's me. Can you let me in?'

'Louise ... Ten o'clock, you said.'

Nicola was already off the sofa, gathering up her clothes.

'I fell out with Becky,' said Louise.

'All right, all right.' He pressed the key and turned to Nicola who was hurriedly putting her clothes on. She threw him his T-shirt.

'Sorry,' he said, putting it on. 'She's completely unpredictable.'

Nicola shrugged. 'It's a girl's prerogative,' she said and ran into the bathroom with her socks and trainers while Lee quickly picked up the blanket, folded it and laid it on the back of the sofa. He turned on a couple of lights just as Louise knocked on the door.

'Hiya!' she bounded into the flat and gazed around open-mouthed, her fight with Becky apparently forgotten. 'Oh, it's *brilliant*,' she said, clasping her hands together. 'A bit bare, but *gorgeous*. See? I told you, didn't I?'

Lee looked around the long, thin, open-plan living room and kitchen. He had to agree, it was a great pad. Or it would be once all his stuff arrived from storage the next morning. It was travelling overnight from London – books, CDs, videos and DVDs, shelves and wall pictures, his crusty old armchair – everything he'd invested in over the years.

Louise dropped a couple of bags at her feet as the bathroom door opened and Nicola emerged. Louise stared at her curiously.

'This is Nicola,' said Lee, 'we're erm ... working on a case together.'

Louise gasped. 'Really? Wow, is it a murder?'

Shaking his head, he put his arm on Nicola's back to guide her to the door.

'Wait!' Louise said, holding aloft a small clear bag towards Nicola. 'Can you sew?'

***

Half an hour later, Louise and Nicola were stooped with their faces frowning in concentration over the red tartan and black satin fabric spread out on the dining table. They laid out a piece of tissue pattern over the fabric then Louise picked up the instructions and read to Lee.

'C please, Dad, for view A.'

Lee looked at her. *What?* He looked down at the tissue paper lying at his feet, bent down and held up a piece while Nicola and Louise shared a 'he's hopeless' look.

'C!' they said in unison.

'Well, bloody hell, I thought you were bringing homework,' he said, his feelings hurt.

'This is my homework,' said Louise. 'Dur.'

'Yes, all right, clever clogs. If you don't want my help then I'll just watch the news, okay?'

Nicola and Louise bit back their smiles.

'Listen, I really have to go,' said Nicola.

'Ahhhhh,' said Louise like a kid who had to leave the playground.

'I'll give you a lift,' said Lee.

'No, no you stay here: help Louise.' She smiled mischievously at him and he sighed his 'okay.'

'I'll see you out,' he said. 'And, Louise, do not use those scissors until I come back.'

Louise narrowed her eyes at him: *don't tempt me*, they said.

On the landing, Lee dug into his pocket and unravelled a scrunched-up tenner.

'Get a taxi,' he said, 'there's a place on the corner, that way.' She held her hand up, but he pushed the money into her pocket. 'I want you to be safe, that's all I ask. Please. Don't put yourself in danger.'

She reached up and kissed him. 'Thank you, you're sweet.' She turned to leave, but he grabbed her hand and pulled her back. They kissed again until she pulled away.

'When can I see you?' he asked. 'What the hell will I do with myself?'

'I don't know,' she said. 'I don't know how this works.'

'I'll get you another panic alarm.'

'Okay, yes.'

He kissed her again, he couldn't stop. 'Shit, Nicola, don't go.'

Nicola smiled at him tenderly, put her arms around his waist and hugged him tight. Resting her chin on his chest, she looked up at him and he winked at her. Everything was going to be okay.

TWELVE

'Wake up.'

Louise pulled the quilt over her head and grunted while Lee stood over her, rubbing his unshaved jaw. How was it possible for someone to sleep for twelve hours?

'It's eleven o'clock, I thought you were going to help me.' He gave the dead form on the futon a little shove with his foot and another irritated growl emerged from beneath.

'I'm tired.'

'Ten minutes, then Abba's going on.'

He heard a mumble.

'What?' he asked, bending in her direction.

The quilt was dragged down by a pyjamaed arm. 'I said you haven't got any Abba,' she said, then turned to face the wall, flinging the quilt back over her head.

Lee sighed and left the room, climbing the slim, spiral staircase to the mezzanine level and his bedroom. He'd been up since the early hours – slept badly on the spongy bed that dipped in the middle. He made a mental note to speak to the landlord about that and the leaky shower in the en suite that sounded like a waterfall in the middle of the night. He missed the hotel's crisp sheets, dry towels and solid mattress.

His stuff had arrived at bang on eight o'clock and he'd spent the last four hours unpacking and assembling the shelves that had once adorned his living room wall in Islington. He'd hoped the sound of the hammering and the electric screwdriver would rouse Louise from her bed. He was wrong. He'd been looking forward to them spending time together, sorting out the flat, and his disappointment stuck in his throat every time he put his head around the door and peeked at her sleeping face. She didn't move a muscle, didn't respond to his voice or his gentle pokes, so he'd returned to the living room to hammer that little bit louder.

After he'd emptied his suitcases and filled the wardrobe, he lay across his bed, his arms stretched above his head. He wondered what Nicola was doing right now. Was she thinking about him as much as he was thinking about her? He couldn't imagine anyone so different to Anita. Anita whom he'd wanted to marry, Anita who'd said yes, Anita who'd worn the cheaper-than-would-have-been-expected ring, though only now and then when she remembered. Anita, the badass Iranian-born lawyer with the sleek face of a racehorse, who'd made partner at the age of twenty-eight, earning five times what he did, sleeping four hours a night at best to get where she needed to be professionally. But where she needed to be geographically was anywhere but London. The place was dated, dirty and dangerous, so when the offer of the job in Vancouver came up, she'd said yes on the spot. No consultation. He was pleased for her. He'd hugged her, lifted her off her feet, taken her out for Japanese food.

'You're coming with me, darling, of course,' she'd said, her arms around his neck.

'Of course,' he'd claimed, nuzzling her hair. Who would turn down an opportunity like that?

***

Nicola held onto the bags of grocery shopping as she sat on the packed bus, its final destination the airport, full of people trying to keep hold of their overexcited children and suitcases full of PG Tips, on their way somewhere hot, foreign and beachy. The schools broke up yesterday, and Nicola dreaded the long days ahead in the refuge, the kids climbing the walls, the mothers right behind them.

She'd spent the morning reliving the night before. It had felt so natural, being in his flat with his daughter. She was astonished at their close bond, formed already after so many years apart. She saw a lot of him in her, though he was blind to it. Determined, pragmatic and somewhat argumentative. She had his eyes and his height, his slightly protruding ears. She'd felt their ease with each other as they'd concentrated on the patterns and the pins, so much so that she'd begun to wonder whether she could have a relationship with her own mother after all these years. It had been almost twenty years since she'd seen or heard from her. She actually didn't know if she was alive or dead. If her mother walked back into her life, would she love her, just like that? Would she even recognise her? And moreover, would her mother love her? She'd felt a flurry of excitement at the prospect. A mother in her life. Not a very good one, but a mother nonetheless.

But as she'd filled her shopping basket with the cheapest, on-offer produce, she'd realised her mother wouldn't know that Mark was dead, and the reality came at her like a bulldozer. Her mother's voice had stayed with her all these years, slow and unfaltering, the words long and incomprehensible, the pitch getting higher and higher as she lost control of her emotions. Nicola had always taken the blame, she was too quiet, too loud, too soft, too cold. She could hear her mother shouting at her now: *You didn't take care of him, you let him get out of control, you allowed him to die.*

Louise might have forgiven Lee, but Nicola had no forgiveness in her. Mark was damaged by it all, and now he was gone. Illness or not, her mother could rot in hell.

Looking through the bus window, Nicola let her mind drift back to the night before, to happier memories. As she relived the feel of Lee's naked flesh all over her, his mouth on her breasts, her hands pulling him further into her, she felt her own arousal and blushed fiercely. The woman next to her shuffled in her seat, and Nicola wondered if the woman could sense the sex oozing from her skin, just like Nicola could still smell the sweat on the back of Lee's neck, could feel it trickle from the small of his back onto her hips.

She bit at the inside of her cheek to stop herself smiling, coughed to hide a chuckle, and glanced around her. But no one was taking a blind bit of notice of her. She was completely invisible, and that's how she wanted to stay.

As she climbed down the steps of the bus and headed to the refuge, the bags felt light in her hands. She felt stronger, physically and mentally. At last she wasn't alone. She could grieve for Mark, Margy, even Micky, but now that she had Lee, she wouldn't have to do it on her own.

She headed for the back lane that provided a handy short cut to the refuge, but as she turned the corner she was thrown roughly against one of the backyard gates and she felt familiar hot breath against her cheek. She pulled in her breath as the gate's padlock dug into her spine.

'Micky, what ... what are you doing here?'

'D'you think I'm some kind of mug?'

'No, no—'

'Is it tattooed on my forehead here, eh? Mug?' He jabbed at his forehead so hard that the fingernail left an imprint in the skin. 'Will I have it tattooed on yours? Because you'll be one if you don't get home, I mean it.'

'I don't want to come home.'

'I'm not asking you what you want, I'm telling you what you're gonna do.'

'It's my life—'

'There's no life without Micky, there's only life with Micky, right? Life with Micky, sweet as a nut. Life without Micky doesn't exist. I'm waiting.'

Nicola tried to catch her breath, the lock of the gate digging further into her back.

'And what if I don't?'

She heard the flick of the blade by her ear and she tried to squirm away from him, but he pushed his body against hers harder, making her cry out as the lock dug deeper in. She couldn't move, her head rigid with his arm against her throat. Her terrified eyes darted down to the blade and she held her breath, her head light and woozy.

'Put it this way,' Micky said, the blade touching her cheek, 'you'll not want any mirrors around the house, because if I can't have you, I'll cut your face to shreds.'

'Just give me a breather, Micky, I don't want it to be like this. Please, Micky, you're really hurting me.'

She felt his body give, and as her throat became less constricted, tears of relief ran down her cheeks.

Micky sighed and bashed the ball of his hand against his forehead, two, three times. He panted, folded the knife away and put it in his pocket then took her chin in his hand and forced her to look at him. Nicola stared into his eyes with a look of judgement that made Micky's pupils contract. She put her hand to his face and his eyes closed at her touch.

'Why are you doing this?' she said through her tears. 'This isn't you, Micky. This was never me and you.'

There was a moment's silence.

'Because I love you.' His voice cracked

. 'You won't listen.' He gripped her arm tightly and spoke through gritted teeth and brimming tears. 'Why won't you listen?'

She put her arms around his neck and pulled his head to her shoulder. 'Okay,' she said, 'it's okay.'

***

Lee sat at his desk, looking at the cracked clock on the wall. He'd left Louise still asleep at one o'clock, unmoving, unforgiving for being disturbed. He'd called Debbie at work and she'd laughed at him when he asked how she got their daughter out of bed. Instead of furnishing him with parental wise words on the subject, she'd asked him if he would like to come for dinner at the house one evening. Lee had frowned. Well yes, he said, he supposed he could, and then he waited for the answer to his original question. But Debbie hung up and he was left none the wiser on how to raise the living dead.

The clock clicked five past two. DC Thompson had arranged it. She was picking the kid up from his house on the pretext of questioning him over a break-in at the transport yard at Central Station. CCTV evidence was her devised weapon. Of course his brother, Gerry, would put up a fight, call her every bitch under the sun, but inside Gerry Woods would be delighted and somewhat relieved that his soft little brother was finally getting some proper work done. You're not an Irish Woods unless you've done some time.

Lee flicked the plastic band that held Mark's file together and waited. He was looking forward to checking out Tyrone Woods for himself. When the desk sergeant rang to say he had a visitor, he promptly picked up the file and marched through the office to the front of the station. But he couldn't see DC Thompson or Tyrone. Instead, Nicola stood anxiously, a look of relief falling over her when she saw him. Lee smiled weakly at the desk sergeant and pulled Nicola by the elbow into an empty interview room where she sat down, waving away a plastic cup of water.

'I've got to go back,' she said before his backside hit the chair.

'Back where?'

'To Micky. I have to go back.'

'No, Nicola. Let me help you. Don't do it.'

Nicola sat ramrod straight in her chair, her face set in determination. 'If I go back, I'll be able to get information, I'll get whatever you need to put him away.'

'No way – it's too dangerous.'

'So is this.' She leant forward, her eyes level with his. 'It's the only way. I'll never be safe until he's locked up.'

'You can do it without going back. If he tried to kill you and the kid—'

'I can't prove it.'

She was right. He'd hit a brick wall with the garage. The CCTV 'broken', the owner uncommunicative, frightened even. No one was grassing on Micky Kelly.

'I won't let you,' he said.

'Yes you *will*.' She threw his hands back at him and sprang to her feet, knocking the chair to the floor. 'I'm sick of being a piece of property, Lee. Don't start this.'

Shit. He rubbed his head and gathered his thoughts. 'Are you sure?' He looked up at her, a bruised, helpless look.

She nodded and smiled weakly, a flicker of hope in her eyes. 'You better be worth it.'

Lee stood slowly, confused about where his fear was coming from. He was afraid for her safety for sure but, more than that, he was afraid that she still loved her husband, that he could lose her when he'd barely found her.

She grasped the handle of the door.

'Wait,' said Lee, his hand over hers. 'When?'

'Tomorrow,' she said.

He conceded and allowed her to open the door, and she walked out just as Tyrone Woods signed his name at the front desk. Nicola stopped and did a double take, then threw Tyrone a hard stare, looking back at Lee as she headed for the main door.

Lee held out his hand to his next interviewee. 'Detective Sergeant Lee Jamieson,' he said.

Tyrone sank his hands deep into his pockets, shooting an uncertain look at the back of Nicola's head as she ran down the steps of the station.

'Come in,' said Lee.

Closing the interview room door, he picked up the toppled chair and held out an arm inviting Tyrone to sit.

'Am I under arrest?' asked Tyrone coldly.

'What's that?' asked Lee pointing at Tyrone's coat pocket, the top of a can of beer peeking out.

'I'm eighteen, so I am.'

'Nah, you're not. I can tell you your birthday if you want, Tyrone Aloysius Woods. Now sit down.'

Tyrone stared back at him, like he had the power to make him back down, but when Lee stood firm and folded his arms, Tyrone sunk down into the seat and Lee continued.

'I know everything about you.'

Tyrone blinked nervously.

'I know your brothers, and your mam and your dad, where they're from and what they've done. But there's something puzzling me.'

Tyrone looked off into the distance like he gave a shit.

Lee rested his hands on the table. 'How come every lad in that youth club, if I was to ask them one by one what they thought of Mark Redmond, would say he was *pure gold*? Were you the only one he offered drugs to?'

Tyrone didn't answer.

'Or were you the only one prepared to grass him up?'

'I'm not a grass.'

'But you are, Tyrone, you are. I'm surprised anybody will have anything to do with you. You're just a snotty little grasser. Why would anybody want to mix with you?'

'They're me mates.'

'Some fucking mate you are: who you going to grass on next? I'd rather shit in my hands and clap than have you for a mate.'

'Fuck off, you know nothin'.' Tyrone looked towards the door, expecting something, someone to save him.

'You know he killed himself,' said Lee, sitting down and leaning forward. 'I pulled him loose, did you know that? He was purple. He killed himself because he couldn't face going to prison again, couldn't face letting his sister and his wife and baby down, hated life without his job, down there, at that centre. He loved the lads there, too, tried to keep them from getting into trouble like he had.' He leant forward towards Tyrone. 'But you know all this, don't you?' He could see Tyrone's eyes filling up. 'You must have had some big reason to do that.'

Tyrone stood up, breathing deeply, and Lee stood, too, grabbing onto his arm. 'Hang on, you've got blood on your hands.'

'What d'you mean?'

A tear escaped, falling down Tyrone's cheek. He looked frightened and Lee softened.

'You know what I mean. You've been used, Tyrone. Who by?'

Tyrone put one arm over his eyes and yanked the other from Lee's grasp. He stood by the door, his crying eyes still covered. 'You can fuck off, you can't keep me here.'

'No, I can't,' agreed Lee. 'You're free to go, Tyrone, but I'm onto you.'

Tyrone threw the door open and tore out of the station.

A lead at last.

THIRTEEN

'Greedy night! Greedy night!'

Liam and Michael Jnr were on their knees, jumping up and down, clapping their hands, joy seeping from their excited faces. Micky emptied the plastic carrier bag of goodies onto the floor between them all. It had been so long since Nicola had had anything indulgent to eat, her eyes bulged and her mouth watered more than the kids'.

They all stared at the mound of sweets, crisps and drinks and waited for the first one to dive in. Nicola caved in first. She tore at a packet of Mini Cheddars and poured them into her mouth, chewing and spitting bits out as she laughed. The kids were hysterical, pointing at her, tears rolling down Michael's face. Micky smiled and nudged her gently so she fell onto her side, choking and coughing bits of biscuit into her hand.

She'd been home for four days and was back in her old routine before she knew it. The house was spotless, the garden pristine, and the great pile of Micky's clothes washed, dried, ironed and put away within forty-eight hours. She'd spent an afternoon at Kim's, cleaning, washing and stocking the fridge while Kim either stared unseeing into the fireplace, or helped feebly, wishing she could be left alone to let her energy ooze into the sofa rather than into something as meaningless as keeping house. Micky, too, felt his stress easing as the house got back into order.

After weeks of sleepless nights, he slept for hours now in his unburdened self.

Micky had been working nights until tonight. Nicola had made sure they weren't in bed together at the same time, rising at five just before he got home, getting Liam up and dressed, making sure he needed her attention. She'd shrug at Micky as she sat at the kitchen table in the early hours holding mashed-up Weetabix in front of Liam's red, tired face.

But Micky was running out of patience. He was getting hard just thinking about her. Four days and he still hadn't had her. Tania would put out no bother, but it was Nicola's soft flesh he wanted to feel under him, not the leathery skin and bones of wife number two. Tania was a great shag, he couldn't deny that, but Nicola turned him on proper. She was young, looked after herself, not like Tania who'd become grey and saggy, especially since little Michaela was born last year. Tania's appetite for sex was unquenchable, but he'd made his excuses the last few days, feigning a bad back, a dicky belly, and a job to be done in Glasgow. When it came down to choice, there was no choice. He hadn't felt his wife's skin under his hands for nearly two months, and his groin ached to be against hers. Like a starving man getting his first whiff of sizzling bacon, he felt the saliva in his mouth and he savoured the anticipation of the passion, tearing at each other just like they used to. His eyes locked on her mouth now, her hands, her nipples just visible through the white vest top.

As Nicola sat up, wiping the crumbs from her face, Micky nuzzled into her neck, and her muscles seized as if nails were being torn down a blackboard. She pulled away, asking if there was anything to drink in the house.

Micky grinned and sprang to his feet.

She couldn't fault his conduct since she'd come back. He'd given her space, played football with Michael, given her money to replenish her wardrobe and make-up. He'd only slept four hours today and they'd spent their Sunday afternoon at the beach. Liam loved riding the Metro. *Stand clear of the doors please.* It made him hoot with excitement when they all made the long *beeeeeep* sound of the doors closing.

'Are there any sharks in the sea, Dad?' Michael had asked, snuggled on Micky's lap. Micky shook his head to reassure him. 'Have you ever seen a shark?' Michael's eyes were wide, hoping the answer was a resounding 'Yes'.

'Known a few, son,' Micky said, 'but not in the sea.'

They'd walked along the beach hand in hand, while the boys ran in and out of the water in their underpants, kicking water at each other and collecting shells and stones in buckets. Micky seemed to be well-heeled. There were takeaways, another mobile phone she couldn't work out how to use, and a new widescreen TV was on order, big as the cinema, he'd said. There was a great roll of cash, hundreds of pounds, permanently in his pocket.

Micky came back from the kitchen with a bottle of champagne and two wine glasses. He held them up like trophies and Nicola smiled half-heartedly. She hated the stuff, the fizz got up her nose and made her eyes water.

'Bloody hell, Micky,' she said, 'it's a bit flash, isn't it?'

Micky brought his arms down, disappointed, and when Nicola saw the sinking of his eyes she held her hands out for the bottle. She smiled a big smile and pulled him down to her side, plonking a kiss on his cheek.

'Thank you,' she said, 'it's all lovely.'

'Gweedy night!' Liam smiled a chocolatey smile as Michael sat quietly, munching his way through a bag of Haribos.

'Must've come into some cash?' said Nicola indifferently as Micky twisted the bottle carefully in his hands. It popped loudly and he smirked, patting the side of his nose with the cork.

'Right then, lads,' he said, poking Michael out of his Haribo heaven, then pouring champagne into the wine glasses. 'To us,' he said, and raised his glass. Michael picked up his glass of fizzy Coke with both hands and Nicola clinked her glass against it.

To us.

***

Nicola could sense Micky's confusion as she came into the bedroom wearing an old pair of pyjamas she'd found in the drawer. She rubbed cream into her trembling hands. It was only nine-thirty, but their sugar-hyper children were finally asleep, and Micky had insisted on an early night.

'Howay man,' he said, agitatedly, lifting the quilt for her to get into bed. She saw he was naked, and she hesitated before climbing into bed next to him, feigning cold and pulling the quilt around her neck.

He turned on his side and put his face next to hers. 'God, I've missed you so much,' he breathed, his hands cupping her buttocks and pulling her hips to his.

'Micky,' she said, moving her head back so she could focus on his face.

'Hmmmm,' he said, moving his eyes from her face and down to her breasts as he undid the buttons on her pyjama top.

She caught his hand with hers and he looked up at her, trying not to look annoyed. Why did women always want to talk at a time like this?

'I just need to know where the money's coming from.'

'Ah man, Nicola, not now.' He turned onto his back and she held herself up on one elbow, caressing his vast chest. She felt him relax a little.

'I won't go on about it, I swear, it's just – I hate not knowing what's going on – it gets me all upset, then I lose my rag, and you lose yours, and it just goes bad from there, you know?'

Micky grunted in agreement.

'I've really been thinking about it, and if we're going to be happy, then I think you should just tell me, then I might not get so stressed. I'm willing to accept it. Compromise.'

Micky thought about it for a moment. Maybe if he gave her a few titbits, she'd make his life a bit easier. But he also knew that her nature was delicate. She couldn't watch violence in films or on TV. She shielded her face from *ER*, for God's sake. No. She couldn't know everything. The protection money, the bullets, the broken bones and slashed faces. The threatened wives and children.

Nicola kissed his neck and ran her finger across his collarbone and down his arm. He closed his eyes, turning to face her and reaching his arms around her back, melting into the sensation of her hands stroking the back of his head.

'It's simple,' he said, 'I'm part of a syndicate. We chip in, we buy the stuff cheap, divvy it up and sell it on.'

'It's drugs then?'

He held up his hands in defence behind her. 'I don't touch it, and I don't sell it on the streets.'

She nodded and looked into his eyes. He saw something in them. Concern, love. He hoped it was love. It made him want to say more, the hope of the love.

'I'm moving up, Nicola. I'm getting a bigger stake, ploughing everything I make back in. Every month, there's a shipment to a party boat on the river. Just quadrupled my money a couple of weeks ago. If I can get one of these boat jobs every month, then in a year we can buy a house. Anywhere you like. Away from this shithole.'

Nicola frowned. 'But what if you get caught?'

'What me? Never,' he laughed.

'I don't want you to do it, it sounds dangerous.'

'Nah. It's like a floating cash and carry, man. And this time, I'm using my nous.' He touched his temple with his finger. 'This time, we're selling it on the boat to prearranged buyers, as well as collecting it. That was my idea.' He looked at her proudly and she smiled at him.

'Okay, as long as you're careful, because I don't know what I'd do without you.' She put her arms around his neck and his hands moved to the inside of her pyjama bottoms, pulling her to him, lifting one of her legs over his. Eyes closing at the pleasure of feeling her naked flesh, he ran one hand up her spine, clinging to her shoulder as he kissed her sweet, minty mouth. His breathing became heavier and his unshaven chin pushed coarsely into her lips. As her top rode up and her stomach touched his, he could contain himself no longer, and his hands yanked down the pyjama bottoms. He was so horny, the foreplay might have to wait for round two.

Nicola was no match for his sheer size and weight. She felt his hard-on crush into her groin. He ate her face. She tried to meet his tongue with hers, but her mouth was too full of him. He squeezed at her breast hard with his fingers, his other hand beneath her bare buttocks as he tried to fish for her with his dick. His eyes were closed, his face reddening. He couldn't get in, and he was getting frustrated. Nicola was completely closed to him, everything tightening and forbidding entry.

'Sorry, Micky, I don't know what's wrong,' she said shakily, her palms against his chest, trying to force him upwards to get some air.

Raising himself up Micky looked down between her legs, watched her reach down with her hand and take hold of him.

'Here, let me just—'

'Fuck that.' He pushed her hand away and rammed into her, her gasp wedged in her throat as he started pumping ferociously, the headboard banging noisily against the wall. She could hear his thighs slapping against hers as he ground deeper and deeper into her, breathing frantically, grunting with each powerful thrust. She tasted the bile in her mouth, and shame wash over her as she swallowed it back down again. Clenching her eyes shut, she put her palms flat against the headboard, forcing her body towards the foot of the bed, frightened her neck would break.

On it went. On and on and on.

It had to stop. She had to stop it. Her head screamed, *no, no, no.*

'*Yes, yes, yes!*' she cried.

It worked. He pounded faster and faster, getting closer and closer and she kept crying out, his grunts climbing higher in pitch until one final thrust and he groaned loudly, sweat running to the end of his nose. She felt him pulsing inside her, felt his arms buckle and he fell onto her with another groan and snorting laugh, his heart pounding in double time against her squashed breasts. She couldn't breathe. She shifted uncomfortably under him and he rolled off her, leaving a pool of sweat in her belly.

He wiped his mouth and nose, still panting. '*Whoosh,*' he said, half-turning to her, reaching for her face and kissing her before turning away.

'I fucking love you,' he said.

She swallowed the rest of the bile. 'Love you, too,' and her eyes closed to contain the tears.

A few minutes later she slipped out from under his heavy, sleeping arm and stole into the bathroom where she threw up as quietly as she could into the toilet. When there was nothing left to purge, she flung a towel around her shoulders, sat against the bath and wept.

***

While Nicola and her family devoured treats, Lee sat on Debbie's sofa, nursing a glass of red wine. Louise was standing on a chair in front of the fireplace with her arms outstretched as Debbie, her mouth full of pins, moaned that the dinner would be ruined if they didn't hurry up.

Louise whined at her. Debbie was doing it wrong. Higher up or it would rip! 'Ow, you're *stabbing* me.'

Debbie stood back and stretched her back. 'Jesus, Louise,' she mumbled through the pins. 'Why do you bother asking me to help if all you do is screech at me?'

'Because I can't *sew.*'

'Well, neither can I!'

'This is really nice, thanks for inviting me,' said Lee.

Debbie turned round and spat the pins into her palm, offering an apology as Louise jumped down from the chair and trounced out of the room.

'I told you to keep it simple!' Debbie called after her.

Lee cringed, knowing Louise well enough by now to know she always had to have the last word. Sure enough, she reappeared at the living room door.

'Yeah, but then it wouldn't be the best, would it?' she said.

'It's not going to be anything if you don't get it finished,' said Debbie as Louise stomped up the stairs. She turned to Lee. 'Hope you like dry fish.'

'Love it.' Lee smiled, and she smiled back.

'Here, sit at the table, I'll get our starters.'

Lee sat where he was told and looked around the room. Travis played on the CD player, and he hummed along to a tune he knew well from the radio. Pictures of Louise peppered the room. A faded baby photo, a naked toddler in the paddling pool, and a more recent, soft-focused professional shot of the two of them, their heads together, smiling happily and looking like best friends. Lee had yet to hear them speak a civil word to each other.

'Come on, Louise!' Debbie called as she brought in two plates for her and Lee.

'Mmmmm,' said Lee, taking in the aroma.

'Bruschetta, then cod in butter sauce with baby potatoes and honey-roasted carrots, followed by homemade cheesecake with fresh strawberries and whipped cream.'

Lee rubbed his stomach and looked up at her with hungry eyes, Debbie returning his stare with a sweet smile before turning towards the living room door and screaming, '*Louise!*'

It made him jump with fright, and he saved his glass of wine by the skin of his teeth, quickly dabbing at the red splashes on the tablecloth with his napkin.

Debbie threw the tea towel over her shoulder, mouthed *Sorry* to him and plodded off into the kitchen while Louise hammered down the stairs. She sauntered in, some black lace and tartan fabric falling out of a carrier bag that she dumped by her chair as she sat down. She looked completely calm and smiled at Debbie as she put Louise's plate in front of her.

'Yum,' Louise said, 'looks fab.'

'Dig in,' said Debbie happily, and Lee looked from one to the other, wondering what had happened to the out-and-out conflict he'd just witnessed.

'My mam is the best cook.' Louise bit into her bread, eyes on Lee. 'You don't know what you're missing.'

'It's lovely,' he replied, looking at Debbie with what he hoped was gratitude.

Louise swallowed a mouthful of food. 'Will Nicola be going to yours again? I could ask her to help. *She* can sew,' she said, looking at Debbie.

'Who's Nicola?' Debbie poured herself another glass of wine.

'A detective. She's really nice,' said Louise.

Debbie looked from one to the other. *Tell me more*, her face said, though she didn't want it to.

'They're working on a case together.' Louise swung her legs under her chair and looked at Lee, blinking innocently. 'Will you ask her, Dad?'

'Louise,' Debbie warned. 'Don't be rude.'

'I'm not being rude. I'm just asking. Dad, am I being rude?'

Lee had his last piece of bruschetta near his mouth, and Debbie looked at him, eyebrows raised while Louise's eyes implored.

'It's, erm, well, it's rude … ish,' he said, then popped the food into his mouth.

Louise reached for his arm. 'Please ask her. I don't know how to do it.'

'She's really busy,' he said, wiping his mouth with his napkin.

Louise did a fractious little jump on her seat and looked up to the ceiling, her face in torment. 'Ohhhh!' she said, her voice cracking.

With a sigh, Lee looked to Debbie for the right answer, his brow furrowed in confusion.

'Why are you looking at me like I should be able to sew?' said Debbie. 'Can you?'

He shook his head.

'Don't be so sexist then,' she said bluntly.

Lee's confusion deepened and Louise's eyes pleaded with him melodramatically.

'Okay, okay, ' he said, 'I'll ask.'

'Cool.' Louise smiled a winning smile. *Kerching.* 'What's her surname?' She sprang from her chair and rummaged on a shelf for a pen and paper.

'Erm. Kelly. Nicola Kelly,' said Lee, scratching uncomfortably at his forehead.

'Nicola. Kelly.' Louise wrote the name on the paper, stuck it onto the plastic bag with a pin, and handed it to him triumphantly.

'You know what I like best about this?' she asked, sitting back down.

'Cheesecake?' said Lee.

'No. We're like a proper family.'

Debbie pointed her knife at Louise's plate. 'Eat,' she said.

FOURTEEN

Lee's jacket and work bag occupied the empty seat next to him in the school hall. He'd made sure to arrive early so he could get a good view, and he was keeping everything crossed that Nicola would turn up. After all, she'd taken quite a risk to finish the dress that was about to be paraded on the makeshift catwalk that jutted out into an audience full of parents and fellow pupils. He looked at his watch: five minutes to go.

He hadn't seen her since Tuesday and it was killing him. She'd come to his flat late morning to work on the dress while Micky slept, and Lee took an 'early lunch'. She'd walked into his flat and flung herself at him, pulling at his clothes and walking him backwards to the bottom of the spiral staircase. He wasn't complaining, he wanted her as much – more. They'd giggled and fumbled up the stairs and into the bedroom where he lay on his back, his shirt open, holding out his hands to bring her to him.

She'd straddled him, her back arched, her nails clawing into his torso.

Afterwards they'd lain, semi-clothed, their flushed faces gaping at the ceiling. She'd curled into him and told him about the coming Friday night, the riverboat party that was planned to sail from the Quayside in Newcastle to Tynemouth and back again. It would be Micky's first time in charge. There would be drugs, money, guns, coming in from Amsterdam. Lee held onto her and hope enveloped them both. If Lee could get the foot soldiers to squeal, Micky would get at least ten years for dealing in arms and heroin on that scale. She could get witness protection, they could disappear. They would be free.

Half an hour of entwined limbs and fingers later, Nicola donned Lee's dressing gown and took the dress onto her lap, sewing the hems while Lee dozed next to her on the bed. He should be at work, she knew he had to get back, but the sound of his metrical breathing was soothing, giving rhythm to the needle passing through the cloth and the lace. She couldn't let him go back. Not yet.

When she was finished, she put the dress on a hanger, hung it on the door and lay down next to him. She curled into a ball, her forehead on his, her hands under her chin, and she closed her eyes for a moment.

The sound of Lee's phone had startled them both awake. He was late for the team meeting, and Thompson's voice was low and urgent. If he wasn't there in five minutes, Meadows would have his neck on the block. Nicola, too, was off the bed in seconds. Micky was a creature of habit; she'd have to get to the nursery for Liam then back by three o'clock.

Lee watched her pulling on her shoes, hopping on one leg and hanging onto the door frame for balance. She stumbled over to him while he zipped up the fly on his trousers, kissing him eagerly before running down the stairs. She snatched her bag and headed for the door, needing to flee, desperate to stay. Lee managed to grab her arm just as she was opening the door, the responsibility of what they were about to do hanging like lead around his heart. She recognised it, she felt the same weight in her own chest and she nodded her head faintly as they both acknowledged how close they were to being either part of each other's future, or part of each other's past.

'Come on Friday?' he'd asked hopefully.

'I'll try,' she'd said, then turned and fled down the stairs like her life depended on it.

It was Friday now. The riverboat would set off at eight o'clock that night, but for now Lee needed to concentrate on Louise. He waited in anticipation, the hall jam-packed and full of chatter. He'd had to tell several pissed-off people that the seat next to him was taken, even though the show was obviously about to start. He could see movement in the wings, and he turned his head to the back of the hall, getting out of his seat to look over the heads of the audience. And there she was, straining her neck to find him and he waved his arm high in the air until she saw him and smiled. Then he saw Debbie, just behind Nicola, waving back at him, both of them winding their way towards him, oblivious of each other. He felt himself fluster. Nicola was ahead of Debbie and she climbed apologetically over the legs of grumbling parents and grandparents, sitting down next to him with a relieved thud. Turning his head, he saw Debbie standing at the end of the row, a look of mortification on her face. He could do nothing but shrug ruefully at her and she turned away just as the lights went down.

'Sorry,' Nicola said.

In the darkness, he safely took Nicola's hand as the curtains opened to reveal half a dozen girls in a pose under spotlights, felt her fingers squeeze his as they recognised Louise, wearing the Vivienne Westwood-esque tartan dress. She looked stunning, her black eyes dangerously striking, and her hair, now red again, sleeked back into an androgynous wedge. She was the first to break free, and she strutted confidently in her 'slut shoes' to the end of the runway, posed, then strutted back. Looking around the hall, Lee saw Debbie standing to the side some way back, camera poised. When she lowered it, he tried to catch her eye, but her face was hard and cheerless.

As the applause started, he turned back and clapped furiously, then whooped loudly, his hands cupped around his mouth, glancing at Nicola who sat with her fingers joined under her chin, smiling at the stage, her eyes reflecting the lights like sparklers. He'd never wanted anything more before in his life.

After the show as they stood outside, Lee was a little relieved that Nicola had to run off home so quickly. They'd stood and whispered in low voices about the operation that night. She was scared: he was like a greyhound in the trap. Now she was gone, Lee could alleviate some of his guilt, hang out with Debbie for a while, and wait for Louise outside the front of the school. But Debbie was distant, giving yes and no answers, refusing to look at him. Lee shuffled his feet awkwardly and was relieved to see Louise bounding towards them, squealing with delight.

'Wasn't it *amazing?*' she said, her face blazing with excitement.

Debbie hugged her. 'Oh, Louise, you were *so* beautiful.'

'Ah, Mam, don't cry, please.'

'I can't help it.' Debbie wiped her eyes. 'It was incredible.'

Louise looked at Lee. 'Did Nicola come? Did she like it?'

'She loved it, you were brilliant.'

Louise was grabbed by some friends and she yelled at Lee and Debbie as she was dragged away, 'See you later, parents!'

The silence was clumsy and graceless.

'So, is she your girlfriend?' asked Debbie, her hands in her jacket pockets, her eyes looking at something in the distance over his shoulder. He noticed she wore make-up, lipstick and had a new haircut.

'No. I mean, yes. I don't really know.'

'You are so weak,' she said and walked away.

***

As Nicola walked towards her house she felt a mixture of dread and excitement. She smiled shyly at familiar faces from the estate. Drunk men with red faces and huge noses carrying cans of cider. Women with squirming kids in buggies, a hunchback old woman taking teeny, tiny steps behind her checkered shopping trolley, dressed for the middle of winter, even though it was the height of summer. She was beginning to experience the life she could have, a life free from Micky and from Valley Park. She liked it. She liked Lee. She thought she loved him. She certainly fancied him like mad.

She heard Michael Jnr's laughter as she opened her front door and stepped into the hallway, stopping in surprise to see Kim getting up off the sofa when she walked into the living room.

'She's just going,' said Micky.

'No, stop for a cuppa.' Nicola smiled at her, but Kim avoided her eyes.

'I've got to get Amy from next door's.'

'You okay?'

'Fine, see you later, Micky. Tara, kids.'

Michael responded with a wave, and Liam squeaked a *byeeee* to Kim while Nicola took off her jacket, trying to ignore the atmosphere.

'Go and watch telly in your bedroom,' Micky ordered the children.

'Why?' whined Michael.

'Just do as you're told. Liam, go with Michael.'

The kids knew not to answer back, and they both shuffled off upstairs.

Nicola sensed trouble. 'Cup of tea? I'm gasping,' she said.

'Sit down.'

'Micky, I didn't ask her to come.'

Micky stood up, pulled a gun from under the cushion of the chair and pointed it at her.

'Sit down.'

She did as she was told.

'We're going to play a game,' he said, sitting on the arm of the chair and placing the gun to her temple. Nicola swallowed, fear pinning her to her seat. 'There's one bullet in here, and every time you give me the wrong answer, I'll pull the trigger. Don't know where the bullet is, though: could be right at the beginning or at the end. But it's not half going to make you answer some fucking questions, right?'

'Micky, please, I didn't ask her—'

He put his hand over her mouth. 'I don't think you're getting the message. You only talk when I tell you to. Right, let's start with where you went – today.' He took his hand off her mouth.

'I went to see Margy.'

Click. Micky pulled the trigger, and Nicola started, her terrified hands shooting down to grab the fabric of the cushion. She gripped, her knuckles white.

'Wrong answer. Start again.'

'I went to see someone.'

'Someone called ...'

'I went to see about a job.'

'What do you want a job for?'

'I just thought a job might—'

'A job might be a bad idea.'

'Look, what do you want me to say?'

'Just tell the truth.'

'I went into town to see about a job.'

Click.

Nicola strained her neck back. 'Micky, stop it, please stop. I'll tell you anything you want to know. Don't, please.'

'It wasn't town you went, was it?'

'Jesmond. That's near town.'

'But it wasn't *in* town. Be careful what you say, think carefully.'

'I went to see about a job in an office, answering the phones.'

Click.

Her lips quivered, but the tears were too terrified to escape.

'By, you're lucky. Three down. It's going to get you soon if you don't start telling the truth.'

'It was a school. I went to a school.'

'Posh school. So you were there for an interview? Carry on, I'm enjoying this. Tell me what time your interview was then.'

'I ... two ...'

Click.

Nicola held her breath, her body shaking and her hands starting to go numb as they clung to the chair's cushion. Micky tutted and shook his head, and Nicola struggled to drag words out of her mouth.

'I didn't have an interview, I just heard they wanted someone, I just called in on the off chance.'

'That's a bit of a long shot, isn't it?'

She nodded.

'Don't move, Nicola, I can't trust myself with this: could go off any minute.'

The tears came and she gasped back air, her body rigid with fear. 'Why are you doing this, Micky? I didn't do anything wrong, I promise.'

'Oh but you did, didn't you?'

'Honest, Micky. I just heard about a job.'

He leant into her face. 'You lied to me.'

'I thought you wouldn't let me go.'

'You didn't even have the decency to ask.' Nicola didn't speak, couldn't speak. '*Did you?*'

She whimpered, 'No, I'm sorry.' She gulped, tears swamping her cheeks.

'So did you get it?'

'What?'

'The job, you fucking idiot.'

'It had gone.'

'Then why did you take so long?'

'Eh?'

'Why were you in so long?'

'Because there was some kind of show on, I had to wait to see the head teacher.' She sensed he'd got the information he wanted and felt the muscles in her neck loosen. Her eyes shot him a glance. 'Were you there?'

'I'm everywhere, sweetheart.'

She nodded. 'Okay.'

'And it's a fucking good job you weren't seeing a bloke, or you'd be dead by now, d'you understand?'

Another nod and a tiny, 'Yes.'

Leaning back, Micky pointed the gun at the floor.

'*No!*' Nicola cried.

He pulled the trigger. *Click.* And again, and again, laughing as he got to his feet, clicking the empty barrel as he walked out of the room.

Wrapping her arms around her stomach, Nicola bent forward and put her head on her knees. Thank Christ it was Friday. Tonight he'd be on that boat. Tonight the police would point a gun at *him.* With any luck they'd shove it in his face. They'd tell him to get on his knees, tell him to shut the fuck up. They'd glide the cuffs on his wrists, read him his rights, throw him into the back of a van with all his scum mates. They'd take his prints, kick him in the kidneys – and that hurt, she knew all too well – then boot him into a cell that stank of someone else's piss. Let him rot. Let him starve.

Tonight was Friday. And Micky Kelly would be out of her life by midnight.

***

Micky lay in the bath, his stomach and knees protruding from the crusty, grey water like fleshy islands. The bathroom suite was green – he hated it, hated the black crevices in the grouting, the dripping tap, the fractured, dried-up bar of soap hovering on a plastic dish of scum. Tania did her best with what the Council had given her, but it was a dump and she'd rather spend her money on earrings and underwear than her house. If he complained, he'd get a tirade of how she was sorry she wasn't Little Miss Frigging Perfect, and if he wanted a wife or a housekeeper, he'd better start making the commitment, better start working closer to home so they could have a proper life together with their kids. He couldn't even knock it into her. She'd been around the block a few times, and her great, articulated lorries of brothers would break his legs before they saw any man lay a finger on their sister. Not after Norman Myers, the first husband. Had six pins in his shins after his legs were crushed like eggshells in a hit and run. Marlon Brewis, husband number two, found in the middle of the Town Moor with two dislocated shoulders and only one bollock. No. You didn't beat up on Tania Brewis. She had no loyalty to thugs that weren't blood relatives.

He sometimes wished Nicola had the same will to defend herself. He wanted her to fight back – self-preservation was the only way he could control himself – knowing he might not win, having too much to lose. If she'd retaliated on that first night, clobbered him with the frying pan, or kicked him in the balls, she could have nipped it in the bud, but no, she just lay there, even let him help her to her feet, hugged him back, told him everything would be okay. *She* apologised. Sorry for doing absolutely fuck all wrong. He didn't beat up Tiger, or the lads or Tania. They wouldn't let him. They would hurt him back.

Nicola had no one to defend her. She had a lot of front, though: she could argue with the authorities, the police, even him sometimes, but she didn't hide her softness either, you just had to see her with the kids to know that. She was the only person other than his parents he'd ever known who genuinely cared about what happened to him, who worried about him, frowned in sympathy when he was sick, stroked his head and willed him to be better. He'd never admit, even to her, that he needed anyone or anything, but he knew he needed Nicola. If she left him, he would go to pieces, because then there'd be no one to care or worry about him. He'd made the mistake of getting used to it, of letting her take care of him. But he'd failed her, and now the only way to make her stay was to frighten her into it. Why else would she? Look at the state of this. He rubbed his hands over his vast stomach.

He missed her. She didn't smile at him anymore when he walked in the door. She stiffened in his arms. She cried after sex. If only she would be like she used to be and love him every minute of the day, every thread of her dedicated to him, everything she did, done with him in mind. *If only she would fight back.*

He sat up in the bath, grabbed a nail brush and began scrubbing his head, fiercely scouring away the self-awareness he wished he didn't have. He saw her, Nicola, on the floor; he watched her crumble, giving up the fight for fear of the pain and humiliation of the bruises. It gave him a whole new level of superiority, the kind he hadn't had since he was in the ring. But that was about to change, because tonight he was in charge. Tonight there'd be money. And money was everything. Money was change. Money was life.

Tania opened the bathroom door and walked in with a lit joint. It was some of the new Dutch shit – strong as hell, and the best hit she'd had in years. She wore a leopard-skin dressing gown, so short as to hardly hide the fuzz that she let grow wild. Her permed hair straggled in dry, purple-black ribbons around her shoulders, the white roots showing her age more than she'd like to let on.

Sitting on the edge of the bath she handed the joint to him. He wouldn't normally, not when he had a big job on, but he was feeling the nerves, and this was just what he needed. His first night as the gaffer and he was shitting himself that something would go wrong. At the same time, his heart skipped with exhilaration at the thought of the handshakes and the slaps on the back he'd get once he'd pulled it off. Micky Kelly. Made us all a mint in three hours.

Micky's your man. Micky's the bollocks. Get Micky a drink, will you? Bring the wife, come to ours for your dinner, Micky.

He took a long drag of the joint and inhaled, holding his breath and closing his eyes as he felt the muscles in his legs float. When he opened his eyes again, he saw Tania's smiling face. She, too, was anticipating a windfall. She'd got the catalogues open downstairs. Shoes. Knickers. Jewellery. She wanted a Siamese cat, she said. Get us one, will you?

Taking another drag he pulled her head towards him, blowing the smoke out of his mouth and into hers. He undid the belt of her dressing gown and she shrugged it from her shoulders onto the floor. Her body was thin, brown from years of sunbeds, her breasts flat, the nipples pointing towards her knees over a line of flesh that sank into her belly button like a deflated balloon. She put one leg into the bath, and his eyes moved from her stomach to between her legs. The water spilled onto the floor as he sat up, passed her the joint and put his fingers inside her. She threw her head back with a barking laugh and started to move her hips back and forth, her free hand over her breasts. He loved watching her come. She screamed, she yelled, she swore like a whore.

They finished the joint lying on the unmade bed amongst a pile of washing. Half an hour and he'd have to get himself into town. It was Friday at last, and he was about to become the biggest earner the syndicate had ever seen.

***

The concealed radio felt sweaty in Lee's palms as he brought it to his mouth: 'Positions,' he said.

His earpiece gave him two *Rogers* and a *Good to go, Sarge* from DC Thompson who was on the boat with two other plainclothes officers.

Lee checked the time: it was eleven p.m. The fireworks at Tynemouth were over and the doors to the boat were being closed ready for the journey back to Newcastle. Music blared, and people stood on the deck doing the dance moves to 'Tragedy'. A couple were necking on one of the benches, his hand up her skirt and hers up the back of his shirt. Lee gave orders quietly and confidently. As soon as any money changes hands, give me the word.

Copy that.

Fifteen armed officers sat in the back of the unmarked van. They were hot and sweaty in their bulletproof gear, most of them fidgeting and trying to keep the adrenalin going in the silence. Two hours they'd been sitting, waiting for their moment, all eyes on Lee as he raised the radio to his mouth and asked if Micky Kelly had shown his face yet.

No sign of him, Sarge, came Thompson's reply.

Lee slammed his hand on the steering wheel in frustration. Where the hell was he? Waiting at the other end? Not much point in all this if you can't get the commander. The real bosses would be at home, or in a bar, waiting for the call to say the business was complete. But this wasn't about them. This was about Micky Kelly, and Micky Kelly had turned into the Scarlet Pimpernel.

Okay, Sarge, here we go.

'Stand by,' said Lee. 'Remember, secure the doors first, I don't want any of this stuff going overboard.' He waited for the code word. It came about ten seconds later.

Riverdance.

The officers piled out of the van and down a creaking metal ramp onto the deck of the boat. They shouted above the music.

'Everybody down. Everybody. Get down, sir, thank you.'

They poured through the doors into the boat, knocking sausage rolls and vol-au-vents from the buffet table onto the floor while women screamed and men looked dazed, herding together like cattle. The officers knew who they were looking for and headed straight for some of Tiger's known associates, a police helicopter overhead making sure there were no opportunities to escape.

Within a couple of minutes, Lee had the all-clear and he headed onto the boat. The inside was bright now and he scoured the place with his eyes, watching some of the officers turning out the pockets of half a dozen handcuffed men, the rest searching under chairs, under the DJ's table. Thompson threw an anxious look his way and shook her head a little as the officers turned out nothing but cigarettes, condoms and loose change from the pockets of the dealers. He gritted his teeth. *It's here somewhere.*

'Cordon the whole place off as a crime scene, nobody goes home till the place has been picked apart,' he said. 'Get everyone's details.' He indicated the partygoers, huddled in corners or sitting on the floor, their heads between their knees. Amongst them he saw Mooney sitting with his back against the wall, legs sprawled, his thick curls heavy with sweat and his crutches strewn by his side. Lee got down onto his haunches and put his face next to Mooney's huge, watery eyes.

'Where's Micky Kelly?' he asked, his voice low and threatening.

'Fucked if I knaa,' croaked Mooney, his voice strained, his breath rank, his legs on fire with the pain of being thrown to the floor.

Lee stood up and looked around him. He wasn't there.

He wasn't fucking there.

FIFTEEN

Micky kept his groans to himself as another blow hit his left ear and sent his face reeling to his right shoulder. He kept it there, the droning in his head becoming louder with each strike. His hands were tied together behind him, his feet tied to the chair legs. He felt his blindfolded eyes closing behind swollen flesh, his pummelled ribs stifling his breathing as his head rolled forward and hung on his chest like the dying Jesus. He'd given up goading them, telling them he'd have them, have their mothers. An hour of constant pounding at his head and body, and he was in no doubt that something had gone horribly wrong the night before.

Nicola had been up, waiting in her big, white dressing gown downstairs when he burst into the house before the sun had even come up. He'd hardly made it up the stairs when they'd kicked the door in and he'd heard her shouting his name frantically. Then her voice was stifled by the hand of one of the heavies sent to haul him in. He didn't make it to the bedroom, his hand didn't make it under the bed to the box covered by the spare quilt where his defence lay. Four hands were on him, brought him to the floor, kicked him in the ribs, face, head.

Dragged to his feet, his arms up his back, he'd tripped down the stairs, Nicola struggling to get free of an orange-faced bull of a man with slits for eyes. She'd kicked backwards with her bare feet, eyes bulging, arm outstretched towards her husband. Micky couldn't look at her, all he could do was try to maintain some dignity as he was pushed down the last few stairs into the hallway. As soon as he let her go, Nicola was on the orange one's back, pummelling his shoulders. *Let him go!* Micky had opened his mouth, lips already swelling up, to tell her to stop, that he'd be back soon enough, but his face was smashed into the full-length mirror that hung on the hallway wall, and she was thrown backwards into the living room, knocking a full ashtray from the arm of the sofa over her face and white dressing gown. He'd glimpsed her powdery face before all he could do was allow himself to be bundled into a waiting car which sped off before the doors had even closed.

His face took another blow. *Something had gone wrong?* That was the understatement of the year. Raided, they said. Armed police – undercover. Knew everything. All down the Swanee because of Micky Kelly. The voice of the first assailant was low and gravelly, the other was strained and high-pitched like the Godfather. Both were Mackems – brought in from outside to do the job then piss off.

Micky raised and lowered his eyebrows in an attempt to loosen the blindfold. It moved enough for a little light to squeeze in under his eyes. It wasn't natural light, a yellow bulb of some sort, and he remembered carpeted stairs and a banister, felt the walls around him, heard the echo of his own voice - a small room, an empty bedroom. There'd been no talking until now. Just the flushing of a toilet, then the hammering of his face and legs and chest.

Micky mumbled downwards to his chest. 'It wasn't me, man. I swear it wasn't.'

'Funny that, coz everyone was there except you. Some people lost fifty grand's worth. All had to be sent back once the tip-off came.'

Micky knew these suppliers. Once they were let down and the police got the sniff, they'd be off. There'd be no refund. Obviously he'd have to speak to Tiger himself to do the explanations. These two were hardly here to listen to his excuses. He only fell asleep, for Christ's sake: it wouldn't happen again.

'Why was everyone there if there was no gear?' Micky panted.

One of the men leant in closer to Micky, making him flinch and breathe blood in and out of his one working nostril. 'Had the tickets, might as well have the party,' he said. 'Sell a bit of leftovers.'

'See Tania,' said Micky, trying to sound like he was in charge, but his lungs were too tight to hold any oxygen and it came out like a whisper. 'Get some of ... my gear. Have it.'

'Fucking guilty conscience.'

'Just sharing,' said Micky, 'with me mates.'

The two men laughed. 'Don't worry, son,' said the gravelly one. 'We've got it all.'

Micky raised his head, even though it felt like a bullet was lodged in his brain. 'All?' The resonance of his voice brought more pain. 'What ... what am I supposed to do?' He swallowed his rising anger. 'I've got a business to run, you twats.' He felt the men's breath, one on each ear.

'You've ceased trading.'

'Sold up.'

'Retired.'

'Through ill health.'

Tweedle Dee and Tweedle fucking Dum.

He didn't know what he heard first, the swish of the baseball bat, the brittle crack as another rib shattered, or his own scream. He coughed, he forced himself not to throw up, he spat on the floor. Who did they think they were?

Managing to lift his head he smiled a bloody, delirious smile. 'I was on this scene long before you, you fucking amateurs.' He gave a half-laugh and waited for the next blow.

Instead, he heard the cocking of a semi-automatic pistol.

***

In Carole Meadows' stuffy, overheated office, Lee sat in one of the leather chairs opposite the DI's empty one. His knee bounced uncontrollably. It was eight o'clock in the morning and he'd been up all night, the coffee forcing his eyes open and keeping his nerves on edge.

Nicola had been hysterical, and rightly so. He'd had to take the risk and call her mobile and, thank God, she'd answered it. What had happened? she'd asked. Why hadn't Micky been picked up? You said you'd get him, you *promised*. He could almost see her, chain-smoking, her green eyes flashing through the fear and exhaustion, her thinning face pale and drawn.

He wasn't there, *he wasn't there!* He'd tried to explain, but he knew it wasn't enough. He should have made sure Micky was there. He should have had him tailed – should have tailed him himself if Meadows wouldn't give him the resources. His failure shrouded him like a heavy, black cloak. How was he going to protect her now?

Lee stood and walked to the 1970s-style shelving unit that ran along one side of the wall of Meadows's office. He ran a finger along the neat row of framed awards and photographs. DI Meadows shaking hands with the Chief Constable, him old and stout, her fresh and youthful-looking in the same grey suit and white shirt. The unit was a light, teak wood and reminded him of a similar piece of cheap crap that had hugged the wall behind the sofa in his parents' house. It had come with them to Valley Park from Kenton, along with the drop-leaf table and TV unit that matched it. On it, his mother had displayed ornaments of women lifting their flouncy Victorian dresses with a delicate pinch of finger and thumb, plates illustrating the four seasons, family photographs and a collection of ceramic and china Beatrix Potter thimbles. A dusty coffee set of blue Wedgwood lounged lifelessly behind smoked glass doors. At the base of the unit in Meadows's office, Lee noticed three long, thin, vertical sections, here used for the storage of her various strategy documents, but in his mother's house, crammed full of vinyl records – The Beatles, Neil Diamond, Val Doonican and his dad's collection of Derek and Clive albums. Lee recalled fondly the drop-down drinks cabinet, mirrored at the back and lined with bottles of whisky and Martini alongside crystal wine and whisky glasses, opened only at Christmas and New Year before Frank's accident. And opened pretty regularly thereafter.

Lee was bending down to look closely at a framed press cutting – *£26 Million Pound Jackpot for Valley Park* – when the office door opened abruptly and DI Meadows entered, harassed and carrying two shoulder bags laden down with files. Her face glowed with the effort, and he noticed several broken veins appearing on her cheekbones.

'I'm afraid I've got a meeting,' she said as the bags fell with a thud to the floor by her chair.

Lee walked to her desk. 'I need to talk to you about the riverboat arrests.'

She waved him away with her hand. 'Thompson's already briefed me on the way in,' she said and started logging onto her computer.

He hovered, affronted at her indifference, raising his chin. 'I wasn't your first choice, was I?'

'Absolutely not,' she said without taking her eyes from her screen.

'Can I ask why?'

'You're a loose cannon, and I don't have time for it.'

'Six arrests, and you can't even say Good job?'

'There was nothing. A few grams of weed on Kevin Moone and Stevie Grahame. They've all been released. Not enough on them to warrant intent to supply. CPS would never go for it.'

Lee bit his tongue. The other two had had wads of cash on them, thousands, but deep down he knew it wasn't enough. Meadows waved a finger at him.

'You bring me the investors who're cutting the deals and supplying en masse and you'll get your pat on the back. Now if you don't mind.' She pointed her head towards the door.

Lee felt his face redden. It was no wonder nobody gave a shit about the job in this place. Most of them had long forgotten the vocation, or the thrill they'd felt all those years ago when they'd first stepped out on the streets in their crisp new uniforms. Job satisfaction had done a runner years ago.

He made sure the door didn't slam behind him. He wouldn't give her the satisfaction.

At his desk, Lee put his head in his hands. His illusions of a night face to face with Micky Kelly in an interview room were shattered – running rings around him, tripping him up, breaking him down like a scene from *Cracker*. Fantasies of Kevin Moone shivering in the cell next door were crushed to pulp. Mooney squealing like a pig, telling Thompson everything, then, as the sun came up, Lee reading out the charges to Micky, telling him he would be going down for a very long time and, once everyone was out of the room, putting his face next to Micky's and telling him, 'I love your wife. She's mine now.' Micky lunging at him, but falling over, shackled and unable to move, helpless.

Fiction. All of it.

SIXTEEN

Lee held the steaming mug of tea in both hands as he sat at the window of the greasy spoon, staring out at lead-coloured clouds that seemed to almost touch the tops of the redundant chimney pots. The sky was about to open its jaws and tip its contents on Valley Park. He wished the rain would drown the damned place, sweep it away into the Tyne and out to sea.

Smiling weakly at the humming Turkish woman who put his full English breakfast in front of him, he pushed his work papers to one side and took a mouthful of warm black pudding. Another meeting awaited him at the civic centre. Another Valley Park regeneration meeting with the developers, the master-planners, politicians, education, housing, the job centre, social services – you name it, they were there. Lee looked at his papers. He counted forty-three professionals listed as attending the last meeting. How anyone could get anything done with forty-three people sitting around a table, their own agendas displayed like Post-it notes on their foreheads, he didn't know. He had meetings coming out of his ears. While they took two years to write their anti-poverty strategies and education improvement plans, dozens of new babies had been born into the very poverty they were strategizing to eradicate, the political administration had changed, and the whole thing started again. New strategies with new political messages. In the meantime the people got poorer, the babies grew up and they all got nowhere fast.

The cafe overlooked the dual carriageway onto the eastern edge of Valley Park. He could have gone to the little Italian place by his flat, had a Swiss cheese croissant and a cappuccino. But, aside from needing comfort food, this place was opposite the little supermarket that he knew she shopped in. She'd called him from the payphone there many times – just to hear his voice, she'd said, no doubt blushing at the soppiness of it. But he missed those calls, the simple feeling of happiness he felt when he saw the familiar number light up the screen of his mobile. He looked now at the dead screen. He was losing her.

Lee ate quickly and, when his plate had been taken away, looked out of the window and took in the row of terraced housing on the other side of the dual carriageway, a third of it boarded up, the rest looking weary after a lifetime of hard labour housing people who didn't give a crap about them. Their façades slumped like stroke victims' faces. Their front paths reached out like gnarled, arthritic fingers, punctuated by broken, peeling wooden gates like the bitten nails of anxious teenagers. It seemed to him that Valley Park had taken a deep breath and screamed, *Stay out.* But the meeting papers in front of him told a different story. This was a place of outstanding community spirit, parents who wanted a better future for their children, a place with huge potential, a land of opportunity. If only they could get the right ingredients. A KFC, a Tesco and considerably more people with disposable income.

Lee sat back in his chair, trying to penetrate his gaze through the houses and down the hill to Elm Street. And Nicola, waiting for her husband to come home from the hospital, a gaping hole in his right foot. The bullet must have gone straight through his trainers and the floorboards, because there'd been none of it left in him.

Micky Kelly was keeping his mouth shut. Lee had questioned him in his hospital bed the day before, the glint of recognition in Micky's swollen, black eyes lasting only a second before he turned them back to focus on the bandaged foot in its hoist. Lee stood by him, looking him up and down with the curiosity of a kitten. He lobbed questions at him. Who would want to torture and shoot him? Did he know where it happened? Did he see them? Hear them? Micky's eyes clouded over and he continued to stare at his foot, drinking orange squash through a straw. Lee clicked his pen on and off, on and off, the spiral pad suspended in his other hand while Micky stared ahead, coughed, winced, then lifted a butt cheek and farted.

Lee could only take Nicola's word for it that he had once been a handsome man. Sought after, clamoured after even. He'd asked what she ever saw in him and she'd said she'd felt lucky to have him. He sensed her defensiveness and didn't like it, so he stopped asking the questions, but that didn't stop him wondering how two people could live together for so long with such disparity. The successful couples he knew had always been finely matched. He remembered his parents. Both working-class, good-looking people who'd met at a street party celebrating England winning the World Cup in 1966. They weren't young, both of them approaching thirty, waiting for the right person and working at careers, he as a linesman, she as a hairdresser and beautician. She'd had plans to open her own shop, but Frank's accident had put paid to that. Still, they never grew apart. Instead, they grew ugly and bitter together, synchronised their regret and dissatisfaction, almost as if convergence were the only option.

Lee had spotted Nicola at the hospital after his futile questioning of her husband. She'd been wrestling a can of Coke from a drinks machine as he emerged from Micky's room. But gone was the delighted smile that had greeted him at Louise's fashion show. The smile that left him breathless. The sight of him was no longer a pleasure, and all he saw was fear, confusion and resentment walking towards him down the corridor.

'What are you doing here? You shouldn't be here,' she said fretfully.

'My job,' he replied. He knew it was a ridiculous thing to say before he'd even said it. She wasn't stupid, so why would he treat her as such? She actually scowled at him. *As if.*

'Nicola ...'

'I can't talk now.'

'When then? When can you talk?'

She bowed her head. 'He's coming home tomorrow. I don't know if I can do this, Lee.'

He had no words. He'd let her down. He'd promised. And now there was distrust and uncertainty.

As Nicola passed Lee and walked into Micky's room, Mooney's oily face shone a spiteful smile at itself in the glass of the drinks machine. He hovered on his crutches, the clean dressings stinging his seeping wounds. He'd just spent half an hour cursing the stupid, foreign bitch who'd cleaned and re-bandaged his legs with the delicacy of a trainee plasterer. But now there was another bitch who warranted his attention. Micky's lass. And a fucking copper. Oh, life didn't get much better than this.

***

Nicola waited impatiently in the taxi, the meter ticking, the twenty pound note burning a hole in her hand. It had to last them all weekend, and Micky had been in the gym ten minutes already. The kids were getting fractious, hungry, punching and scratching at each other, Liam howling as Michael's nail caught the edge of his eye. She separated them, putting one on either side of her, a finger pointing in their faces as she told them to calm down or there'd be no telly and no football tomorrow. Liam screamed louder and Michael joined in: *That's not fair!* Life's not fair, thought Nicola, glancing again at her watch as the meter clocked up another pound.

Inside the gym, Micky waited outside the office for Tiger, whose laughing voice seeped under the closed door. A minute later, Stevie's bald head appeared and indicated for Micky to come in. Micky veered himself towards the door in a hospital-issue wheelchair, his bandaged foot sticking out like a giant cotton bud. Tiger sat behind the desk, his dark glasses reflecting the white of Micky's foot to four times its size, his thumbs dancing with each other on his stomach. Stevie stood next to him, his forehead falling over his eyes like a bloodhound's, and Micky felt himself flush as they watched him struggle in silent amusement.

Straightening his tie and removing his glasses, Tiger took on a look of mock sympathy, his slightly crossed, albino eyes glittering in his crinkly face. 'Micky. What can I do for you?'

Micky was well rehearsed. 'I've come to see you about the bit of bother. I want you to know that it had nothing – and I mean nothing – to do with me.' He looked at Stevie, expecting some backup. Micky would never grass: solid as a rock, Micky. But Stevie stared straight ahead.

'Doesn't make any odds to me,' said Tiger, 'it's the lads who lost out.'

'I lost out an' all, Tiger. They took all my gear and I had nothing to do with it.'

'Still got to be paid for.' Tiger's eyes turned from playfulness to stony indifference.

Micky creased his brow in confusion. 'But I can't sell gear if they've taken it, can I? I sank everything into that.'

Tiger looked bored and shifted in his seat, crossing one leg over the other and wiping fluff from the leg of his suit. 'You know the score, Micky: easy terms, fifty per cent cash upfront and the rest a week later. It's already overdue.'

Micky looked into the blank faces of the two men. 'Have *they* paid?' he asked.

Watching Tiger pick at his trousers, Micky felt panic welling in his chest. 'Well, can I have more time to pay?' Stevie's smirk said *You're joking,* and Micky racked his brains for more suggestions. 'Can I have some more gear, then, and I'll pay it all at once?' Tiger shook his head slowly, pursing his lips, and Micky leant forward, exasperated. 'Howay man, Tiger, how long have I been working for you? I'm hardly gonna run away, am I?' He nodded towards his foot with a forced smile.

With a glance at Stevie, Tiger stood up. 'You're off the team,' he said, taking his jacket from the back of the chair and putting his glasses back on.

'What?'

Tiger blanked him and indicated with his head to Stevie that the meeting was over, barely hiding his revulsion when Micky pointed a finger.

'I'll prove it wasn't me,' he said.

'Don't bother,' said Tiger, nodding again at Stevie who took the back of Micky's wheelchair and spun him around, pushing him out the door and letting go.

'I will, *I fucking will,*' Micky yelled, trying to stop the wheelchair hitting a tall tower of stacked plastic chairs. The pain in his arms was excruciating, and, when he was stationary, he turned in the chair awkwardly, trying to mask the agony as he watched Tiger walking towards the door of the gym. He called after him, '*Look at the state of this, man.*' But Tiger was gone, and the gym fell silent. 'There's no call for it,' he muttered, fighting back tears of anger and humiliation.

He wheeled himself slowly to the door of the building. So Stevie was on the team now, got what he wanted – his job. Well, he'd make sure they knew it wasn't him. Micky Kelly grass? Never in a million years.

Nicola watched Micky's profile from the back seat of the cab. He stared to his left out of the passenger window, computing, the theories clocking systematically through his head like the meter of the taxi. If the clock stopped at her name and it all added up, she was finished. Micky was capable of murder, of that she was sure. He'd promised to kill her many a time - if she left him, if he ever found her with someone else - *if, if, if.* She feared not her own death, but the lives her children would lead without her. Left with Micky, what would they learn? To be tough, to take no shit. Violence. Who would teach them please and thank you, the value of money and the importance of justice and friendship? They would end up like Mark, but with no big sister to vouch for them in court.

Taking her phone from her bag she checked the sent and received call lists, making sure for the umpteenth time that she'd deleted all communication with Lee. Only Micky's and the hospital numbers were displayed and some unanswered calls she'd made to Kim that morning. It was sad. Less than half a dozen numbers on her phone. Who did she have left in the world whom she could trust?

She felt sweat prickle her brow. Lee knew never to call the mobile number, but the fear that he might crack just for the need to talk to her made her feel sick. She was finding it more and more difficult to live with the constant anxiety. She didn't sleep more than three hours a night, and her appetite was gone, the food sticking in her gullet and making her retch. And now that Micky was coming home and his activities had been shut off by Tiger, she saw no end to the nightmare. How could she get information on him if he wasn't working?

Names, Lee had said. Get me names. Names that will drop him in it. She swallowed hard, wondering if it was all worth it.

Getting Micky up the steps into the house was a feat in itself. Michael stood by, embarrassed at the spectacle and Micky's irreverent use of language. With so many broken bones, hopping his hulk up the steps on one leg was impossible. Neither arms would take his weight, so trying to get him up the steps on his backside was equally unworkable. Scotty, the pub's barman, had to be fetched from over the road to get Micky into the house and back into his chair. Scotty's nervousness was palpable. Word had got around, and he made it clear that he was doing the favour for Nicola, not Micky, and that there was a condition – she was to tell no one he helped. He heaved Micky unceremoniously back into his wheelchair without word or gesture, making sure the coast was clear before he crept back over the road to his house.

Once inside, Nicola moved the armchair and wheeled Micky to a position opposite the TV. He sat dead still, swallowing the shame and mortification, and she felt her stomach pitch when his hand covered his mouth, concealing a trembling lip. Michael and Liam sat together on the displaced armchair, not quite knowing what to do with themselves. Micky looked up and held out his best arm as wide as he could to them, but they blinked at Nicola, unmoving, not wanting to commit to anything.

'Howay man, I need a cuddle,' said Micky.

Eyes down, Michael cautiously made his way over. 'Come on, I've missed you,' said Micky, easing Michael towards him by the arm. Michael climbed onto his lap and Liam, seeing all was safe, leapt off the chair and ran to his daddy. Micky held onto them both and kissed their heads.

As she closed the front door, Nicola heard a familiar barking and spotted two small, brown eyes looking through the bars of the garden gate. She held her hand to her heart and ran to open it, Rufus bounding around her legs, filthy, skinny and absolutely beside himself. She picked him up, held him out at arm's length in front of her and took him into the house. Seeing Liam and Michael, he twisted to be free and she set him down on the floor of the living room.

'Rufus!' the boys cried in unison, falling off Micky's lap and charging over to the dog. Nicola smiled happily, but when her gaze met Micky's, her smile faded to nothing. His eyes were shrunken, his posture hunched, defeated. He looked away from her, out of the window, and the guilt ate her up like the hungry dog.

***

As the week went on, Micky became more and more withdrawn. His unshaven face aged and great bags of pink, wrinkled flesh appeared under his eyes. He filled a bottle with his piss and made his way slowly and excruciatingly up the stairs to the bathroom every morning for a crap and a flannel wash. His breath reeked. He slept on the sofa: he came nowhere near her. He accepted the food, tea, beer and kind words with silent tolerance. He kicked grumpily at the dog and stared vacantly at the TV, the remote control untouched on the table next to him. He had no visitors – for all the mates he had just a few weeks ago, they'd deserted him now. Not a phone call, not a Get Well card. Nothing.

She held his hand – sometimes he grasped at hers as she said goodnight to him. She would lie beside him, teetering on the edge of the sofa. He never touched her, never asked her to touch him, and she wasn't sure how to take it. Perhaps he knew exactly what she had done and was lulling her into a false sense of security. Perhaps he was so depressed he'd lost his sexual appetite. Perhaps he just didn't fancy her anymore.

She looked at him now, sleeping, snoring, the bruises turning green and yellow. She'd never known him so quiet and introverted and she wondered if it was possible he'd got a taste of his own medicine. The punches and kicks, bruises and battered limbs.

She settled herself on the floor in front of the sofa, her face next to his. He was supposed to take care of her. When she married him, that's what she'd expected. She couldn't remember her father, but perhaps he would have taken care of her had he been able to stomach her mother's dreadful moods. Nicola would feed herself and Mark out of tins when her mother went AWOL, too embarrassed to ask for help from the neighbours or a teacher. She would steal money from her mother's purse, save it in a jam jar under her bed for the eventuality when her mother would forget she had children at all. The absences became longer and longer until one day their mother didn't come home at all.

After several weeks, the money and the tins of food ran out. They would watch adverts on the TV for Super Noodles and McDonald's with hungry, dinner plate eyes. The truancy officer who found them had covered her mouth and gasped back her tears. A big, buxom, bouncy castle of a woman, soft as clarts and posh as the Queen. She'd held them both to her soft pillow of a chest and said no, they couldn't stay here, they needed to be taken care of, they were too little to take care of themselves. Care. Something she'd never really had. Foster parents tried to care, but Mark wouldn't let them. He spat and kicked and screamed. He broke their heirlooms, hit their children, pissed in their plants and in their beds. And when he went back to the home, she went with him because she was the only one who could take care of him.

Micky's face twitched, and he grunted, wriggling himself into a more comfortable position. It struck her then that she'd never thought about having to take care of herself for a very long time. But she knew now that she had been doing it for years, and was going to have to do it forever. She thought about Lee. She missed him. She thought of him every hour of every day. She had almost called him several times, but fear overshadowed desire.

Micky's eyes opened sleepily, and he reached out for her hand, muttering something she couldn't hear. She put her ear next to his mouth.

'I'm sorry,' she heard.

***

Depression turned to paranoia. A few days later, Micky was eyeing her every move, even from one side of the room to the other. He timed her trips out to the shops or to Kim's. Every minute had to be accounted for. Her phone was confiscated. No money for phones. He'd banished the dog to the back garden, telling her he wanted rid of it, she could take it down the cat and dog shelter, tell the kids it got run over. She'd offered to take him to the gym, and he'd looked at her with such disgust that she felt it pierce her skin and poison her blood. Sometimes he looked at her with infinite tiredness, daring her to sympathise, then lashing out if she so much as touched him.

Still he slept downstairs, like a Bullmastiff, guarding the front door should she mean to escape. Her nights swung between wide awake and stressful dreams. Any trip to the bathroom in the middle of the night, and she'd find him standing on one leg at the bottom of the stairs, looking up, making sure she got back into bed.

Tonight she was in a deep sleep for a change, when she woke up in the pitch dark, wondering whether the loud thud had been part of an instantly forgotten dream or reality. Hearing another clatter from the boys' room, she dragged herself out of bed, and swayed towards the bedroom door. She squinted against the landing light as she made her way across to the opposite bedroom where Liam sat on his bunk whimpering, 'Bottley, Mammy,' and Micky lay on the floor, holding himself up with one elbow, trying to right himself. She helped him sit up and Liam cried louder, *'Bottley!'*

Micky was breathless with the effort, 'I didn't want him to wake you up—'

'It's all right, I'll get it.' She ran downstairs and put some milk in a bottle, bringing it back upstairs, Liam grabbing it from her desperately and lying down on his pillow, sucking furiously, rubbing his head with his fingers. She pulled his quilt up to his neck and kissed his head.

'*Bastards*,' she heard Micky swearing under his breath. She sat next to him, her arm just stretching around his massive shoulders. 'They think I grassed them up. Jesus, if I was gonna do it, I'd do it big time, not a stupid riverboat party.'

'At least you're out of it, eh?'

Micky held a piece of paper in his hand. 'They're all here,' he said, holding it aloft, hate oozing through his clenched teeth. 'The whole syndicate – it's got to be one of them. I'm telling you, I'll find out who it was, you watch. And when I find out. They're dead.' His hand started to shake, and it fell to the floor as if the paper weighed a tonne. Half turning to Nicola, he stared at the floor, not able to look her in the eye. 'I can't even fetch for me own kids. What am I gonna do?' His shoulders shook, and Nicola swallowed the lump in her throat. 'Me foot, Nicola, they nearly took off me foot.'

Her arms went around his neck and he buried his face in her hair, his hand still limply holding the piece of paper in front of him. She felt him sob and she held onto him. The man was in pieces, and it was all her fault. What the hell had she been thinking? *This* was her life, her husband, her house, her children. Kim and little Amy. Perhaps if she was good to Micky, he'd make sure Margy and her family could come home. But his power was gone, he held no sway with the big boys now. She sighed. No matter. She'd been a fool. What did she think she would do with Lee? A copper's wife? Hanging around with other coppers' wives? Dinner parties with coppers? Living in a place where she knew no one, always looking over her shoulder, her children living with a new dad who didn't even know them? She needed to be near Kim, but would Lee ever be accepted? *A filthy copper?*

She rested her cheek on Micky's head and closed her eyes. Christ, she'd been a stupid, stupid cow.

***

Lee's legs became heavier with every step as he left the cemetery where they'd first kissed, Nicola still sitting on their bench, head bowed, with relief or sorrow, he wasn't sure. She couldn't live with herself, she'd said. She'd done a terrible thing. He was never to contact her again. She'd meant it, too, every word. There was no persuasion, no reassuring hug, the panic alarm back in his possession.

Never. That word again.

SEVENTEEN

The pounding in his head started just seconds after consciousness reclaimed him. The room was outrageously light, the long white voiles no defence against the streaming sun that shone directly into the room – directly onto his face. Lee crushed his eyes shut against the fiery heat then snapped them open again, staring at the ceiling, rigid, as the realisation of where he was dawned on him. Lying flat on his back with one bare foot on the floor, he turned his head slowly to his left. Debbie lay with her back to him, her shoulders rising and falling rhythmically under the quilt. Was she naked? *Shit!*

He pulled back the duvet silently, relieved to see his boxers, one sock and his T-shirt still on his body. The night was a fog of red wine and malt whiskey and he didn't remember going to bed at all. There'd been music, dancing in the living room, The Specials, The Pogues, the rest he couldn't recall.

His work trousers and shirt lay sprawled over the back of a chair under the window. He moved like a sloth, painstakingly slow, until he was on his feet. His head was in a vice, his mouth full of dough, and he thought he might fall off the edge of vertigo and straight to hell when he stood up. Swaying, he steadied himself on the cast-iron bedstead then snuck out of the room on tiptoes, his clothes held tight to his chest. In the bathroom he took a long piss, swilled some mouthwash and pulled on his trousers and shirt, wondering where the hell his shoes and other sock were – please God, not the bedroom. If she woke up, he couldn't bear the shame.

He found the shoes strewn by the sofa in the living room and thirty seconds later he was pulling his jacket from the coat hook and closing the front door as quietly as he could. He was still over the limit, he was sure, but needs must, and he had to get out of there.

***

'You're early,' said Thompson, sitting with her coffee at the station reception. Lee grunted and headed to the office, chewing on a piece of minty gum he'd found at the bottom of the glove compartment – not his, must've been Louise's, and for once he was glad she chewed like a horse all day long. Anything to get rid of the sickly taste of his own mouth. Lee glowered at Gallagher at the filing cabinet, wondering why he was in an hour before he actually needed to be, and two hours before he normally was.

'Shit the bed?' asked Gallagher with a wink, eyeing Lee's crumpled shirt. Lee ignored him and picked up a bunch of messages from his desk, quickly throwing them back when he realised none was from Nicola. 'Shit on the pot or get off,' continued Gallagher, 'that's another one of mine. Either get it off your chest or move on.'

'Has anyone ever told you what a disgusting little moron you are?' asked Lee.

'All the time, Sarge, all the time.'

The day went from bad to worse. In his Great Escape, he'd left his wallet at Debbie's house – no money, no cards. A pubic hair greeted him with a bristly wave from the bacon and egg butty bought with a couple of quid borrowed from Thompson. The CPS hounded him all day with phone calls and emails, questioning the legality of the raid on the riverboat while one of the dealers arrested that night brought a counter charge of assault against the arresting officer. Bruised ribs and a swollen wrist were worth thousands to some scrawny scally, thanks to Lee's little midnight swoop. It pissed down outside all day, the office roof leaked; the pit-pat of water dripping into the empty bins irritated his slow-cooking hangover. He drank a sea of coffee, his stomach and heart churning, wishing the day would be over so he could crawl onto his sofa and sleep until it all went away. Debbie called him twice, but he didn't have the guts to answer the call, not today. He felt like the biggest coward that ever walked the earth.

Five o'clock was almost here, not before he'd had to drive to the edge of the cemetery and have half an hour's sleep in the car. Still he felt revolting. The words on the computer swam in front of his eyes. *Ten minutes,* he thought, *and I'm out of this wretched place.*

But DI Meadows had other ideas. Out she swanned, that poker-face again, a red, birthmark-like stain creeping up her neck. She cleared her throat aggressively and stood a few feet away from Lee. He peered at her over the report he was pretending to read.

'Had the commissioner on the phone,' she said. 'My office, now.'

He sat slumped in a chair in her office, legs crossed, watching her pace and wishing she'd floss the annoying piece of black debris that was wedged in an incisor. He wiped his tongue over his own teeth, hoping she'd get the message. She didn't, and his irritation had no limits. The arrests weren't enough, she was saying, staring at his feet, avoiding eye contact. They needed more, so now was his chance to get that pat on the back. His informant needed to come up with something more solid. Who was taking the bulk of the goods. Delivery dates, distribution networks, cash deposits, where the money was being laundered. She stood over him, staring down at his shoes rather than his face.

'No can do,' Lee said. 'She won't do it anymore.'

'Make her,' said Meadows going back to her chair, 'and put both socks on tomorrow, will you?'

***

As he dragged his feet up the stairs to his flat Lee tried doubly hard not to roll his eyes when he saw Louise sitting outside his front door, legs spread-eagled, headphones blaring. He stepped over her and opened the door without a word.

'You should give me a key,' she said, pulling her earphones off and following him inside.

Lee threw his keys onto the dining table. 'What is it, Louise?'

'Mam says do you want to come for supper, she wants to talk to you.'

'I'm too busy.'

'You've just got in.'

'I've got stuff to do.'

'Like what?'

'Louise, do you mind? I want to be on my own. It's not you, honestly.'

Louise tutted and walked up to him, his wallet in her outstretched hand. He took it, embarrassed, and sat down heavily on the sofa.

'I'm sorry,' he sighed, 'some ... bad things happened.'

'You should've just said.' Her voice softened and she sat next to him. 'What sorts of things? Work things?'

Lee shrugged.

'Dad?'

Lee looked up, still not used to the title. 'I was ... Nicola ...'

'Oh my God, what's happened?' Louise touched his arm.

'Nothing, nothing, we just ... it's finished, that's all.'

Louise looked confused. 'What? You were going out with her?'

'Sort of.'

She stood up. 'Nicola?'

Lee squinted up at her. 'What's wrong with that?'

'You slept with my mam!'

'Hang on, I—'

'Last night. You did.' Lee struggled to speak, and Louise tried to stop her voice from shaking. 'She *loves* you,' she shouted.

'What?'

'You're horrible.' She headed for the door.

'Louise, wait—'

'I *hate* you!'

As Lee heard the echo of the slamming door resonate through the whole block he threw himself back onto the sofa and covered his head with a cushion. The world needed to go away and leave him the hell alone.

***

The next morning, Lee waited resentfully in his car outside the decrepit supermarket on the outskirts of Valley Park. The conversation with Debbie wasn't going well. What did he mean, did anything happen? He couldn't remember? *He couldn't remember?* Lee closed his eyes and moved the phone away from his ear. The hangover was extending into day two.

'Louise seems to think we had a night of passion,' he persisted. 'Did we?'

The silence made him nervous.

'I need to go to work,' she said.

'No, no, no ...' said Lee, his frustration spilling out into the handset. 'Come on, Debbie. I'm sorry, I swear I am. But I need you to be honest with me. No more games. Please, Debbie.'

'Well, if we did, it was obviously completely forgettable,' said Debbie petulantly.

'Oh my God,' Lee whined, exasperated.

'Oh, all right then,' she snapped. 'No, nothing happened. Happy now?'

Lee exhaled and his head fell to his chest. He grinned a little, half relieved, half amused at Debbie's false anger. Despite the years, he still knew her little tantrums rarely amounted to anything.

'We should talk ...' he ventured, only to be cut short.

'Whatever, Lee, but not now. I've got better things to do with my time. Goodbye.'

She was gone. But Lee understood the subtext. He was forgiven, and the conditions of their relationship had been met. There was no future, they would remain parents, potentially friends, but nothing else.

He looked at the windowless supermarket with its fed-up security guard at the door, the paint peeling from the sign, and a row of yelping dogs tied up outside. He turned his focus back to the street that stretched downhill into the distance, watching in the hope that she would turn the corner at the bottom of the hill as she usually did on a

Tuesday morning. A few more seconds passed and there she was, a little dog on a lead pulling her forward, her arm getting a break as the dog stopped to sniff at something on a front yard gate. She wore grey jogging bottoms and the pretty pink hooded top he'd bought her. Moreover, she was alone. When she bent down to fuss the animal, he jumped out of the car and hurried into the supermarket, heading for the little office at the back. Thompson was already there, supping from a polystyrene cup and avidly watching a row of silent black and white TV screens on the wall just above her eye level.

Lee sat next to her. 'She's coming,' he said, eyeing the brown envelope on the table in front of Thompson. He turned his eyes to scour the TV monitors while Thompson leant forward to get a better view of the screens. They sat in silence, their eyes darting back and forth for several minutes.

The office door opened with a crash, making Lee turn his head, but Thompson didn't flinch, her eyes remaining on the people hovering around the store's entrance. Bacon sandwiches and tea had arrived from the cafe opposite. Elaine, the store manager and a notorious nosy parker, put the greasy paper bags in front of them then stood at their shoulders, eager to be part of the drama and have a story to tell her friends.

The screen showed 09.10 a.m. when Nicola walked through the door.

'That's her,' said Lee, pointing. Elaine stifled a theatrical gasp with her hand and Lee, indulging her, commanded her formally to tell the store detective that they were *all systems go.* She gave a little salute and ran from the office.

Lee and Thompson shared a smile then stared at the screen, tucking into their sandwiches. After several minutes a short-haired woman in a frumpy jacket and comfy shoes took Nicola by the arm and spoke to her. They watched Nicola pull her arm away and step back, angry, gesticulating with her arms. The security guard appeared behind her and she looked up to the ceiling then down to the floor in defeat, her hands on her hips. The store detective touched Nicola's arm again and she wrenched it free before following the security guard to the back of the store.

When they were off-screen, Lee and Thompson fixed their eyes on the door of the office. They heard her before they saw her. She'd done nothing wrong, why would she want to nick any of that rotten crap? The door opened, and Nicola stopped dead, Lee freezing mid-bite, and Elaine making a reappearance with a face eager for more action.

Blood rushed to Lee's head, and he felt his palms begin to sweat, the food in his mouth taking on the characteristic of chalk. He stood, swallowed dryly and spoke to her politely, 'Take a seat please, Mrs Kelly.'

Nicola's stupid cheeks flushed red, and she tried to cover her humiliation by pulling her fringe down over her forehead, her eyes following the outstretched hand that pointed to a plastic chair.

'What do you want?' she asked coldly.

'To talk to you.' He pulled the chair out and leant on its back with his hands.

Nicola sat. 'Have you got any idea how embarrassing this is?'

Thompson indicated to Elaine that it was time to leave the room, which she did reluctantly, giving a final glance back as she closed the door very, very slowly indeed. Lee and Thompson waited impatiently until the door was finally closed, then Thompson leant forward.

'We didn't want to blow your cover,' she said.

'Cover?' Nicola peered at Thompson, incredulous.

'As an informant.'

Nicola laughed, cynically. 'Get real,' she said, opening her cigarette packet and lighting up, shaking her head.

'We made six arrests on the information from the riverboat party,' said Thompson, her face serious, intense.

Nicola looked at Thompson over the exhaled smoke then turned her gaze up to Lee. 'I don't know what you're talking about,' she said, 'can I go now, please?'

His initial trepidation overcome, Lee took his seat and observed her. 'You were going back to get free, now you're deeper in it than ever, aren't you? He won't let you out of his sight.'

Nicola continued to smoke, glancing at Thompson, wondering how much she knew while Lee continued in a flat tone: 'I suppose you think he can't be up to anything while he's laid up? But there's the other wife and kids. Probably keeping the business going.' He nodded at Thompson who took the photographs from the brown envelope and placed them face-up on the table. Nicola looked scornfully at Lee. He was talking rubbish, this was seriously desperate. 'Common-law wife,' he went on, 'Tania Brewis, and two little girls. Bobby Anne and Michaela.' His eyes guided hers to the table.

Nicola looked down at a photograph of Micky kissing Tania at an open front door, a little girl about Liam's age perched on her hip. It was a recent one, hardly a few months old, she guessed. She picked it up, bringing it closer to her face. Underneath was another photograph of a smiling, happy Micky with the same toddler sitting between his legs and a baby of about six months in his arms, Tania falling against his shoulder, her eyes closed tight, her mouth laughing widely.

'Got a look of your boys, haven't they?' Lee said, trying to catch her eye.

Nicola's appalled face looked up at him: *Why are you doing this?*

With a glance at the door, Lee's eyes indicated to Thompson that he needed some time alone, and she left the room, leaving a dense silence behind. Lee's tone changed, became softer, more reassuring.

'Tania's the one who picks up his supplies and divvies them up to the dealers. People like Mooney and Mark.'

'Mark was not a dealer. Micky would never use—'

'He uses Tania, the mother of his children. In fact, Tiger Reay has probably given her Micky's place in the syndicate.'

'So, arrest her, what do I care?'

'Oh, I'm sorry, I thought you did care. About people like Mark and Kim and the kids on your estate.' Nicola looked away guiltily. 'I need to know who else is on that syndicate.'

Nicola scoffed. Fat chance. She put her cigarette out, not able to look at him, not wanting to see his face. As long as he was out of her sight, her resolve remained strong. But seeing him: well, that was different. She pushed her fringe back from her face. She looked a state. No make-up, her hair greasy and messy in a bobbled ponytail. She'd stopped caring. But now his eyes were on her and she felt ashamed of her unplucked eyebrows and rat-tailed hair. She looked again at the photograph of Micky with this wrinkled, rough-looking woman, older than her by twenty years, it seemed.

Lee picked up on her insecurity. 'Does he make you happy, Nicola?'

'I want to go.'

He reached his hand out and put it over hers. 'I miss you.' The touch was like sunlight itself moving up her arm and into her head, chest and belly, settling in her legs. She pulled her hand away, knowing that allowing herself one tender move would be her downfall. 'So much, Nicola. I'm a mess.'

She opened her mouth to speak, just as an alarm rang in the office and a red light flashed on the wall above a sticker reading *Customer Service*, the CCTV monitor displaying two lads at the cigarette kiosk, hoods up, scarves around their mouths, golf clubs at the ready. Lee scrambled in his inside pocket and took out his radio.

'Robbery in progress, Safeways, Ellington Terrace. Two youths, possibly armed.' He turned to Nicola. 'Sorry. Wait here. Please wait here.'

When he'd gone, Nicola watched the line of CCTV screens, fascinated at how many there were for some two-bit supermarket. She saw Lee and Thompson holding up two-for-one advertising boards as defence against the golf clubs that rained down on them while the security guard and a warrior-faced Elaine pitched canned vegetables at the two youths with sports-like precision. The youths started to back away, and Lee and Thompson joined in with the can throwing, the robbers reaching the exit just as a stream of police cars lined up outside.

Looking around her, Nicola noticed the fire exit sign at the other end of the office, took the photographs and hurried out the back exit of the store. Outside, she could see Rufus tied to the drainpipe on the corner of the building, barking at the commotion. Clutching the envelope, she scurried to him, quickly unfastening his lead before shooting a glance at Lee who stood with his arms folded as a uniformed officer cuffed one of the thieves across the head and shoved him into the back of a police car.

As if feeling her eyes on him, Lee turned and squinted as he saw the arse end of the dog disappearing behind the wall.

She was walking away from him again, and there was nothing he could do about it.

***

'*Detective* Nicola Kelly?' Meadows bristled as her anger stewed. 'That's who this daughter of yours asked for when she was brought in.' Meadows stood over Lee's desk in the open-plan office, arms folded, little bits of white foam at the sides of her mouth. She was beginning to repulse him. The Titless Wonder. 'It doesn't take a brain surgeon to work it out,' she said pompously.

'She's just a kid, she got it wrong, that's all,' sighed Lee. 'Can I go and see her now?'

'Are you having a sexual relationship with this woman, Detective Sergeant?'

'No. She's an informant. Was an informant.' Lee felt his face warm as he imagined the eyes of the team shooting glances at each other.

'*Was* is no good to us. You want your strategy to work, you better start getting information. I mean, that is the basis of your strategy, yes?'

'Can I go and see my daughter now?' Her condescension was embarrassing him beyond belief.

'I suppose so.' She walked towards her office. 'Gallagher, get me a coffee, will you?'

DC Gallagher sprang from his seat and marched over to the kettle, tutting and shaking his head as he passed Lee. 'Got a right little tearaway there, eh?'

Lee sneered. 'Just do what the boss-lady says, tea boy.'

***

In the interview room Lee sat opposite Louise who sucked in her cheeks and looked anywhere but at him.

'Can't you get them to drop it?' she asked the wall.

Lee shook his head. 'Why did you do it?'

'Why did you?'

Lee looked puzzled. 'Do what?'

Her eyes were on him, almost cutting him in half. 'Come back here, make me think you loved me and everything.'

'I do love you. Now can we stick to your little shopping spree?'

Louise looked away again. 'No you don't. And you used Mam.'

'I didn't.'

'You're a user. You use people and then you dump them. I bet you've done it to loads of people.'

Her eyes were filling with tears despite herself and Lee sat back in his chair with a tired sigh. 'I came back to try and face up to things. To – I don't know – make it up to you.'

'I never want to see you again.'

'So why did you do this, then? If you needed anything, all you had to do was ask.'

'I needed you to get back with my mam. So I could be normal, like everyone else.'

'So, if I can't give you your wildest dreams, you don't want anything?'

Louise squirmed and pulled her sleeves down over her hands, clinging to the cuffs of her blouse with her fingers. 'What's wrong with Mam?'

'Nothing. And in my wildest dreams I thought I could come back, mend everything, and we'd all live happily ever after.'

She leant forward to him. 'We *can*.'

'Louise, we can't. I love someone else.'

She grabbed his hands. 'But she doesn't want you. We do.'

He didn't know what to do or what to say. How could he have got it all so very wrong?

'Dad?'

He leant into her. 'Louise. I don't love your mother. I'm sorry, but I don't. But I love you and I want you in my life. Take me or leave me. I don't know what else to say, I really don't.' Her face fell from hope to misery. 'It's up to you.' He got to his feet.

'Where are you going? You can't leave me here,' she said anxiously.

'Stealing is a serious offence. You'll face the consequences like everyone else.'

'Dad!' she cried as Lee closed the door.

He approached the desk sergeant. 'Leave her for five minutes then give her a warning and send her home,' he said. The officer nodded, wondering why some jumped-up detective was telling him how to do his job. Obviously, first offence, verbal warning, off home to Mummy.

Buzzing himself through the door Lee walked through to the reception area to catch his breath but stopped as he heard laughing voices on the other side of the reinforced glass. He strained his neck over the desk sergeant's head, and spotted Tyrone Woods, hands cuffed behind his back, head bowed, flanked by two male officers who shared a joke. Lee turned away and messed with some papers on a desk while Tyrone was booked in, then watched the desk sergeant escort him to an interview room. When they were both out of sight he sidled over to the clerk.

'Tyrone Woods?' he asked, looking over her shoulder.

'Aye,' she replied, 'only a matter of time with this family.'

He hmphed in agreement and peeked at the charge note. *Gross indecency.*

'Jesus,' he said.

'I know, and with some other young fella an' all crying rape.'

Lee turned to see Gallagher strolling through reception filling his face with a packet of crisps. Gallagher cleared his throat and grinned a little as he opened the interview room door, Lee catching a glimpse of Tyrone for just a few seconds. Tyrone's eyes blinked upwards at Gallagher with wounded scorn before the door closed.

***

The photograph in Nicola's hand distinctly showed the name of the road on the wall of the house. Cathall Ave, NE9. She'd spent half the milk money on an A-Z. and she'd found the street quickly – Gateshead. Jesus, it was only five miles from her own house as the crow flies. She'd managed to get the leather jacket, gold jewellery and make-up out of the house without Micky making a fuss. She sat on the Metro now staring at the photograph of Micky and Tania kissing, Liam's half-sister sniffling in her mother's arms. The jewellery was on, the black eyeliner pasted around her eyes, and her hair was loosely stacked on her head, straggling tails hanging around her face. She'd picked some white heather from the roundabout by the bus stop.

She arrived at Cathall Avenue in about ten minutes. It was a long road, but within a few minutes she spotted the house at the end of the terrace. There were no front gardens or yards, just the doors opening straight onto the pavements. She checked the photograph, the location of the road sign, the front door with the canopy over and the dried-up flowerpot on the windowsill. She knocked on the door, and Tania answered with the toddler in her arms.

'Buy a piece of lucky heather?' Nicola asked in her best witch's voice.

'No thanks.' Tania's accent was thick and drawling, and Nicola took in the tattooed knuckles, the gold rings on every string-like finger. She smiled at the child.

'What lovely hair, what's your name?'

'Tell the lady, Bobby Anne.' The child repeated her name shyly.

'Ahh, that's nice.' Nicola looked back at Tania. 'Want your fortune told?'

'No, I'm busy—'

'See if you're gonna have any more?'

Tania hesitated. At forty-four she didn't hold out much hope for any more kids, but she was always grateful to hear the contrary. She held out a tentative palm which Nicola took eagerly.

'You've got two girls?'

Tania nodded suspiciously.

Nicola shook her head. 'No more with the man you're with. His name begins with M?'

'Yeah, Micky.' Tania was hooked.

'Your love line's all broken up. Does he leave you a lot?'

'He works away, but we're still together.' Tania leant into Nicola. 'Are we going to move soon?'

'Ahh, he's promised you a big house.' Tania nodded, wondering how this Romany hag could be so on the nose. Nicola frowned at Tania's palm. 'He can't be trusted, love. You look after yourself and your children. And don't get involved in anything that would harm them. Even if he says you must. Do you understand?' Tania stepped back, stunned by what she was hearing, and Nicola handed some heather to Bobby Anne. 'To keep you lucky.'

She walked slowly to the house next door and pretended to ring the doorbell as Tania closed her door, then she dumped the heather on the pavement and scurried down the street. Utterly betrayed, she bent her head against the rising wind and made her way back to the Metro station. It must have been going on for at least three or four years, probably longer. How many others were there?

She tore the earrings from her lobes, tears of rage smudging her eyes blacker. Everyone must know about it. All of his boxing mates, Tiger, Mooney. Who else? Kim? They were all laughing at her. The humiliation swallowed her whole as she fought the tears and climbed the stairs to the approaching train. It was one thing to bruise her skin, but to bruise her dignity was unforgiveable.

EIGHTEEN

Lee looked out to the distant lighthouse, his hand shielding his stinging eyes from the sand and salty air. A blustery wind swarmed around him, lifting his shirt so it billowed out around his torso like a balloon, making the buttons strain in their holes. The beach was virtually empty except for a few tourists in shorts, sandals and bum bags, holding their fleeces tightly closed, heads bowed as they fought their way against the torrent of air that twisted around their ears, making their hair stand upright. He blinked and saw her shimmering form approaching him at some distance, the little dog running excitedly in and out of the water. She'd tied her hood around her face by the tassels and was struggling to push the buggy through the sand. She waved to him. He smiled, his nerves wrapping themselves in knots, and waved back a hopeful hand.

Eventually they stood, face to face, hardly able to open their eyes against the raging wind. He held out his arms and she offered no resistance, falling against him with an acceptance that felt as natural as air. They kissed, ignoring the sand grinding its way into their mouths and noses, Rufus running rings around them, barking, *Play with me!* Lee's arms tightened around her as her chin fell onto his shoulder. She clung to him and it felt right, like she'd come home.

He kissed a fresh cut above her eye. 'I can't believe you want me to rescue a dog when you're in so much danger.'

'He was going to shoot him,' she said.

Lee saw the paranoid look in her eyes as she glanced to her right at someone walking along the sea edge.

'Come on,' he said.

They sat in a deep cove beneath the rocky stairs that led to the road above, the wind whistling past, Kim's baby, Amy, asleep in the buggy, and Rufus dozing with his chin on Nicola's lap. She sat nestled between Lee's legs and rested the back of her head on his chest, his arms locked around her waist. His breastbone was solid and smelled sweet, not like Micky's spongy sourness. His cheek rested on her head and they sat for a while just breathing in unison before she told him everything that had happened over the last twenty-four hours.

***

She started with Kim.

Kim wasn't answering the door, hadn't done so for several days, so Nicola had gone around the back and let herself in, Michael and Liam following behind, eating orange ice lollies. The kitchen was a disaster. It stank of stale bins and rot and she'd held her breath as she headed down the hall to the living room, the ticking clock of *Countdown* seeping through the crack in the door. When she opened it she saw Kim lying with her back to her, curled up on the sofa, her shoulder blades piercing through her vest top like scalpels. Mooney was slumped in the armchair facing the TV, his head lolling on his chest, a little bubble of saliva ballooning and retreating with each breath. The overpowering smell of stale beer and smoke had her covering her mouth with her sleeve, but there was another smell in the air, the liquorish stench of something unfamiliar.

She kicked away the cans that littered the floor and shook Kim to no effect, then shuffled towards Mooney through the mess. She kicked at his little boy legs, still in braces.

'Eh? Wha ...?' His head rolled back and he prised his eyes open into glassy slits.

'What's going on?' demanded Nicola.

Her face was like the blinding light of a torch in Mooney's eyes. 'Eh?'

'What've you given her?'

'Nowt, man, fuck off.'

Looking around her, Nicola spotted a syringe peeping out from under a newspaper on the floor. She moved the newspaper with her foot and saw a pile of half a dozen syringes, burnt spoons and foil.

'My God.' She turned and realised Michael and Liam were watching from the door, open-mouthed, the last of their lollies dripping to the floor. 'Michael, take Liam out the back to play.'

'But, Mam—'

'Now!' she yelled, and Michael pulled Liam away, Liam crying, his lolly stick outstretched to the gloop of ice on the carpet.

When she turned the emaciated Kim onto her back she gasped. Kim's cheekbones jutted from her snow-white face, and her eyes rolled back in her head. She was barely breathing, and Nicola could only feel a hint of warm breath on her cheek when she put her face to Kim's mouth. She faced Mooney, spitting fury.

'You fucking idiot, she's got a baby.'

'Nowt to do with me,' he sniffed.

'Oh yeah? Last time I saw her she was smoking a bit of weed then suddenly it's heroin? Where else would she get it?'

Mooney belched and rubbed his stomach. 'Don't pretend you don't know,' he sneered, fishing about beside the chair and dredging up a curly sandwich.

'Know what?' she asked, hands on hips, thinking he couldn't possibly put that food in his mouth. He did, and she felt her stomach heave.

'You mean, she didn't tell you?' he chewed with his mouth open then swallowed hard, 'that she was dealing for Micky?'

Nicola laughed bitterly. 'Liar. She couldn't stand Micky: why on earth would she do that?'

The rest of the sandwich was in his mouth. 'Coz he gave her the money for the funeral.'

Her face drained, and, after a stunned second she turned to look at Kim, sorrow overwhelming her. Then her blood boiled, and she picked up the newspaper from the floor, hitting Mooney on the head with it, swiping it across his ugly face. He lifted his arm and leg up in defence, laughing.

'How, man! Pack it in, you fucking loony.'

Eyeing the phone on the windowsill, she threw the paper at him and stormed towards it. 'I'm phoning the police,' she said and lifted the receiver. But the phone was dead.

'What, your boyfriend?' Mooney grinned slyly at her, his head jerking and his face twisting. She put the receiver back in its cradle without looking at him, heard him clear his throat and spit into the fireplace. 'You shop me, and I'll tell Micky about your Private Dick.'

She felt the knife in her gut, but she kept it hidden, swept her hair from her face and looked at Mooney with contempt. 'Where's the baby?' she asked.

'Fucked if I knaa.' Mooney stood up and stretched like he'd just had a pleasant afternoon snooze.

'Get out,' she said icily.

'Nee worries.' He yawned past her and, with a final contemptuous grin, picked up his crutches and expertly swung himself out of the house.

When the door was closed, Nicola covered her mouth with her hand, willing herself to stay calm. Amy. Oh Amy, that gorgeous little girl.

She headed up the stairs, images of Mark's hanging body and bulging eyes flashing before her. As she approached the cot, she held her hand to her stomach and breathed deeply. She peeked over the edge, not sure if she was ready for what she was about to see. Amy lay on her side with her back to her, just like Kim downstairs. Nicola reached out a trembling hand and turned the baby over sharply, a blue-veined face and stiff body in her mind's eye. Amy jolted awake, her eyes wide and startled at being disturbed so roughly. Her face twisted, turning crimson as she drew in breath and belted out a long cry. Nicola's eyes were wet with relief as she picked the baby up and held her to her neck, bouncing her up and down and patting her on the back. 'I'm sorry, I'm sorry,' she cooed. But she wasn't sorry. Mark's baby was alive, and she was going to make sure she stayed that way.

She'd hurried downstairs, put Amy in her buggy and sat next to Kim on the sofa, shaking her and calling her name. She felt for a pulse, but she didn't really know what she was looking for. Kim's lips were turning blue and panic welled up in her throat. She'd put her cheek to Kim's mouth once more, but the breath was gone.

***

The wind was dropping now, the air less chilly as Lee pulled Nicola tighter to him. He allowed her to take a few moments to gather her thoughts and wipe her tears away.

'Go on,' he said, 'take your time.'

She continued, her breathing shallow and her fingers picking at the skin of her thumbs.

***

It was nearly midnight last night. They were in the kitchen and Micky was holding up a plastic carrier bag, the one containing her leather jacket and hooped earrings.

'What've I done wrong now?' she'd asked, looking defiantly into Micky's enflamed face.

'You tell me, Gypsy Rose Lee.'

She'd been back from the hospital for less than five minutes and was overwrought with exhaustion. The doctors had managed to revive Kim, but she'd been without oxygen a long time and Nicola had left her in Intensive Care, a machine breathing for her. The staff nurse had taken care of Amy, fed and changed her, soothed her frantic cries. Micky hadn't batted an eyelid when she got home. He was livid, she could tell, and she stood in front of him now, draped in fear, but hiding it well. If Mooney had opened his mouth, she was dead. She clutched the panic alarm in her jacket pocket, knowing it would be useless against a strangling hand or a bullet.

Micky backed her into the corner of the kitchen, manoeuvring her expertly into the space between the table and the fridge. The bag was thrown at her, and a crutch lashed across her face. The sound of the dog's incessant barking from outside the back door made her ears thrum, and Micky moved in, his back arched, his stomach touching hers. He'd spoken to Tania – she'd had her fortune told, she said. Some green-eyed, Geordie traveller who knew everything – knew all about his long absences and empty promises.

'Who told you?' he growled into her face.

'I don't know.' She shook her head, looked down, felt the blood trickle past her eye onto her cheekbone. She let it run. She had no fight in her tonight.

'Don't fucking lie to me.'

She didn't move, didn't flinch. Tired. So tired. 'Just some woman, all right? She phoned here and said you were having an affair.'

'Eh? Who the fuck would do that?' Micky wasn't sure how to handle Nicola's indifference, it made him want to hurt her again, at least that would get a reaction.

But she kept her voice steady and monotone. 'I don't know, Micky, it was just some woman. Maybe it was her, your ... other woman.'

Micky hobbled backwards and stared at her. Jesus Christ. They'd got to Tania, told her everything. Told her he was married, kids, house, garden, and she'd gone apeshit. He rubbed his hand over his unshaven mouth, frustrated at the absence of fear in his wife, but knowing that he couldn't catch her if she ran. He leant back into her, one hand against the wall.

'I'm sick of people stabbing me in the back and not doing what I say. What did I tell you about that dog?'

She glanced at the back door, Rufus beyond it, still barking his failed attempts at protection. She remained silent.

'If it's not gone by tomorrow, I'm gonna shoot it, and you can bury it, right?'

She stared ahead, not doubting his intentions, the blood dripping down her neck and onto the collar of her jacket.

'Right?'

Amy had started to twist in her buggy, hungry, alone, confined. Micky pointed behind him. 'And *that's* not staying with us. Get it to social services or something.'

Eyes empty, Nicola looked at him and then at Amy. There was nothing Micky hated more than a screaming baby. He moved back to let her past so she could stop the screeching.

Micky watched her pick the baby out of the buggy and take her into the living room, calmly wiping the blood from her face with the baby's blanket. Her hands weren't shaking. No matter how defiant she managed to make her face or her body language, her hands always shook. Always. But tonight they didn't, and he noticed something in her he'd never seen before. It took him a while to realise what it was, to put a name to it.

Courage.

And there it was again – a rising dread that made his legs weaken and his palms sweat. This wasn't right. She had to fear him, otherwise what was he? Who was he if he wasn't the man scaring Nicola? Wavering, he sat down at the kitchen table, his thoughts frozen, his plans crashing in.

Nicola held the dummy in Amy's mouth and rocked her gently as the baby's eyes glazed over and started to succumb to sleep. There was no movement from the kitchen. Maybe he was working on his list. She had seen him, two or three times over the last few days, bent over the pad of paper, a pen chewed to a grizzly nub in his mouth. The list grew and diminished, was ripped out, torn to shreds and started again. He drew diagrams and ran arrows from names, noting motives, incentives, family ties.

Every now and then, a name would be roughly crossed off, the pen cutting through the paper. He'd sigh and start again, muttering to himself: 'Ray McKewan.' He'd stare at the name, pen in his mouth and continue to mutter: 'Brother – Sonny. Ten years – Acklington. Wife left him. Took the lot.' He'd sit back, lift his head and stare at the wall. She'd seen him slip the pad of paper under the sofa cushion when someone came to the door or if she walked into the room. She'd only need five minutes to copy the names down: she just needed to get him out of the living room, but he was still sleeping downstairs. She'd do it tomorrow when he trudged upstairs to use the bathroom: that was a fairly predictable morning occurrence and it would give her just enough time. Tomorrow, if she could muster the nerve.

The next morning she walked unsteadily to the payphone at the supermarket before anyone was awake. Lee agreed to meet her at the coast. He'd wait for her however long it took. He loved her, he feared for her, he wanted her to be safe.

Back home, the wind hummed through the windows and made the back door rattle. She'd spent the night reeling between spells of euphoria and fits of mouth-drying anxiety. Micky's tea and bacon and egg sandwich had been consumed, and he stood up with a groan and a sniff. She sipped at her coffee, watching him over the mug as he hobbled towards the living room door. He was moving more quickly now. Maybe she'd miscalculated how long he would be out of the room.

Her heart battered her ribs as she listened to each foot on every stair. With the kids outside playing with Rufus, and the shot of the bolt on the bathroom door still in her ears, she ripped the cushion off the sofa to retrieve the writing pad. She felt around with her hands but all she'd found was a pen and a red plastic Monopoly hotel.

Shit!

She put the cushion back and looked around her, listening at the same time for the sound of the toilet flushing. The other sofa cushion and the chair yielded nothing. She checked under the sofa, under the chair, inside the magazine rack. She rattled her brains. Where had he been other than the living room? She ran upstairs, rummaged through the bedside drawers, peered under the bed at a hot-water bottle, a dusty pair of trainers, moving the spare quilt to one side and pulling the shoe box towards her. She knew what it contained – the gun that had been pointed at her head just a few weeks ago. There it lay, alone, and she felt her stomach tie in knots at the sight of it.

She got to her feet, walked onto the landing and knocked tentatively on the bathroom door. 'Everything okay?'

'*Piss off, man.*'

Back in the living room, she put her thumbs to her jaw and rubbed her temples with her fingers. *Think, woman, think.* She paced, her eyes closed, tripping over the rug in front of the fireplace. She felt something under her foot, under the rug.

They were all there – her salvation. On the front page were about a dozen names, some crossed out but legible, and at the bottom of the page, scribbled and circled many times – *Tania???*

She snatched a pen from the mantelpiece and started copying the names down. As she started writing, the toilet flushed, the bathroom door opened, and her pounding heart made her face drain, and her hands shake. It would take him about thirty seconds to limp down the twelve stairs that stood between her and freedom. How many times had she counted the stairs taking Michael and Liam to bed, helping them learn their numbers? She heard Micky's foot and crutch thud on the first stair. *One.* She wrote as quickly as she could.

Two. Three.

Ronnie Jaques – Durham South.

Davie Hannon – Durham North.

Five. Six.

Micky Morris – Middlesbrough.

Eight. Nine.

Tim Fletcher – Hexham and Ponteland.

Tommy Peacock – Sunderland.

Eleven. Twelve.

Billy Angus – Blyth.

She ripped the page from its spiral binding and threw the pad under the rug, just as the door swung open. She folded the piece of paper in her hand and put it in the back pocket of her jeans.

Micky was breathing heavily. 'What's that?' he asked.

'Just the shopping list.' She kept her palms against her lower back, but he held out his hand, still panting, exhausted from the exertion of the stairs.

'Here, let's see it.'

'It's just some bits—'

'For Christ's sake, just give it here, man.' He motioned with his hands. 'I don't want you spending money on stuff we don't need.'

The piece of paper stayed steady between finger and thumb as she passed it to him. He opened it and studied it line by line. She swallowed as he nodded without looking at her, sniffed and handed it back to her. 'Get us a paper, will you?'

She'd taken back the shopping list she'd prepared earlier that morning and put it back in the pocket where the piece of paper that would change her life still lay hidden.

***

Amy stirred in her buggy, and Nicola tucked the blanket more firmly around her. As she sat back against Lee, she took the paper from her pocket and pressed it into Lee's hand. He sat up with his chin on her shoulder, his arms still around her waist, and unfolded it in front of her.

'This is perfect,' he said, 'they'll be known to us anyway, we'll find them.' He kissed her on the temple. This woman was brave, and he felt somewhat humbled.

'That's not all,' she said, reaching for the bag that hung over the back of Amy's buggy. She took out a mobile phone and gave it to him. 'It's his, he gave it to me this morning. Wanted me to phone the house when I got to the hospital, when I left the hospital, when I got to the dog shelter, when I left the dog shelter, the shop, everywhere.'

'And have you?'

'No. It's switched off – he'll be going mental. But they're all in there.'

'Nicola. Do you realise what you've got here?' He turned on the phone.

'I don't want to know. Just do it.'

'You can stay with me,' he said, waiting impatiently for the screen to light up. But he knew what the answer would be. The children would come first, no question.

Amy stirred again and Nicola got up to shush her and put her dummy in her mouth as Lee scrolled through the phone, copying down names and numbers. *Fletch, Tommy P, Woodsy* – Gerry, no doubt, thought Lee, not much of a surprise there. *Plod.* Lee stared at the entry, his forehead creased. *Plod:* someone on the inside.

Nicola watched him, feeling strangely composed and content, as if a story was reaching its inevitable conclusion.

As Amy settled back down, and Lee handed Nicola the phone, the piercing sound of the ringtone hacked into the air. *Home* flashed up on the screen.

'I better go,' Nicola said, standing up and letting it ring. 'He likes cat food better than dog food,' she said, giving Rufus a final stroke as Lee stood and put a hand to her cheek. She covered it with her own, and her voice became urgent. 'Mooney, if he knows about us ...' she said. Lee began to speak but Nicola put a finger to his lips. 'Just hurry.'

Lee nodded silently, and watched her as she walked away, pushing the buggy over the spiralling sand, her head bent against the wind. He braced himself for the night ahead.

He had to get it right this time.

Later that day, Lee bumped clumsily into DC Gallagher as Gallagher emerged from DI Meadows's office. They exchanged brusque nods and Lee entered the DI's office without knocking, his features indicating he was ready for battle.

Carole Meadows dropped her pen and sat back in her chair, a little alarmed at the manic look on Lee's face. A crumpled piece of paper landed in front of her, and she sat forward, looking down as Lee's finger jabbed at the list of names and numbers. She pulled it towards her quickly. 'Is this it?'

'Micky Kelly's contacts, and all twelve of the syndicate.'

She could barely contain her smile as she smoothed out the paper, took off her glasses and picked it up to look at it close up. 'Well, well, well,' she said faintly.

Lee stood at her shoulder and ran his finger down the list. 'See here?' he said. 'Plod.'

'Plod,' she repeated.

'Only one way to find out,' said Lee, snatching the paper from her and taking his phone from his inside pocket.

'Hang on ...' She reached up for the paper, but Lee had walked away, impatient, the musical bleeps of the phone's keypad the only sound in the office. He turned to look at her expectantly as he waited, their eyes rotating in unison to the mobile phone on her desk as it lit up and started to ring. Lee stared at her, his mouth slightly open as he cancelled the call and the ringing stopped. The knock on the door turned both their heads, and Meadows quickly opened her top drawer, dropping the phone into it. Gallagher put his head round the door, his frowning face scouring the room.

'Sorry, ma'am. Did I leave my phone in here?'

Lee's mouth closed, and he and Meadows regarded Gallagher in silence.

''Fraid not,' said Meadows, forcing a smile.

Hesitating, Gallagher gave them a tense nod then closed the door behind him. Meadows reached into the drawer, retrieved the phone and turned it off, looking up at Lee with a wry smile.

'In your dreams, Detective,' she said.

Lee smiled back and looked to the ceiling in relief.

'Get rid of him,' she said firmly. 'He can't be involved in this.'

'With pleasure. But how—'

'Just do it.'

***

Lee fiddled distractedly with paperwork on his desk, watching the clock as it ticked its way towards home time. Gallagher had turned his desk upside down, his cheeks shining blood red. His hand went through his hair as sweat rings swelled under the arms of his faded blue shirt. He threw himself onto his chair, his fingers pulling at his top lip as he delved into his mind to the last time he'd used his mobile. Lee watched with mild amusement as Gallagher picked up the desk phone and dialled a number, waiting a few seconds before slamming it down crossly. The riverboat raid: of course they were ready for them. Of course they'd found nothing but the dregs. Gallagher was the anonymous tip-off.

Lee wheeled his chair closer to his desk, tapped his fingers on his forehead. He had to get rid of Gallagher so they could plan the next stage without the information leaking. His eyes fell on his in-tray, and he grabbed the flyer for the Equalities Seminar, scouring the front page. *Valuing Diversity: Your role as a public sector servant in ensuring equal access to grass roots services. Harrogate, 20 and 21 July 1999.* An ironic smile brewed.

Bingo.

Lee walked casually to Gallagher's desk and put the flyer in front of him, Gallagher starting slightly and closing his computer screen.

'Can't go to this anymore,' said Lee. 'Boss said you should.'

'Eh?' Gallagher took a few seconds to look at the flyer. 'You're fucking joking like.' He looked up at Lee's indifferent face then threw the flyer across his desk. 'No way. Bunch of lezza ball-breakers? I'm not going.' He looked around him, smiling, expecting endorsement from his colleagues. When none came, the smile faded and he turned to the blank screen of his computer, playing with the mouse and eyeing Lee out of the corner of his eye.

'Well,' said Lee, retrieving the flyer and putting it back in front of Gallagher, 'she *specifically* said that you would be best placed to go.'

Gallagher snorted. 'Send *her*,' he said, indicating Thompson. 'Or one of the darkie coppers from Uniform.'

Lee bent down, his mouth a few inches from Gallagher's ear. 'You're going. Or else my recommendation to Detective Inspector Meadows is that you get transferred to court filing duties. Like that now, me and her,' he crossed fingers in front of Gallagher's nose, 'and your performance leaves rather a lot to be desired when it comes to solving crimes.' He lowered his voice further. 'Targets. That's what the commissioner wants.' Gallagher's eyes glazed over as compliance set in. 'So, you'll get the train later, stay at a nice hotel for a couple of nights, and come back on Friday with a whole new vocabulary.'

Gallagher stared straight ahead. 'Yes, Sarge.'

Lee straightened up and patted Gallagher on the back. 'Good man. Now why don't you go home early so you can pack?'

Without looking at Lee, Gallagher rose from his chair, grabbed his jacket and took himself out of the office. When the coast was clear Lee sat at Gallagher's desk and reopened the screen on his computer. Tiger Reay's lily-white face stared right at him – his police file, previous convictions, current surveillance and activities. Lee clicked the back button, and there was Micky Kelly. The latest entry read: *Nicola Kelly, Wife. Potential Informant. Key contact: DS Lee Jamieson, West End.* Paul Gallagher knew how to use a computer all right.

DI Meadows's blunt voice called his name, and he looked up to see her head peering around the door of her office. He clicked back one page quickly as he stood up, and there were Mark's sad eyes peering at him. Lee looked closer at the word 'DECEASED' written in large letters underneath Mark's photograph. What interest would Gallagher have in Mark Redmond now? Gallagher's desk phone rang, and Lee started: Meadows, impatient that he hadn't leapt to attention immediately. He moved back to Tiger's page and minimised the screen, skipping lightly across the room towards Meadows's office.

Meadows indicated for Lee to sit opposite her. She passed him Gallagher's phone and he stared at a text message – *Need some stuff xxx. Joe and Sandy's party on Saturday. Will need warming up! xx.* And another: *Mr and Mrs B short. Asking for more Tuesday xx.* Lee looked at the sender – Joyce.

'It's full of them,' said Meadows.

'Who the hell is Joyce?' asked Lee.

'His wife.'

Lee raised his eyebrows. Gallagher had a wife?

Meadows turned her computer screen around, and before his eyes was a web-page from the Council's housing department, and a picture of Joyce Oduwu, Director of Housing, the striking hazel eyes smiling at him in a posed shot. Lee grinned to himself and shook his head.

'So, what now?' he asked.

'You better be ready for an early start tomorrow,' she replied.

NINETEEN

Lee had been pacing Meadows's office for an eternal five minutes before she appeared at six o'clock the next morning. The dawn raids had been in operation for half an hour, but Micky Kelly and Tania Brewis still slept soundly in their beds. Their front doors intact, their children's slumber undisturbed. Lee stuck to Meadows like a leech as she walked to the coffee maker and switched it on.

'I want Nicola Kelly out of there.' He'd thought after yesterday's revelation about Gallagher that she would be on his side, that they would crack this together.

'You're too close to it now, you need to back off, let me handle it.'

'She's in danger, you can't use her as collateral damage.'

'It's too personal, you'd be best to get off my back if you value your career. I'm not as daft as I look.'

'I don't give a shit about my career.'

'I know you don't so I'm doing it for you. Bringing her in would simply attract more attention to her, I'm not authorising it,' said Meadows, opening the bag of coffee with her teeth.

'Well, get him out, then!' he seethed.

Meadows took in his unshaven, tired face through the corner of her eye. She didn't like people raising their voices at her, and most certainly didn't like being told how to do her job. But she sensed his volatility and spoke calmly through the chugging of the percolator.

'I thought you said there weren't any drugs in there anyway.' Still she didn't look at him.

'*So?*' he blurted with the half-laugh and wide eyes of a man on the edge.

'We're not bringing in Kelly until the others drop him in it. I want evidence and corroboration.' She sat at her desk and stretched her arms above her head in preparation for a sixteen-hour day.

Lee clenched his jaw and leant his hands on Meadows's desk. She leant back, away from his face. 'You promised me a safe house. Him out first, her out and into safety, then the rest.'

'Now, you know I can't make promises like that.'

'She could be *dead* by now.'

'Don't shout at me!' Meadows sprang up, her knuckles resting on the desk in front of her, their faces now less than a foot away from each other. 'What's up? Soft southern boy can't take the pressure?'

'We're talking about people lives—'

'If you want out, you know what to do.'

'Why is everything so fucking bureaucratic? Just do it!'

'*No.*'

As they squared up to each other over the desk Lee looked into bloodshot eyes, smelt the stale whisky on her breath then stood up straight, regaining his poise. 'This place stinks,' he spat, and left the room a desperate man.

The main office was empty aside from a couple of uniformed officers drinking tea and doing crosswords. He walked to the door of the control room where the raids were being overseen. He'd have to find a way of overriding her instructions. It would cost him his job, probably his career, but his priority right now was to make sure Nicola was safe. This was their one chance, and if Micky put two and two together, that chance was over. His hand held the knob of the door to the control room for a moment, then he thought better of it and walked out of the station.

***

He knew the address: it was on the Pembrook Estate about a mile from Valley Park. A fair number of his schoolmates had come from the Pembrook. It consisted of three high-rise blocks and four streets of three-storey, prison-like structures with concrete balconies that sunlight never reached. The streets were laid out like a crucifix, with the three towers at the centre. Kevin Moone lived on the tenth floor of Falcon Rise, which contained mostly bedsits and one-bedroom flats, a flytrap for the mentally ill, alcoholic or just downright lonely. He pounded on the door several times, the sound echoing in the early morning quiet, waking the dogs of the neighbourhood, who belted out their warnings to their snoring masters.

Mooney only had to open the door an inch before Lee kicked it back, throwing Mooney backwards into the hall and over a mound of boxes full of computer keyboards and mobile phones. Mooney held his arms out in defence as Lee bent down, picked him up by his T-shirt and threw him against the wall.

'How man, gerroff! I'm disabled, me!' screeched Mooney.

Lee's voice fizzed. 'You sad, evil bastard.' He pinned Mooney to the wall by his throat. Lee thought for the first time in his life he could kill a man.

Mooney frowned, recognition creeping over his face. 'I know you,' he gurgled. 'You're the one shagging Micky's lass.'

'And you're a murderer.'

'Am I shite,' Mooney scoffed, saliva running down onto Lee's curled hand.

'You will be when Kim Redmond dies. And she will die. And she'll die because you gave her heroin.'

'No I didn't.'

Lee let Mooney go, only to push him harder against the wall, lifting him off the floor so only the tips of his toes touched the filthy grey carpet. Mooney's bulging eyes grew even wider.

'Kim's house is sealed off. There'll be bits of you all over the place. Nicola's agreed to testify as a witness.'

'Fuck off, will she. You can't prove nowt.'

'Wanna bet? Coppers can do anything. Framed Mark, didn't they? He was about to do a nice little ten-year stretch.' Mooney swallowed hard and Lee continued. 'I'll make it my lifelong ambition to put you away, even if it means a little white lie here and there. My word against yours.'

Mooney's face twitched violently. He'd already done just short of a year in Durham in his twenties. His short-arse frame had been the undoing of him, having to act as gofer for several of the lifers just to keep the soapy hands of the shirtlifters off him for a few months. But he couldn't keep them off him forever. He tried to blink away the memory and the dread, and Lee took full advantage of the change in demeanour.

'I'm prepared to bargain with you,' he said, loosening his grip so that Mooney slid slowly down the wall. 'Twenty pence could buy you your freedom.' He reached into his pocket and took out a twenty pence piece, holding it so close to Mooney's face he had to cross his eyes to look at it. 'Here's what you do with it. You go to the phone box, you ring Tiger.'

'What for?' Mooney looked at the coin as if it were about to bite his face off.

'All you have to say are three little words. And they're not *I love you.*'

Mooney looked Lee in the eye as Lee said, 'Micky. Kelly. Grassed.'

***

Micky stood at the bedroom window, scouring the street. Stevie's teenager of a wife had been on the phone, effing and blinding at him. Half the syndicate's doors had been driven in. *They'll be coming for you, Micky!* she'd barked at him. Micky had hung up, raging. If Stevie had any brains he wouldn't be storing any gear in his own house. Only twats played that game. But if a load had just come in the night before, and they were holding it before distribution, they were all fucked. But there was a silver lining, he realised, and it brought a small smile to his face. At last, he'd know who the grass was. Wouldn't the filth spare their own informant? The grass would be somewhere safe. The grass wouldn't be arrested. He'd be able to point the finger with confidence, prove it wasn't him. A simple process of elimination. So he waited for the police to come, with pleasure.

But twenty minutes passed, and Micky's unease mounted. The phone rang again, and he picked it up cautiously. *They're all gone,* Stevie's wife sobbed hysterically. *Every single one of them. Why haven't they picked you up, Micky?* Micky dropped the receiver angrily. Every single one of them? So the grass was outside the syndicate.

Hearing Nicola yawn at the bedroom door, he turned furiously towards her, grabbing her by both arms. 'Why did you have to go upsetting Tania, eh? Why?' he accused her.

'I had a right to know if it was true.'

'Putting all sorts in her head. The whole thing's blown – it'll be *her*.' He pushed her away. 'Get the kids up and out the way.'

'What for?' Her eyes were flitting everywhere, then they rested on the window. But he saw no fear in them, only expectation, hope even.

He followed her gaze to the window. 'No, forget that.' He dropped to his knees, unrolling the spare quilt from under the bed and pulling out the shoe box. 'Leave them in bed. Don't go out.'

Nicola saw the gun and panicked. 'Micky, what's going on? This'll just make it worse...' But Micky had stopped listening. The gun was just in case; his instincts were telling him to keep it close, and he always listened to his instincts. He stood at the window once more. *Come on, you fuckers.* Micky would rather spend years behind bars than be thought of as a grass. No competition.

But the police didn't come, and Micky was breathing heavily now as Nicola stood in the doorway, watching his neck redden, his face set in hostility, the gun firmly in his hands.

'Micky, who are you waiting for?' Maybe she could persuade him to relinquish the weapon. But Micky had seen something, and his eyes stared straight ahead like a cat who'd caught sight of a flightless bird. He waved his arm behind him to get her out of the way but she walked into the bedroom instead, just as she heard glass breaking downstairs, and footsteps walking down the hallway into the kitchen. Micky spun round and lunged towards her, pulling her into the room and closing the bedroom door.

'*Get back. Get in there,*' he hissed, pointing at the wardrobe.

'No! The kids, Micky!' she cried. But he thrust open the wardrobe door and pushed her inside, locking her in. She stood, frozen with fear, praying with all her might that it wasn't Lee's feet she heard coming up the stairs. She peeked through the gap between the doors. Micky's gun was pointing at the bedroom door, but something had caught his eye and she watched his lips part.

Micky's stare was fixed on his wife's fluffy, white dressing gown hanging from the back of the door, small streaks of grey still evident on the lapel, where Nicola had knocked over the ashtray the morning Tiger had had him kidnapped and tortured. It had been about five a.m. The ashtray was overflowing, the house stank of cigarettes. She'd been up for hours, chain-smoking. The smoking of a person on edge, nervous, waiting for something. His gun dropped for a second as the realisation hit him, and he turned to see one frightened eye peering from the crack between the wardrobe doors. The eye met his as the bedroom door came crashing in, his gun uselessly pointing at a pair of slippers instead of the torsos of his assailants. He was face-down on the bed a second later, a pistol at his head, his face twisted towards the wardrobe.

Inside, Nicola held her heart, mouthing, *I'm sorry, I'm sorry ...* His eyes stayed on hers, even as the gun went off and the men were gone as quickly as they'd arrived. Nicola stood rooted to the spot inside the wardrobe, Micky's eyes still looking at her, a great stillness enveloping him, the stillness of time. No regret, no recrimination, no fear or pain. No feeling at all. As his eyes slowly began to look through her rather than at her, and the blood mushroomed onto the white quilt, she started to shake, her body wracked with terror and guilt. She slid down inside the wardrobe, her hands shuddering at her face as she heard the drone of police sirens.

They were too late. He was too late.

***

Lee opened the wardrobe doors and looked down at Nicola, her body curled into a ball among the coats and dresses. He held out his hand to her, but she ignored it and moved herself forward onto the floor then stood up. She backed away from him and looked at her husband's dead body.

'Can I?' she asked DC Thompson.

Jane shook her head. 'I'm sorry, no one can touch him, not yet.'

Nicola walked slowly to the bed and stood over Micky, her palms on her cheeks. Lee watched uncomfortably. 'The kids?' she asked blankly.

'In the car,' said Thompson gently. 'They don't know anything, they're fine.'

Lee, unable to watch any longer, walked out of the room, head bowed in remorse. Meadows had been right. They were all bleating like frightened goats already, and the police had been on their way to arrest Micky Kelly. Fear and impatience had overruled his reason, and now the price had been paid.

TWENTY

The rain thundered off the caravan roof like a shower of stones. It had been unremitting for two days, thunder and lightning splitting the world open, water pouring down the windows in streams. Outside was colourless and dark, and Nicola and Margy sat under blankets with their steaming Cup-a-Soups, Michael Jnr and Liam hunched on the floor playing Hungry Hippos while Amy slept in the bedroom. Little Jimmy sat on a beanbag, book in hand, glancing now and then covertly over the pages at the two playing brothers, pretending not to be interested in such childish games.

'Not really the weather for caravans,' Margy said as she frowned at the condensation on the windows.

'No,' Nicola muttered, not sure how she was going to break the news. 'I was thinking in bed last night about going back to the refuge. I could get the bus down tomorrow, I've only got a couple of bags.'

'What for?' gulped Margy, a mixture of shock and hurt. 'They'll not have you, the man's dead.' She pursed her lips to shut herself up for once.

Nicola sighed. 'Margy, you've been dead kind, but I can't live here, I need to get myself sorted.'

'I'll get you sorted.'

Nicola answered with a half-hearted 'No,' trying not to sound ungrateful.

'I'm managing the biggest bloody community centre in Berwick, man. I can give you a job, you can stay here until we sort a house for you. The school's lovely, isn't it, Jimmy?' Jimmy's huge, bespectacled eyes didn't leave the page, but he nodded. 'In fact, come and stay at the house, with us. It'll be ready in a couple of days.'

'No, I couldn't.'

'Of course you could.'

Nicola was firm now and her face pleaded with her friend. 'Margy, I've got things to do. Kim's on life support, I need to be near her. I've got three kids to get settled, I can't live in your pockets, I have to get on with my life.'

'Why can't you get on with it here?' Margy asked bluntly, then she softened. 'I'll miss you. *Again.*'

Nicola set her cup down, put an arm around Margy and hugged her like she was her mum. 'I love you, you're the best friend anyone could ever have. But you can't sort everything all the time.'

Margy felt somewhat guilty. She'd committed a cardinal community work sin – instead of empowering people to do things for themselves, her natural instinct was to do things for other people. *Give a man a fish and he'll eat for a day*, she'd been taught. She rebuked herself with a sigh. 'I know. I just take over, don't I? I can't help it.'

Nicola nodded and kissed Margy on the cheek, comforted by her friend's devotion. But in the silence that followed, gloom came rushing over her like the deep grey waves she could just make out through the misty window, and her stomach churned as she thought about what lay ahead.

She was dreading the funeral. Margy had said she didn't have to go. Didn't have to do anything she didn't want to. Margy was right, too, and Nicola had even thought about it

– about not going to her own husband's funeral. But the thought had lasted a mere second before it drowned in a mixture of loyalty and guilt. Besides, someone had to organise everything, pick a coffin, hymns, readings, send invites, someone had to make sure there was a headstone for her boys, and his girls, to go to when they were grown-up and missed the dim memory of their father. No, she would give him a proper funeral and lay him to rest with the dignity she'd watched fade away from his proud life.

'You should take her up on her offer,' said Margy, reading Nicola's thoughts. Nicola blew into her mug and took a sip of the salty liquid. She might not have any choice. Micky had left nothing, and she had nothing. Tania's letter lay in its envelope in her bag – the offer of money, Micky's money, to pay for the funeral. There was nothing warm about the letter. An acknowledgement that neither knew the other existed, that Tania had loved him and wanted to make sure he got a decent send-off. She still couldn't believe he would betray his friends like that. She would never believe it, and neither should Nicola.

Margy peered at Nicola, whose eyes were taking in the interior of the big old caravan that had served as Margy's home for the first weeks of her move, provided by the police after the death threat, just until they could get something more permanent from the Council. The threat had come from Micky, Margy was sure of it, in which case it would be okay for her to go back now. But her loyalty to Valley Park was fading. Little Jimmy was coming out of his shell. Joe was drinking less and laughing more. She hadn't realised the stress the place had put them under. You've done your bit, Joe had said, now let's concentrate on us.

'What about lover boy?' Margy asked, making Nicola's eyes dart to Margy's face then down to her own toes, wriggling under the tartan blanket. Nicola shrugged and sighed.

'We killed Micky, Margy,' she said in a low voice while the kids shrieked at the start of a frantic new game of Hungry Hippos.

'No, you didn't.'

'Yes, we did. I should've just left him. Gone to live somewhere else, started a new life.'

'You know he would have found you, wherever you went. This lovely new life of yours wouldn't have been worth living.'

'But the kids, Margy, look at them, they loved their dad. And I should know what it's like to be, well, dadless.' She held a palm up to her forehead and stared sideways out of the steamed-up window.

'They'd've grown up just like him,' said Margy.

'They still might, Margy,' said Nicola sadly. 'Look at the people around us on that estate, it's full of Mickys, they're everywhere.'

Margy took a gulp of soup and smacked her lips. 'Exactly why you should move here,' she said chirpily.

Nicola grinned at her. '*Margyyy*,' she said warily. But the caution in her voice did nothing to stop Margy smiling widely and giving a little victory shuffle, spilling some of her chicken soup onto the shelf of her chest.

'Shit!' she spluttered under her breath, and Nicola giggled as Margy swiped at her white T-shirt, her chin multiplying several times as she strained to see what she was doing. 'I knew you'd see sense,' she muttered.

'I'll *think* about it.' Nicola sipped her soup. 'You know, when he's near me, I'm a wreck,' Margy stopped wiping and looked at Nicola with sympathetic eyes. 'My thighs tingle and everything.'

Margy nodded. 'I know,' she said. 'You could bring him with you?'

But Nicola shook her head. She'd be back in Valley Park tomorrow with the boys to sort out Micky's affairs. She looked at Michael Jnr and Liam playing on the floor. They'd stopped asking about their dad for now, and Nicola thought about the time when they would be old enough to know the truth. Or perhaps they knew it already.

***

Lee sat back casually, eyeing the pouting Gallagher, who squirmed in his seat in the interview room. Gallagher's eyes were fixed on the green light of the tape recorder. It read eight minutes. Eight minutes of this twat grilling him. Joyce was somewhere else, in another room, Meadows having a pop at her. She would keep shtum, that was the deal. But Joyce had been jittery as hell since it all came out. For having a stressful, high-powered job, she wasn't handling the pressure well at all. She'd been drinking. Too much for a woman in her condition. Last night she'd hurled an empty wine bottle at him, her career ruined, her family stunned and her friends silent as night. He didn't exactly know what she had to complain about. She'd done very well out of it: nice new kitchen, fucking shoes pouring out of the bedroom. After she'd calmed down they'd come up with the only plan open to them right now. She'd say nothing, let him handle it. He'd seen people get away with it for years, he knew just how to play it.

'You think you're dead clever, don't you?' said Lee calmly, 'that you know every trick in the book? But we've already pieced it all together so it's pointless, this 'no comment' shite. The joke's on you, pal.'

Gallagher smirked: he didn't think so.

Lee sat forward. 'First rule in detection: look at the evidence, what is it saying?'

'You tell me, Sherlock.'

'Well, it's saying to me that Micky Kelly was supplying you with cocaine for your wife and her friends' seedy little habits.'

Gallagher shook his head, turning his mouth down at the sides.

'We've got your phone records, we've got what you've been looking at on your computer, we've got the scales in her bedside drawer, we've got traces in the glovebox of your car, we've got lists of her mates and what they owe her, we've got the cash, we've got wardrobes full of expensive clothes, handbags, shoes. My God, she makes Imelda Marcos look like Cinderella.'

'My wife has a good job. I don't ask what she spends her money on.'

Lee looked him hard in the eyes. 'Gallagher – you can't argue with evidence, it's fact. Oh, and by the way, one of her mates has done a deal.'

Gallagher stretched back in the chair and cracked his knuckles in a stretch, but Lee could see the sweat mushrooming under his armpits.

'Be a man for once, eh, not the wimp at the beck and call of *wifey*, and tell me how Mark Redmond was involved.'

'You're the genius, work it out for yourself.'

'I'm stumped. Who would bother using their own stash to frame a nobody? Who would throw money away like that? Stakes must've been pretty high.' Gallagher picked at his bottom lip and peeled a long piece of skin from it. He considered it before putting it in his mouth.

'Hate this silent routine.' Lee stood up and walked around the room. 'So, let's have a guess – Mark knows you're buying from Micky, threatens to grass you up. Bad lad made good, doing the right thing for his community. Or maybe he wanted some money, whatever. You use the stash you've bought for Her Indoors, get into Mark's house, leave traces for evidence, then bung it up the drainpipe – that's how you knew exactly where to find it, that's why you did the arrest. So any evidence, any particles of your sad little being that you left behind, wouldn't count. No wonder he was fucking angry, no wonder the poor kid killed himself taking the rap for a bent copper. What a bastard you are.'

'Not even warm.' Gallagher's eyes were fixed on the tape deck. He lifted his gaze to Lee and pulled his finger across his throat.

Looking at his watch, Lee leant across the table. 'Interview suspended at ten thirty-six a.m. for the suspect to use the lavatory,' he said and pushed the stop button on the tape deck and sat down.

'I want a deal,' said Gallagher matter-of-factly. 'I know you're shagging Kelly's wife.'

'So? You'll get no deal until you tell me who framed Mark Redmond.'

'And I know her life won't be worth living if it gets out she grassed on Tiger Reay's boat party.'

'She didn't.'

'She did. Micky Kelly would never grass on Tiger.' He mimicked Lee: *'Look at the evidence, what is it saying?* She informed to you, you informed the boss. There wouldn't have been a raid without pretty cast-iron evidence coming from *wifey*. And if I breathe a word out there, she's dead meat.'

Lee's face hardened. 'Okay, what are we talking?'

'Lose the list, lose anything to do with my wife, her friends. I'll admit it was my habit, fell into temptation due to stress, I need help et cetera.'

'Did you use it?'

'Nah, can't stand the stuff.'

'Why?'

'Why d'you think? You've seen my wife: don't say she's not attractive.'

Lee couldn't disagree. 'Okay, so who did it?'

Gallagher thought for a moment, still weighing up the pros and cons of the conversation. 'Micky Kelly.'

Lee frowned. 'Why?'

'Because Mark wouldn't groom the kids for Micky's dealers.'

'But the Woods kid said he did.'

'Micky found out about Joyce and me, heard Mark telling Nicola that the kid was bent. Bad news in an IRA family – hate gays. Micky told me to arrest Mark or else he'd drop me in it, then he told Tyrone to give evidence that Mark had offered him drugs or else he'd tell his brothers he was queer.'

Lee felt the pieces falling into place like cherries on a slot machine.

Gallagher continued. 'Micky had everyone stitched up like a kipper, that's probably why the lad killed himself, there was nowhere else to turn.' He told it like he was delivering the punchline of a long-winded joke.

Lee's immediate thought was why Mark hadn't told Nicola, but then he didn't know the guy, maybe he didn't want to break her heart, or maybe he didn't want Micky to break his legs. Or hers.

'Cheers for that, Gallagher,' Lee said as he made his way to the door.

'You'll see to the list?'

Lee turned and looked over his shoulder, 'Sorry, mate, submitted it first thing.'

Gallagher threw him a murderous stare. 'You bastard.'

'Takes one to know one,' said Lee, and he closed the door.

TWENTY-ONE

The clouds hung black and threatening over the Tyne, though the sun shone down on the station. Lee had stepped outside for some fresh air after finally charging Gallagher and his wife. The papers would have a field day with this and rightly so. He thought of Nicola. The funeral was that afternoon, and he wanted to be there, at the church. Lee wondered at the irony of it. An ungodly man if ever there was one. But he knew the priest would find good things to say about Micky Kelly, a man who'd spent his life helping old ladies across the street, keeping the likes of Gerry Woods in order and the other East End boys out of the local pubs where they would have caused no end of bother. The sort of anti-hero that stole from the poor and gave none of it back. But Lee knew he couldn't be seen with Nicola, he wasn't that reckless. And besides, she hadn't responded to his letter. He'd kept it brief. Apologised, told her he missed her, he still wanted to be with her if she could forgive him. Even Margy had failed to persuade her to respond. She was tied up organising the funeral, Margy had insisted, and Kim's house and Micky's affairs. There's a lot to do when someone dies. *Be patient.*

***

Nicola stood at the door of the church as she watched a couple of suited men open the mouth of the black hearse.

She'd had to hire pallbearers – none of Micky's friends had responded to her invitations. She'd spent the evening before at the hospital, Kim still breathing through a ventilator, her brain dead, her organs ripe for harvesting. She'd found the donor card in Kim's purse as she cleaned up the house over the previous few days. It would be Nicola's decision in the end: she was her closest family, her next of kin and executor. Once all the legals were sorted, Kim's life was in her hands. Not if, but when to turn off the machines. Mark's wedding ring hung on a chain around Nicola's neck, and she held it now between her finger and thumb, swinging it from side to side across her chin as she waited for the hearse to arrive, the priest at the bottom of the stairs, and Margy and Joe flanking her on either side. There was no one else present and Nicola felt Micky's pain at such a sad spectacle of emptiness. He might have been a thug, but he always boasted that he was more popular than Gandhi.

Ten minutes to go, and a solitary blue car pulled up and parked in the grounds of the church. Nicola looked curiously at the bobbing heads of the people inside, but the tinted windows hid their faces. The doors to the car opened eventually and six people poured out as if they were emerging from the TARDIS. The men were tall, six foot and more, the one woman in a black veil, bent double with grief and holding a small purple handbag with one hand and the shoulder of one of the mammoth men with the other. Nicola looked at the brown, leathery hands with their tattoos and rings and recognised Tania. Her brothers surrounded her like bodyguards, their huge, solid necks almost the size of the heads they held up. They walked towards the church, shook hands with the priest at the bottom of the stairs then stood in a herd facing each other, lighting up their cigarettes.

Tania regarded Nicola through the veil. Their eyes met, at least Nicola thought they did. She thought she saw a faint nod of Tania's head. At least he'd have his two wives here, thought Nicola, with a hint of derision.

They all stood shuffling their feet, only the birds and distant passing cars offering any soundtrack to the afternoon. Nicola nodded to the priest. She was ready. As he nodded back and started to make his way over to the funeral director, Nicola felt Margy's nudge, and heard the wheels of another car crunching over the gravel. She raised her head as another followed behind it, and, as they parked, a crowd of seven or eight people emerged from behind the tall, sandstone wall that surrounded the grounds of the church. Nicola recognised Stevie, his young wife, Annie, and several other faces. Nicola and Margy turned to each other with a curious stare as more cars and people streamed into the car park, Scotty and the staff from the pub, old boxing friends, more shaking of hands with the priest and more cigarettes lit. Nicola's eyes, dry until now, started to tear as she felt an enormous relief envelop her.

She made her way down the steps toward Stevie and his group, but as she approached them, their backs turned and her outstretched hand was ignored. She turned to look nervously at Margy, whose eyes narrowed as she studied the growing crowd and their reaction to Nicola. No one acknowledged her: everyone turned from her as she approached them, but when Tania and her brothers merged into the crowd, Micky's 'other wife' was comforted as keenly a close relative would be.

Margy hurried down the steps to Nicola's side, took her by the arm and led her back to the church door.

'What's happening, Margy? Why won't they talk to me?' Nicola's hand closed in on the ring around her neck again.

'I don't know, sweetheart, let's go inside.' Margy gave the crowd one more suspicious look before leading Nicola up the steps to the church.

'No,' Nicola said suddenly and turned around, pulling herself free of Margy. 'They're not doing this to me.' She put her shoulders back, raised her head held high, and made her way to the coffin which was being slid out of the hearse and onto the shoulders of the pallbearers. Stevie and four other men were shaking hands with the undertaker before Nicola could get there. She elbowed her way through the men and reached the undertaker, the same young, blonde woman, tall and lithe, who'd been to her house twice to discuss the arrangements. She nodded at Nicola and smiled.

'These gentlemen have offered to carry the coffin,' she said softly, 'if that's all right with you.'

Nicola looked at the men around her, their eyes on the coffin, not her, and hated every last one of them. *Where were you?* she wanted to scream at them. *Where were you when he was stuck in that chair? Which one of you pulled the trigger?* But despite their desertion, their gutless actions, she felt Micky's words in her ear. *You've no right. This is your fault, not theirs.* Nicola nodded at the undertaker and, when the men parted to let her through, she knew that they knew what she had done, and she knew that she would never be able to live among these people ever again.

***

The church service was over, and Lee walked purposefully up the uneven path of the cemetery. Behind him, Tyrone

Woods dragged his feet, his hands sunk deep into his pockets, his bowed, hooded head bobbing from side to side with each laboured step. Tyrone's alleged rape victim shivered in a cell awaiting solicitation charges, a known prostitute who'd been in and out the system for years. Tyrone was free to get on with his life.

When they reached the entrance to the northern section of the cemetery, Lee stood, both hands on the wooden gate, and surveyed with astonishment the throng of people gathered around the graveside. There must have been a hundred of them, heads lowered as the priest read from a Bible. He heard a collective Amen and heads were raised back up, backs slapped and sunglasses adjusted on noses. He watched people disperse slowly through the gate at the other end of the cemetery, and as the crowd thinned he saw Nicola at the head of the grave, Tania at the foot. He could see only the back of her head, her black dress fluttering in the breeze, but he could tell she was composed and poised, unlike Tania whose face, contorted and blotchy, screamed anguish and misery. Tania held a white tissue to her face and leant her head against the shoulder of one of her brothers, clinging to his arm. He saw Nicola raise her head towards her and their eyes met over the hollow in the ground that now housed their dead man. Tania turned her face into her brother's shoulder and he turned her away under his arm, leading her towards the exit. Margy stood slightly back with her husband, her arm linked through his, their other hands clenched together in front of them.

Lee nudged Tyrone and opened the gate. As he approached Nicola he looked on in alarm, as an immaculately dressed Tiger Reay walked past her and spat on the back of the black jacket that she'd pulled tightly around her waist. Then someone else did the same, then another, and another. His instinct was to run to protect her, but Margy was there in an instant, flailing her handbag at anyone who came near her friend, but still they spat, if not at her, at the ground by her feet. *Piss off!* he could hear Margy shouting as she ran at them as if they were pigeons scrapping over bits of bread. *Gallagher*, he thought. He'd kept his promise and made the call, probably that very morning.

When the cemetery was empty and Nicola stood alone, Margy saw Lee walking towards them. As she wiped the spit from Nicola's coat with a tissue, she whispered something to her and Nicola turned around. She faced Lee then looked contemptuously at Tyrone. Her eyes were dry, her face sad and vulnerable.

'What's he doing here?'

'Tell her,' Lee said.

Tyrone bowed his head; he couldn't.

'Tell her now or the hounds of hell will be on you, I promise.'

Tyrone muttered to his feet, 'I lied about Mark.'

Nicola looked at Lee then at the boy. 'What? What d'you mean?'

'Micky told me to say Mark had offered us drugs – that he was dealing.'

Nicola was lost, trying to make sense of his statement. 'I don't understand.'

Tyrone sighed sullenly: why didn't she get it? He wanted the ground to swallow him up. 'He wasn't dealing, Micky just told me to say that, I don't know why.'

'Then why the hell did you?'

Tyrone shook his head like he didn't understand, looked at Lee to help him out.

'Okay, go,' said Lee, nodding his head towards the gate they'd just come through. Tyrone didn't need any encouragement and he turned quickly and walked with small running steps towards the exit, Nicola watching after him, wanting answers, but her mouth was not her own.

Lee took Nicola's hand. 'Micky wanted Mark to get the kids to try stuff, groom them, so his dealers could move in. Mark was having none of it, so Micky framed him, got him arrested, got Tyrone to testify – blackmailed him.'

'How?'

'What did Mark tell you about Tyrone?'

The penny dropped. 'That he'd come on to him. Why didn't Mark tell me about Micky? Shit! Why didn't he tell me?' The question was directed at Margy, who shrugged her shoulders sadly. Shaking her head in disbelief, Nicola lit a cigarette, taking a deep drag and filling her lungs, making her head feel woozy.

Lee's glance was all Margy needed. She got the hint and walked to Joe who stood reading the headstones, knowing where he wasn't needed. Lee touched Nicola's arm and they walked side by side to the garden of remembrance, sitting on a bench and staring out across the grass, the wall around it flanked by flowers and wreaths, the lawn marked here and there with ashes thrown on it in the sign of the cross. Peace, for a moment.

'I'm going back to London,' Lee said, not looking at her.

Nicola felt her stomach drop like a stone inside her. She didn't reply. She couldn't. Even when Lee's hand reached for hers. She didn't move but he wrapped his fingers around hers carefully as if she was so precious he was scared he would break her. But he was more scared of the answer to his question.

'Will you come with me?' The shake of her head was like a thorn in his heart.

'You know I can't,' she said.

Lee looked up to the blue sky, a few starlings circling, waiting for dusk so they could sing their evening song.

'You and me,' she said, 'we're not daft. We don't live in a fairy tale.'

'I love you,' he said.

'I know,' she smiled, 'I know you do.' She put her head on his shoulder, and he squeezed her hand.

Fairy tales didn't happen on Valley Park.

TWENTY-TWO

The car park at the front of the great Art Deco flats was virtually empty. Thankfully, he'd been able to park the hire van right outside the door. There was just enough space now for the final box which Lee and Louise pushed into the last inch of space with their backsides. As it slotted into place, they high-fived each other and Lee slammed the doors of the van shut. He wiped the sweat from his brow and stood with his hands on his hips as Louise grinned from ear to ear.

'Aren't you even going to cry a little bit?' asked Lee.

Louise pulled a mopey face, but she couldn't rake up any sadness. Not only did she have a proper dad now, but he'd be living in London. *London!* Once a month and half the holidays. She smiled again. 'You're mad, leaving Newcastle. It's the best place on earth,' she said. 'I'll never, never leave here.' Lee pulled her to him roughly, kissing the top of her head as she hugged him tightly.

'You're a top kid,' he said. 'I think I'll miss you.' She gave a little groan and hugged him tighter. 'Right,' he said, prising her arms from around his waist.

He walked into the lobby and dropped the keys into the white metal box on the wall that read 'Flat 8'. He was running away. Again. He'd thought he was coming back to his roots, but he'd changed too much and Newcastle didn't want him back. Memories that had haunted him for years, though, were fading now. His father's sticks beat him across his back; his mother sat in the corner, silently weeping, her puffy face covered in bruises and scrapes, not from her husband's sticks but from falling over and walking into things, too drunk to negotiate everyday items. Her feeble attempts at martyrdom had hurt him back then. She could have saved him if she'd wanted to, but her yellow eyes and swollen hands and feet told their own story. Give her the option, her son or her gin, and he knew what her choice would have been.

He was well out of it. His granddad had told him so, and he wondered where Tyrone would be by now with a thousand of Lee's pounds tucked in his pocket. Tyrone's freedom from the prison of his family was only a train ride away, and Lee wished him luck wherever he was but pitied the lad's inability to ever come back home and be accepted.

As he came out of the lobby, a familiar, small purple Micra pulled into the car park, stopping some distance away. Lee paused, and peered through the early evening sunlight, blinking. The engine cut out and it was as if the whole world became soundless as he held his breath and waited for the car door to open. When it did, and she stepped out, she did so in slow motion. First a leg, then an arm, then the other leg, and then her lovely face emerged. He felt his hand go up above his head. It waved and she waved back. Then she was walking towards him, and still all he could hear was his own heart, thudding louder as it climbed up his throat. She was smiling, but she wasn't running. She wasn't running into his arms.

The noisy world burst back into life and deafened him when she stopped a foot away from him.

'I needed to say goodbye properly,' she said. 'I'm sorry, Lee. I'm so sorry.' Her voice broke. 'But I can't. I just can't.' Lee glanced behind her at the car and saw Liam's face, steaming up the window with his breath, Rufus's nose next to his. He nodded. Their daddy was gone because of them. Because of him. 'I'm going to Eyemouth, with Margy, I'll be by the sea, it's lovely...' she said, her voice trailing off. She reached around her neck and undid the chain that held Mark's wedding ring. 'Here,' she said, handing it to him.

'No—'

'Shut up and take it.' She pulled at his fingers and put the chain onto his upturned palm, closing her fingers around his hand. 'Thank you. For believing me.'

Lee closed his eyes against the unwanted gratitude, the words twisting in his throat. 'Come with me?'

Nicola took his other hand, held them both to her lips. 'In another life, maybe.'

He released a hand and touched her face, his thumb wiping away a tear.

They heard the car door open, and Nicola turned to see Margy, her arm resting on the roof of the car. 'Howay, man,' she shouted, 'I'm missing *Casualty!*'

Nicola smiled at her friend, then turned to Lee, the smile still playing on her face. 'Goodbye,' she said.

As she turned to walk back to the car, Louise sidled up next to Lee. He put his arm around her shoulder as hers enveloped his waist.

In another life, he thought. *Maybe.*

Finished The Prodigal? Now is a great time to leave a review at Amazon. I appreciate every single one.

ACKNOWLEDGEMENTS

Massive thanks to everyone who has supported the effort to get this book to print: to everyone who's encouraged me and motivated me to keep going.

In particular, thanks to Carolyn Reynolds, previously a producer at Granada TV, who believed in the story even though it never made it to the screen. To my critical friends and readers: Sarah Bidder, Lynn Clarke, Jackie Cotton and Rossana Leal. To Olivia Chapman from New Writing North for supporting the first structural edit, and The Live Theatre for giving me my first opportunity to write. To Laura Lindow for directing those pieces so brilliantly and encouraging me to keep writing.

Thanks to all the loyal Twitter and Facebook followers who have been so patient and positive. You're all brilliant!

Finally, of course, to my family and friends, I love you all.

ABOUT THE AUTHOR

Nicky Black is a collaboration between two friends, Nicky and Julie. Julie originally wrote The Prodigal as a commissioned two-part TV series for Granada back in 2001. It never made it to the screen, but Julie kindly allowed Nicky, ten years later, to turn the story into a novel. This is the result, and much of the dialogue in the book is taken from the original script.

Julie has written for TV in the past, notably Hollyoaks and Casualty, and this is Nicky's first novel. Both met when they worked in the urban regeneration industry nearly twenty years ago.

Nicky was brought up in Northumberland and worked in Newcastle upon Tyne for twelve years before moving to London in 2002, then back home in 2016. Julie is a born and bred Geordie, and still lives in the Toon.

We hope you enjoy reading this story as much as we've enjoyed telling it.

CONNECT WITH ME

X: @AuthorBlackNE
Facebook: Facebook.com/AuthorBlackNE
nickyblack2016@gmail.com

Printed in Dunstable, United Kingdom